EMBER

Eagle Elite Book 5

by

Rachel Van Dyken

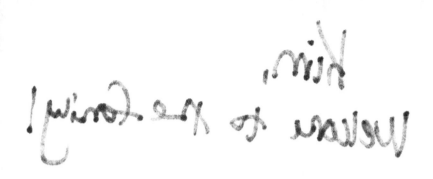

Ember
by Rachel Van Dyken
www.rachelvandykenauthor.com

This is a work of fiction. Names, places, characters, and events
are fictitious in every regard. Any similarities to actual events
and persons, living or dead, are purely coincidental. Any
trademarks, service marks, product names, or named features
are assumed to be the property of their respective owners, and
are used only for reference. There is no implied endorsement if
any of these terms are used. Except for review purposes, the
reproduction of this book in whole or part, electronically or
mechanically, constitutes a copyright violation.

EAGLE ELITE SERIES

Ember: A small piece of burning coal. **Origin:** Old English, Germanic. Example: All it takes is a one tiny piece of ember to start a flame, one small flame to burst forth into a fire. One spark, and a man's world may implode from the inside out.

PROLOGUE

Phoenix

"DO IT," MY FATHER spat. "Or I will."

I looked at the girl at my feet and back at my father. "No."

He lifted his hand above my head; I knew what was coming, knew it would hurt like hell but had no way to fight back — he'd already starved me of my food for the past three days for arguing, for trying to save the girl and her cousin.

His fist hit my temple so hard that I fell to the ground with a cry. The click of his boots against the cement gave me the only warning I'd have as he reared back and kicked me in the ribs; over and over again he kicked. The girl screamed, but I stayed silent. Screaming didn't help; nothing did.

I waited until he was done — I prayed that he would kill me this time. I prayed so hard that I was convinced God was finally going to hear me and take me away from my hell. Anything was better than living. Anything.

"You worthless—" Another kick to the head. "—piece of shit!" A kick to my gut. "You will never be boss, not if you cry

1

every time you must do the hard thing!" Finally, blessed darkness enveloped my line of vision.

I woke up from the nightmare screaming, not even realizing that I was safe, in my own bed. With a curse I checked the clock.

Three a.m.

Well, at least I'd only had one nightmare — that I'd remembered. I'd been living with Sergio for the past week; his house was so big that I'd basically taken the east wing, and he'd taken the West, said he'd hated living alone anyway. I wasn't stupid; I knew the guy wasn't exactly a big fan, but it worked. I needed to stay in the States while I figured shit out.

And I wasn't ready to leave. Not when I needed to learn all I could from Nixon. Not when I had responsibility.

And not when I had those black folders freaking burning a hole in my mind.

Luca hadn't just left me an empire; he'd left me secrets. I wasn't sure what was worse, knowing everything there was to know about those I was supposed to be protecting or knowing that at any minute one of them could turn on us.

"Hey!" Bee barged into my room.

"Damn it!" I pulled the blankets over my naked body, my heart picking up speed at her tousled hair and bedroom eyes. *Tex's sister, Tex's sister.* My body wasn't accepting that — physically it wasn't accepting any information other than she was beautiful.

And it was dark.

I looked away, scowling.

"I heard screaming." Bee took a step forward, her perfume floating off her body like an aphrodisiac or drug, making me calm, making me want something I had no business wanting.

"Yeah, well..." I gave her a cold glance. "...clearly I'm fine, so you should go. Actually, why are you here? You know you live with Tex, right?"

She shrugged and sat on my bed. I clenched my fists around the blankets to keep from reaching out to her. It was getting harder and harder to ignore her warmth — when I lived in a constant state of near-death cold.

"He's with Mo, and they need privacy. I'm not stupid. So I asked Sergio if I could move in for a while."

"You did what?" I asked in a deadly tone, one I was sure would probably give her nightmares later.

She grinned. "I'm your new roomie!" Bee bounced on the bed and sent me a shy look from beneath her dark lashes. "Admit it, you miss our slumber parties."

Forget the nightmare — I was looking at it.

CHAPTER ONE

Bested by a turtle

Phoenix

IF THAT GIRL TEXTED me one more picture of herself, I was going to lose my damn mind.

I drove like an insane asylum escapee back to Sergio's then screeched to a stop right in front of the gate, waited impatiently for it to open while tapping my fingers harshly against the leather steering wheel of my Mercedes C class coupe. Another gift from Luca. I would rather have had his life than the new car every guy on the planet was salivating over.

I wanted a lot of things.

But *want* didn't really belong in my vocabulary anymore.

The gate opened slower than I would have liked since I was pissed off. I sped through the minute I saw an opening, not caring that I could possibly scratch the ridiculously expensive car, and pulled to a stop right before hitting Bee.

"Damn it!" I threw open the door and slammed it as hard as I could. "What the hell are you doing?"

"You curse more now." Bee's eyebrows furrowed. "You

4

know that?"

Yeah, I was picking up bad habits where she was concerned; really, freaking awful bad habits. "What do you want, Bee? And didn't we talk about the pictures? I don't have time to respond to pictures of goats and sheep and ugly dogs. I have a business to run, a family to protect..." My voice trailed as her face scrunched up with hurt.

"I just..." She shrugged. "...thought they would cheer you up."

"How is a turtle making it through traffic and causing a ten-car pileup cheerful?" I challenged.

She smiled wide, hitting me square in the chest. "Because the turtle made it!" She danced around in front of me and clapped, then paused and arched her eyebrows in my direction.

"I'm not clapping."

"It's worth clapping for."

"Turtle power," I said through clenched teeth. "Now, was there anything else? You said something about an emergency?"

"Oh..." She waved me off. "...I need help picking out my first-day-of-school outfit."

"Call a girl," I snapped, walking past her.

I felt warm fingers on my arm, and before I could jerk away, I was rendered completely paralyzed by her tender grasp. Shaking, I swallowed the terror and gave her a pointed look.

Her face fell, but she didn't remove her hand. "I just... I heard they wear uniforms at Elite, and I just don't want to look stupid. I only have a few choices... I mean it's not a big deal, I just..."

Well, damn me to Hell. I sighed and hung my head. "Fine." I'd just try to ignore the way that the clothes hugged her body, and then when she was done twirling in front of me, I'd go puke in the bathroom and run ten miles to get the image out of my head. Sounded like the time of my life. Bring it on. After all, I deserved that type of torture, didn't I?

"Yay!" She clapped again then looped her arm in mine. "Thanks, Phoenix. I knew I could count on you."

Funny she should say that. After all, I wasn't *that* guy. The trustworthy one, the accountable one, the mature one. I might as well be a body without a soul. It's what I felt like most days, and she did nothing but remind me that I'd once had it all and lost it.

"Hey…" Bee nudged me. "…you look like you've seen a ghost."

"Every day in the mirror, Bee, every day."

"What?" Her bright smile fell.

I forced my own. "Nothing. Let's go pick out shoes."

"Awesome!"

CHAPTER TWO

How much can she torture me? Let me count the ways.

Bee

HE HATED ME. I knew it. Everyone knew it. I tried everything I could to get him to open up — to smile. But it was like he'd forgotten how. When I asked Tex why Phoenix was so… cold and indifferent to me, my brother had laughed and said to be thankful.

Thankful? That the man was an ass? Thankful that my only friend couldn't even look at me? And that was the pathetic part, wasn't it? He was truly my only friend, my first friend. The first person who had stayed next to me when I'd cried myself to sleep. The first person who had threatened to kill someone on my behalf, and the first person to genuinely protect me with his life — with no regard for his own safety.

How was I supposed to get past that? How was I supposed to move on from Phoenix when he was literally the only familiar thing I had? The only one I truly knew.

Ever since moving to Chicago, things had been different. I was given freedom I'd never had before, but I couldn't take it. I didn't even know how to use it. Sure, I was given my own car, compliments of my mafia boss brother along with a credit card that I'm pretty sure had no limit. But money didn't buy happiness — that much I knew.

I'd grown up with a cold-hearted father who'd wanted nothing to do with me.

And then been given to a cold-hearted uncle who'd leered at me every chance he'd gotten.

Both had been wealthy.

Both had been powerful.

Both were dead.

Just another gift from my long-lost brother.

"Bee?" Phoenix said from behind me. "You okay? You stopped walking up the stairs."

"Yeah, well…" I kept my voice light. "I was hoping you'd run into me and accidentally cop a feel."

Phoenix snorted. "Keep dreaming."

"Every night," I sang. But his words hurt. They hurt so bad, he had no idea how much. The sad part? I lived for his reactions — even when ninety-nine percent of them were negative, I still held out hope for that one percent. Maybe it was my innocence talking, maybe it was just the need to hold on to one tiny thread of hope that my life would be more than getting passed between family members. I was still waiting for the gauntlet to fall. For Tex to get rid of me, pass me off to another associate or worse, just forget I was his family.

The only constant in my life had been Phoenix De Lange.

And he wanted nothing to do with me.

I shivered, out of loneliness, rejection, then I lifted my chin. I was a Campisi; I was made of tougher stuff. I just wished I felt that way rather than acted that way.

"So…" I made my way into my room and pointed to the three outfits. "Which one for my first day at Eagle Elite?"

Phoenix moved from behind me and stood in front of my bed, his hands on his hips. From this viewpoint I could stare at him without looking like a complete lunatic. His stance was always rigid, like he was just waiting for someone to pull a gun on him or attack. Every muscle taut. My eyes roamed over his muscular back and tight black T-shirt. Muscles protruded everywhere. He wasn't huge, but he wasn't small by any means either. Around six foot two, he wasn't the type of guy you'd mess with, especially with the way he always looked so pissed off. Dark circles almost always framed his eyes. His lips were pulled tight across straight white teeth that I never saw unless he smiled by accident — which was rare.

Phoenix sighed loudly, his dark head bobbing up and down once before he turned and stared straight through me, his dark blue eyes clouding over. "Does it really matter that much, Bee? The reason Elite has uniforms is to make you look like everyone else."

I flinched. I didn't want to look like everyone else — I wanted to look pretty, for him.

Phoenix swore under his breath and pinched his nose.

"Well, how about this one?" I stepped up next to him, my arm brushing his. He jerked away and clenched his jaw tightly.

"No." He bit down on his lower lip, turning it white before he swore again. "Don't wear the skirt."

"Okay..." I drew out the word and looked back at my two remaining options. "I guess I could wear the khaki pants? But pants always look stupid on me."

"As opposed to what?" Phoenix scowled. "Pants are clothes. In order to go to class, you need to wear clothes. I really don't see a problem. Wear the khaki pants, white pullover, and pair it with one of the sweaters. You can't go wrong. We done here?"

I nodded, words getting caught in my throat. I didn't find my voice until he was halfway out my door. Running away. Again. "Thanks," I called.

A grunt was his response.

Defeated, I crumpled onto the bed.

Maybe I should move on. But I had no one to move on to and nowhere to go. My brother and his new wife were living in marital bliss, and I got the hint early on that they needed that alone time, what with him being the new Cappo to all the families and nearly dying.

Drama. That's what the mafia brought my life. Drama and loneliness. I had no place to fit. I didn't fit with my brother in his home, and I didn't fit with Phoenix at the giant house that felt more like a mausoleum than anything.

Bored out of my mind, I lay back on the bed and tried to think of something else.

School.

I could focus on school. Focus on getting my degree. And maybe, just maybe, if I focused hard enough. I wouldn't cry myself to sleep — like I'd done every night since I was old enough to know what tears were.

CHAPTER THREE

Breathing is necessary in order to survive — right?

Phoenix

I STORMED THROUGH THE house, ran down the stairs, and damn near collided with Sergio when I entered the kitchen.

"Where's the fire?" He scowled, arching a brow in my direction before opening the fridge and pulling out a bottle of water.

I didn't trust my voice not to shake, didn't trust myself to hold the scream in. I couldn't deal with her, I seriously couldn't. Her smell, the way she smiled, her body heat. Damn, I couldn't even breathe the same air as her without suffocating with want.

"A man of so many words." Sergio smirked and tossed me a bottle of water. "Tex is on his way."

"His way?" I croaked. "Where?"

"Here."

"Why?"

Sergio rolled his eyes. "Do I look like *Gossip Girl*? I didn't ask, and frankly I don't care."

Clearly Sergio was still bitter that he'd been on the losing end of that love triangle. Mo Abandonato had chosen Tex early on — there was nothing Sergio could do; hell, the man wasn't even on the same playing field. Not that I was going to be the bearer of such chipper news. Like I should talk. I couldn't even look at a girl without getting sick — without wanting to vomit. Without remembering the way I'd treated them in the past.

Without remembering how I'd treated Trace, Nixon's wife.

I clenched the water bottle tighter in my hand.

The doorbell rang.

Sergio didn't move.

I stared at the wall.

Screwed up, that's what we were.

"I'll get it." Bee's voice carried through the house.

I ignored the way it made me feel, ignored the goose bumps, ignored the desire flaring inside. I would not, could not go there. Ever.

"Honey, I'm home!" Tex's booming voice elicited a groan from Sergio and a half-smirk from me.

One thing I could count on? Tex's ability to piss Sergio off just by breathing the same air. Kind of made my constant darkness not feel so dark when someone else was suffering worse.

"In here." I took another drink of water and waited.

Heavy footsteps pounded against the wood floor, drifting in from the foyer. When they appeared in the doorway, Tex had his arm wrapped around Bee. He whispered something in her ear, and then she disappeared, skipping — right, skipping! — out of sight. Her happiness was like a homing beacon for someone like me, a starved man, a man in such desperate need for something light that he'd do anything to take it, to take *her*.

"So…" Tex popped his knuckles and took a seat at the barstool in front of me. "How goes life, Phoenix?"

"Why…" I set the water bottle down calmly. "…do I get the sudden feeling that you're going to ask me to do something I really don't want to do?"

Sergio moved to the opposite end of the table and watched. That was what he did best, watched and waited to make his move.

Tex smirked. I ground my teeth together. This couldn't be good. A personal visit?

"You could have texted." I sniffed, looking down at my hands.

"I text you about this, you read said text, throw your phone against the wall, grab your passport, and hightail your ass out of the country."

"That bad, huh?" I tried to keep my tone light — tried and failed if Tex's sudden dark scowl was any indicator.

"I know you have your own shit going on with the Nicolasi family."

Great, that was just great. Remind me that my mentor was dead, and I was in charge of a multi-million dollar crime family that wanted nothing to do with me. And the coals just keep getting heaped. Oh look, Hell.

"But, I don't feel comfortable about this and neither does Nixon… Chase doesn't get a vote because Chase doesn't feel comfortable about anything these days when it comes to you… no offense."

"None taken." Kinda hard not to be offended when Chase still hated me, but whatever. I couldn't fix it. It was my fault in the first place. I was surprised that Nixon still spoke to me and that Trace looked at me in the eye and had the nerve to invite me to Sunday dinners. I refused all her mass invitations on account that I was pretty confident God would strike me dead for walking on holy ground. Didn't want to test it. Not yet at least.

"Spring semester is starting again. I just need you to find a way to balance your duty with Bee and your duty to the

Nicolasi family."

Dread filled my entire body, making me damn near shake myself off the chair and go into a seizure on the floor. "Speak plainly."

"I enrolled you. Well, actually Nixon did. Sergio helped with the specifics."

I threw my water bottle against the wall and glared at Sergio. He held up his hands. I was going to freaking cut off every finger and feed them to the chickens out back.

Did we have chickens?

Mental note: *Buy chickens. Feed Sergio's parts to them.*

"I don't need to finish school," I said more calmly than I felt. "Can't you put one of the associates on bodyguard duty?"

"She's my sister. The sister to the Cappo." Tex shook his head. "Do you trust anyone else with her? Honestly, Phoenix. Tell me the truth."

"No." I swallowed. "But do you really trust me with her?"

"Of course." He waved me off like it wasn't a big deal that my past consisted of attacking women and almost raping my best friend's wife. "You wouldn't touch her, because you know if you did, you'd find your body parts scattered all over the good old US of A. Don't worry though. I make really pretty cuts. You wouldn't even feel the first slice, or the second... now the third? The third cuts always the deepest, hurts like a bitch." He stretched his arms above his head. "So, tomorrow. Any questions? Concerns? No?" He rose from his chair and then turned, tapping the counter with his knuckles.

I schooled my features, pretending disinterest when he smirked. What now? More threats? Then again, asking Tex to just deliver an order and leave was basically unheard of; the man liked to make sure everyone understood where he was coming from, even if it meant he needed to make graphic demonstrations on his part.

"Oh, and just in case there was any confusion just now...

you watch her. You don't touch her. You never touch her. I don't care if the only way to save the planet is to hold her hand. You keep your damn hands to yourself, or I cut off each part of your body that came into contact with hers. Capische?"

I stared him down, my eyes giving nothing away, even though blood surged through every vessel in my body, causing my temples to throb with both irritation and dread. I didn't respond well to threats — on account of my father had been a sick bastard hell bent on doing just that — threatening me every damn day he breathed air. I knew it was different with Tex, but it didn't make the anger any less real; instead it boiled, swirled below the surface, just begging for release. Snapping my jaw shut to keep myself from saying anything that would make the situation worse, I gave him a curt nod.

His cold stormy eyes begged me to try and say something in my own defense. But I didn't have a leg to stand on.

Tex nodded his head once and then glanced at Sergio. "Walk me out. I have a job for you and your brother as well."

"Watch me contain my excitement," Sergio said dryly.

"Aw, getting me alone makes you wanna break out in song? You should have said something man... Now I'm married."

Sergio rolled his eyes and stormed past me, following Tex out of the room.

Once I heard the front door slam, rage overtook me. I threw the table over, knocking it into the wall, and slammed a barstool on top of it. Wood scattered all over the floor. "Son of a bitch!"

I slammed each piece of wood until it splintered into tiny pieces. I still didn't feel better. Frantic, I reached for another barstool just as Bee charged into the room.

"Phoenix!" she yelled. "Stop!"

I raised the second stool above my head. Bee wrapped her arms around my middle, tugging me back against her soft body. I shook. Everything shook with rage, with so much rage

I didn't think I could control myself. Didn't she know I could hurt her? "Bee, go," I said through clenched teeth.

"No." She held together. "Put the barstool down, Phoenix."

"Bee…" My voice broke. "Please, please just go. Now."

"Put the chair down first."

"It's a stool."

"Fine, put the stool down first."

Shuddering, I lowered the stool slowly to the ground and tried to jerk out of her embrace.

She held firm, tight.

My muscles ached with the need to touch her. "Bee…"

"You calm now?"

"Leave."

"Phoenix—"

"Just leave me the hell alone, Bee. I don't want you." My voice was cool detached; it had to be to make her believe that I didn't want her arms around me, that it didn't cause me severe pain to be touching her but not really touching her the way I wanted to be. I was a mess. And she was ruining everything. "Bee, I don't know how else to tell you." I turned in her arms until we were chest to chest, face to face. "Leave me."

Her blue eyes darted back and forth then filled with tears. "I'm just trying to help."

"I don't need your help." I said with a sneer, my voice cracking. "I grew up all on my own without your help, Bee. You really think a guy like me would ever need a girl like you to get through the day without going bat-shit crazy? How big of an ego do you have?" She flinched as each word appeared to land a physical punch to her body.

Stepping back, she rubbed her arms, and nodded. "Sorry."

"Go to your room."

Her head snapped up. "Seriously? Go to my room? You

aren't my father, and you sure as hell aren't my brother."

"Thank God for that."

"I hate you!"

"Not near as much as I hate myself." I smiled mockingly. "Your hate does nothing to me, just like your care does nothing. Now, go to your room before I toss you over my shoulder and put you there myself."

She stumbled back, her hip colliding with the breakfast bar, before she whirled and ran out of the room. Her stomps were so loud I almost winced. The sound of a door slamming finally had me relaxing. I was able to breathe, able to exist without her scent.

Pushing her away was for the best.

Because the only other option was holding her close.

And nobody wanted the monster to get the girl — that wasn't how stories were told, that was not how happy endings were found. I deserved my darkness, and only a truly selfish individual would be all right with tugging the innocent into hell with them.

She was heaven.

She was light.

And damn if I wasn't going to do everything in my power to keep it that way.

"Whoa," Sergio said, walking into the room. "Barstools and table piss you off?"

"Something like that."

"Maybe you should enroll in anger management."

"Maybe you should mind your own damn business." I shoved past him and made my way to the workout room. I had some anger I needed to deal with.

CHAPTER FOUR

It all comes out in the end. Every time.

Sergio

THE WOOD HAD SPLINTERED and broken, spreading itself all over the floor like a tangled mess. I could just have one of the staff members clean it up. One text and they'd be in the kitchen.

Instead, I sat on the floor amidst the broken wood and sighed. I closed my eyes and waited for my blood to stop boiling; I waited for my heart to start beating. I could always count on my heart. Hearing it reassured me I still had one. Ridiculous, but there it was. I needed to feel the blood pump. Sometimes I woke up in the middle of the night and felt my pulse so I knew I was alive and not living my own personal hell.

I'd come out of hiding weeks ago, and I was already regretting it.

No longer a ghost. Now I had to work for the family out in the open. It was weird. Being surrounded by family, I'd never felt so alone in my entire existence.

My cell went off, the ringtone telling me exactly who it was. I wondered, in that moment, if the deal I'd made was worth it. Because in the end, I knew it was my own death I was staring down.

"Yeah?" I answered.

"Well, well, well… someone's been busy."

I snorted and rolled my eyes. "You need something, or are you just calling me to remind me who has my balls in a vise lest I make a false move and piss someone off?"

He chuckled. "Let's leave your balls out of this."

The line went silent and then crackled… Yeah, talk about a wiretap. Thanks, bastards.

"I heard a rumor."

"You been gossiping about me?"

"Pretty sure we typically have better things to do, but is it true? Has a new boss been named?"

"New boss?" I played dumb. "You know I'm nothing to the family. They don't tell me shit." Lies, all lies, but if he knew how deep I was back into the family — it would be a death sentence.

"The Nicolasi family."

Sighing heavily, I licked my lips and glanced at the door. "I don't see how that's anything you need to know."

"We need to know if they decide to stay and set up house, don't you think?"

"Trust me to do my job and don't forget to do yours. Remember who you report to. Remember who I report to. And don't forget… you may have my balls in a vise, but the five families hold the gun pressed against your temple."

I hung up the phone and threw it across the room. It shattered into pieces on contact with the floor.

I was in some seriously deep shit.

And I had no one to blame but myself.

CHAPTER FIVE

Friendship is the antidote to the mafia's poison.

Bee

PHOENIX WORKED OUT FOR four hours. Not that I was stalking him or anything... I just... sometimes watched. Watched and wondered what made him so angry, so upset that he needed to take it out on a punching bag while sweat poured down his body.

He'd been shirtless. His muscles so tight, so lean, that I kind of wanted to bake him a cookie or at least make pasta for dinner. Thinking it was a good idea to fatten him up, I went into the kitchen, though I had little to no experience cooking, and grabbed a recipe book.

How hard could making dinner be?

Yeah, a bit hard for a novice like me. I finally decided on lasagna, and when that didn't work on account of I didn't know what the heck I was doing and how to layer anything — I went and got an actual frozen lasagna and put it in the oven then cleaned up my mess.

Pretty sure every Sicilian within the country was rolling

their eyes at me and groaning. What Sicilian girl didn't know how to cook for her family?

Well, that was easy. One who didn't have a family. One who didn't know her own mother. One who wouldn't even know how to shop for the stupid ingredients for lasagna because she never been allowed outside — not even to play. One who couldn't even boil water because she'd never been allowed in the kitchen, or out of her room unless it had been to prance around for her father's pleasure.

The familiar pang of rejection hit me square in the chest. It shouldn't affect me in that way. It really shouldn't. I mean, when you got used to feeling it, shouldn't you just stop reacting? But I couldn't. It was impossible not to react, not to feel my chest seize up every time I felt like less of a woman because I didn't know how to cook, how to clean, how to kiss, for crying out loud! I talked a big game, but I was kidding myself. I wasn't even on the bench. I was a complete outsider, just begging for someone to pick me to join their team.

And that's what sucked about wanting to join.

You always got your hopes up that one day someone would point and crook their finger.

And every time my hopes got up, they were shot down.

The timer dinged. I pulled the lasagna out. Nothing burned! I seriously could have done a little dance right then and there but refrained from making a fool out of myself when both Phoenix and Sergio walked into the kitchen.

"Smells good." Sergio grabbed a few plates. "I didn't know you cooked."

"She doesn't," Phoenix answered just as I opened my mouth. There went that rejection again, washing over me, taking my one small triumph and making me feel stupid for even getting excited over the fact that I was able to turn the oven on.

I narrowed my eyes at Phoenix and grabbed some forks. "I thought it would be nice to cook for you guys, and since I don't really know how, I've decided to teach myself."

"How to turn on the oven?" Phoenix said dryly.

I flinched. Like, actually flinched from his statement — maybe because he'd said it once when I'd managed to warm up pizza inside the box and nearly burnt the house down. You'd think I'd be used to his barbs, but for some silly reason, I'd forgotten to put on my armor that morning, and the hits kept coming, aimed at my heart, my soul, my insecurities.

Sergio sighed. "Don't be an ass, Phoenix." His gaze was one of pity when he locked eyes with me. "Thanks, Bee, it looks great."

A compliment.

One compliment, and my eyes were already filling with tears. I hated that about myself. Despised it actually. One compliment, a real compliment, even said in passing, was enough to make me a sobbing mess — probably because compliments were so rare, like jewels or diamonds. I'd spent my entire life being put down, amazing that it only took one ounce of kindness to help me straighten my shoulders and look someone in the eye. I grabbed a plate and handed it to Phoenix.

He looked at the plate then at my hand. "I'm not hungry."

Sergio groaned. "Didn't I just tell you to stop being an ass? What? Four hours at the gym still couldn't work that bad seed out of your system?"

"Once a bastard always a bastard." Phoenix's jaw twitched as he took the plate from my hands and set it gently on the counter.

"You should eat." I found my voice. "You're going to need your strength if you plan on working out for so long every day… you need calories."

"I need sleep," he muttered under his breath. His sweat-clad shirt hugged his body, making his muscles look so sharp, so defined it was hard not to stare. "I'll just make a protein shake and go to bed."

"But—"

"Bianka." Phoenix didn't smile. Didn't pat me on the hand. Didn't do anything, just said my name — my real name, not the nickname he'd given me — and I backed off. Way off. I knew that look. No arguing.

"Right." I heaped a giant stack of lasagna onto my plate and started eating while watching him out of the corner of my eye. Broccoli, spinach, kale, green apples. Seriously the guy had a thing for green. He dumped everything into a blender and added two scoops of protein powder.

"Color." Sergio snorted. "You should try it."

Rolling his eyes, Phoenix reached into the fridge and pulled out two strawberries. He dropped them in the blender and then flipped Sergio off as he punched the switch. Groaning at first, the blender soon began to whir as it chewed the ingredients into a nasty green pulp.

Sometimes I hated living with them, but I had no other choice. Sergio was usually so grumpy I wanted to dump Prozac into his coffee every morning, and Phoenix was so haunted it may as well be Halloween every day of the month.

The sound of the blender did me in.

The cutting growl.

I hated loud noises; my ears had always been sensitive to them, maybe because, when I was locked in my room, all I ever heard was screaming, gunshots, and the sound of a vacuum cleaner hitting my door over and over again. Picking up glass, blood... who knew?

"Excuse me..." I pushed away from the table, hands shaking, and carried my plate to the sink. My feet tangled in something soft, and I fell forward, instinctively reaching out to stop my fall. With a sharp crack, the plate split into my hand, and searing pain exploded through my fingers as the edges sliced into my tender flesh. "Shit!"

Phoenix's hands were on mine in an instant, picking

away pieces of lasagna and plate. Blood spewed from my right palm. Wincing, I tried to pull away but his grip was too strong. He held my hand under the faucet and slowly ran his fingers over the deep cut. "You need stitches." He turned and glowered at Sergio, kicking the dishtowel toward him. "And pick your shit off the floor, jackass!"

I tried to hold the tears in. When I couldn't anymore, I looked away and mumbled, "I'll be fine."

His grip tightened. I cried harder.

"Come on." Showing more tenderness than I knew he could possibly possess, he lifted me into his arms and kept a fresh towel pressed against my palm.

Sergio said nothing, just watched with narrowed eyes as Phoenix carried me out of the kitchen and up the stairs. "Hold the towel tighter."

In too much pain to argue, I whimpered and clenched the towel against my palm as tight as my fingers would let me. I leaned my head against his sweaty chest. It felt good; he smelled good, like man, like a real person, rather than a ghost walking around in someone else's skin.

"Sorry." Phoenix's jaw popped again. "I should have showered but—"

"It's fine." It was more than fine. "I don't mind."

A grunt. Yup, that's all I did to him, made him grunt and hate food.

"Down you go." He set me on his bed then went into the bathroom. Minutes later, he emerged with a small kit.

The bleeding had slowed down, but I still held the towel tight against my hand.

With a wince, Phoenix pulled out a syringe and a small glass vial; he tipped the jar over, put the needle inside, and drew back the plunger, pulling in a bit of the liquid. Then he tapped the end of the syringe before reaching for my hand.

I jerked away. "What are you doing?"

"Making it so you don't cry anymore," he said gruffly,

taking my hand in his and pressing the tip of the needle directly into my palm. I let out a little hiss as the sting burned all the way down my fingertips. A warm sensation flooded me, instantly taking place of the pain. Then my entire hand went numb.

Phoenix eased the needle from my skin, set it next to me, and then pulled something from the kit that looked like Super Glue and white gauze. "I won't stitch you up because I think this should do the trick. He pressed my skin together and then put the liquid on the large gash. When it was covered, with one hand he kept the skin together, with the other started wrapping fast around my palm.

"Where did you learn to do this?"

"Prison."

I smirked.

A ghost of a smile appeared on his lips then quickly disappeared. "Pretty sure in our business its typical to know how to fix a flesh wound. Hospitals ask too many questions."

"It's not like I got shot."

His hands froze over mine then started to shake. When I tried to move my left hand to cover his in a comforting gesture, he jerked away and shot to his feet like I'd just stabbed him.

"So..." He pointed to my hand. "You should be fine... I'm tired."

Right, that was my cue.

I stood on wobbly feet and collapsed back onto his bed.

He swore and then his arms were around me, carrying me out of his room and into mine.

One last smell...

One last memorization of what it felt like to be in his arms.

Protected. Safe. Special. Even if just for one minute in my sad pathetic life.

"Thanks," I whispered once I was safely on my bed and

he was halfway to the door, as though he was late for a meeting.

He paused. "Yup."

And that was it.

CHAPTER SIX

All I'm capable of is pain; all I feel is hurt.

Phoenix

I WENT TO BED early that night. Too many conflicting emotions were pulsating through my mind, and I was sick of trying to constantly control everything. If I was being completely honest, she terrified me. I'd been numb for so long that even her touch was like getting burned. My entire body flared to life, and then I was suddenly reminded of what happened when I was with a woman.

I tok advantage of her.

I hurt her.

Because that's all I'm capable of.

I was dangerous; she just didn't know it. And I didn't know how else to keep her safe other than pushing her away, making her hate me, making her realize that I wasn't anything special.

Nightmares haunted me.

Even the smell of the dank rooms my father had kept the girls in... it somehow found its way into my nightmares, causing me to get sick damn near every night.

Bee was innocent.

So. Damn. Innocent.

Even touching her pissed me off because I could swear I saw the darkness leave my body and try to imprint onto hers.

I shivered and tried to force my eyes to close. Tomorrow was the first day of Hell, where I had to return to the one place I swore I'd never go back to.

The place that started it all.

Eagle Elite.

My nemesis. My curse.

The door to my room softly clicked open. I jolted from my bed, sliding my knife from underneath the pillow and lifting it above my head.

Bee wandered in, lifting her hands. "It's just me."

I dropped the knife onto the nightstand and leaned back against the pillows. "What the hell do you want?"

She didn't answer, but she was moving closer. I could tell by the way the air shifted whenever she was near. My body quivered with both sickness and a dull longing as the mattress sank under the pressure of her body relaxing against it.

"Phoenix..." Her voice was small, weak. "...I just... I have a question, and I couldn't sleep, and I knew you wouldn't be sleeping because you're like a vampire and all."

"I love it when you wake me up at two a.m. with compliments."

"But..." As always, she ignored my irritated tone and just kept on talking. "...promise me you won't laugh."

I sighed. "When have you ever heard me laugh?"

Her breath hitched. "Good point."

Damn, as far as two a.m. conversations went, this one was bordering on suicidal.

"So..." She cleared her throat. "...how do you make friends?"

Not what I was expecting. Was she seriously asking a

murderer, a mob boss, a thief, a rapist, an emotional terrorist in his own right how to make a freaking friend? "Go to your computer, type in *Mr. Rogers,* watch a few episodes, take detailed notes, and you'll be good to go." My hands shook with the desire to comfort her, but those same hands had hurt women — had hurt so many people. How could they bring comfort? When all they ever truly brought was death?

"Phoenix." Her voice was soft… too soft.

I could only see the outline of her body. She reached up to wipe her cheeks, my hand collided with hers. Wet. Her fingers were wet.

Damn it. "Why are you crying?"

"B-because…" She sniffled. "…you're the only friend I have, and even then you don't like me! How do I get people to like me? I must be doing it wrong, because I don't think anyone really does like me. They just put up with me, and I really… really…" Her words slurred together as she hiccupped out. "…could use a friend right now."

She thought I was her friend. How sad that I was her only friend? The idea should have repulsed me, caused me to push her away. Instead, I had this insane desire to pull her close, kiss her forehead, and say thank you. Thank her for being my friend when I was the least likeable person in the universe, when I was the least deserving.

Humbled. My hands continued to shake with the need to touch her. My body went hot and cold all at once.

"Bee, you're going to do fine tomorrow. How could anyone not like you?"

"You don't like me." She shifted, pulling her knees to her chest.

"Hey!" I tried to keep my voice light. "I thought you said we were friends."

"Friends eat other friends' lasagna."

It was dark, so I was totally free to smile without her seeing that, yes, I did, in fact, have a sense of humor and a giant-ass chink in my emotional armor. "Would that make you feel better? If I ate a bite of lasagna?"

"Maybe," she croaked. "But more like a plateful."

"Is this just a ploy to get me to eat a color other than green?"

"If it is?"

"Tears work."

Bee moved closer to me; I could almost taste her. Instinct told me to lean forward, so I moved back, away from temptation. I couldn't trust my instincts anymore. They were evil — like me.

"One plate of lasagna… because you said we were friends, and that's what friends do."

"It's two in the morning."

"Good." She stood and held out her hand. "Then maybe the starch will stick to your body, and you'll go up to three-percent body fat."

I rolled my eyes and took her hand.

The minute our fingers touched.

I regretted it. In a very big way.

Images flooded my brain. Of kissing her, of pulling her into my arms, and then those images turned into something horrific… memories of hurting those girls… memories of their screams, their cries.

I dropped her hand, my own suddenly clammy.

"You coming?"

"Yeah," I whispered, pulling a shirt from the floor and tugging it over my head, careful to keep at least a foot of space between us. We walked in silence down the stairs.

Bee quickly moved through the kitchen, pulled the lasagna out of the fridge, and placed it on the counter. I reached for a plate, just as Bee reached for one; her hand was on mine again, her body pressed tightly against my chest.

Cursing, I stepped back, giving up the plate and my sanity for a brief moment before taking a seat and letting her dish out the food.

Apparently, she thought I was in a starvation camp because the helping she gave me was so large it took up the entire plate.

"Again…" I pointed. "…two in the morning. Not sure I can eat all that."

"You can," she said confidently. "You don't eat enough as it is. It's like you're punishing yourself or something."

"Maybe I am." She wanted friendship; well, that meant honesty.

Bee's hand hovered over the microwave. It dinged a minute later. The smell hit me square in the face; my stomach growled on cue.

She had no way of knowing.

But it was going to be the first real hot meal I'd had in close to three months. Protein shakes and cold eggs in the morning. That had been my life, my existence. It made sense if I really thought about it. Why should I experience any sort of pleasure — even with food — when I was the one who freaking took it from everyone I came into contact with?

My body trembled as I picked up the fork and slowly dipped it into the cheese on top. Damn, I was like a little kid eating his first bite of cereal.

Lasagna officially terrified me.

What if one bite was all it took to send me off the edge? What if that one bite, that one bit of pleasure made me crave what I'd done in the past? What if…

I dropped the fork and pressed my sweaty palms against the cold countertop. "I'm sorry. I can't."

Bee sighed and plopped down on the barstool next to me after a brief glance at the empty spaces left by the two stools I'd destroyed. Other than that look that was so quick I might have imagined it, she seemed utterly unfazed.

Cursing, I put my elbows on the table and leaned forward; sweat started to pool around my temples. I was going to be sick.

"We're friends, right?" Bee asked.

I didn't look at her. But I nodded my head and managed a tight. "Sure."

"Then, I'll help."

I could really do without her type of help.

Bee reached for the fork and put a small bite on it then slowly lifted it to my face.

I turned; the lasagna was steaming off the fork, mocking me, begging me, tempting me. My eyes flicked to hers.

She nodded.

My breathing became erratic.

"It's just lasagna," she whispered.

"No, it's not." I gulped my stomach rolled with the need to puke. "Not to me."

"One bite."

"I don't know if I can."

She shrugged, and then searing pain hit my shin as her foot collided with it.

"What the hell!" I yelled, opening my mouth, and, what do ya know, the fork found its way inside. The minute the food hit my tongue, I damn near passed out from ecstasy. Chewing never felt so good. I couldn't remember a time that lasagna actually tasted so mind-blowing, so explosive. I swallowed and looked greedily at the fork again.

Bee met my gaze and winked, then dipped the fork into the lasagna again. "Here comes the little airplane."

I fought damn hard not to smile.

"Are those teeth I see?" She leaned forward. "Is Phoenix De Lange... smiling?"

"One thing at a time." I forced the smile down. "It's good, Bee."

"The airplane? Because I can do a choo-choo train too."

"No." Damn her! That smile made me want... so desperately. "The lasagna... even though I had to earn a bruise in order to taste it."

"If you wouldn't be so difficult."

"Ha!" I nodded. "I'm good at difficult."

"True." She handed me the fork. "Think you can handle this on your own, champ?"

I nodded, taking the fork in my shaky hand. The second bite was hard because I was doing it on my own. I kept expecting her to make fun of me. What loser couldn't eat food? What loser was tempted to throw up from the idea of pleasure? Me. Only me. I was sick. I would always be sick.

I finished the food in record time, my body stuffed so tight I thought I may actually have to throw up.

With a sigh, I rose from my seat and put my dish in the sink, careful to wash off any remnants of food before placing it in the dishwasher. Bee moved around me in silence; she set the lasagna dish back in the fridge and closed the door.

"So..." Bee leaned against the counter, crossing her arms.

I hadn't noticed how short her shorts were or how tight her tank top was. I looked away, ashamed I was noticing now, pissed that there was just enough light to see the outline of her body.

"...about making friends."

"Bee..." I clenched my jaw and rubbed my face with my hands. "Look, all you need to worry about is being yourself. People will love you. Promise."

"You can't even look at me, and you expect me to believe you?"

Sighing, I slowly turned my head. The minute my eyes found hers I lost the ability to speak. My fingers twitched, my body hummed, I took a step toward her, then another, until my body was almost pushing her against the counter. The heat from her hit me in slow, erotic waves.

"Be yourself," I whispered, placing my hands against the cold granite countertop, careful not to let my arms graze her body. "And they will love you."

"Be myself," she repeated, her eyes darting between my lips and chin. "What if it's not good enough?"

"It is," I croaked. "Got me to eat lasagna... first real meal I've had since..." I shook my head. "In a long time. You have a good heart Bee. Just let them see it."

"And you'll be with me?" Her innocent gaze held mine.

"Yeah." I swallowed the dryness in my throat. "I'll be right there, willing to shoot anyone on the spot who throws that friendship back in your face."

"Like you did."

Caught, I could only stare and give her a pathetic nod.

Bee's hand moved to my chest. I didn't pull away. I should have. But I didn't. The warmth felt too damn good. I shuddered. Then I freaking leaned in.

"Whoa, midnight snack?" Sergio's voice sounded from what seemed like a mile away.

I jerked back and gave him an eye roll. "Yeah, I was... starving."

Bee smiled and moved around me. "Sergio, you need some food too?"

"No. just water." His eyes narrowed in my direction. "It's late. You two should be sleeping."

"He was," Bee said confidently. "Then I forced him to get up, tell me how to make friends, and eat food that had color."

"Wow, you accomplished all that? In the wee hours of the morning?"

"I'm magic!" She threw her hands into the air and then yawned. "And tired... See you in the morning, boys."

The sound of her soft footsteps hitting the stairs finally allowed me to breathe easy. That was until Sergio stalked toward me and said in a cool voice, "What the hell do you think you're doing?"

"I was sleeping..." I rolled my eyes. "...then the princess needed lessons... and force-fed me, and now I'm going back to sleep. Why? That bother you?"

"Just…" Sergio ran his hand through his long dark hair. "Be careful… she isn't yours."

"Trust me." I moved past him and whispered, "I'm well aware."

CHAPTER SEVEN

Phoenix and lasagna: the stuff dreams are made of

Bee

I DREAMED THAT PHOENIX was in a parade riding a giant float of lasagna… he looked at me, winked, handed me a fork, and then we kissed.

Nobody ever said dreams had to make sense.

The kiss had been amazing… warm and passionate. His lips had tasted mine, explored me, really taken time to coax until I was ready. If I could have dreams like that every night, I'd die happy. I wasn't even sure how I'd managed to conjure up such a hot kiss — all things considered. I'd kissed only one guy in my life, and it had been more of a sabotage. He'd kissed me at one of the family dinners. I'd pushed him into the swimming pool, and my father had told me I was a stain on the family name.

A year later that same kid tried to grope me.

When I told my father — he'd asked me why I hadn't given the guy what he wanted, when clearly I'd been asking for it.

Right. I asked for it and wasn't even sure what *it* was.

That was the problem with hitting puberty so early. You looked old when you were fifteen, and at eighteen I already looked like I was twenty-five or twenty-six, a woman of the world — experienced, sexual, exciting.

I was none of those things.

None.

I quickly got ready for the day, careful to do my makeup perfect since it was the only thing I had control over. My uniform looked stupid, but there was no helping that. On top I looked all feminine and girly; my hair was in loose curls; I had bright red lipstick on, and my cheeks had just enough color to look healthy.

From the neck down... I resembled a confused first grader. Khaki pants? A sweater? But I stuck with the outfit Phoenix had picked out, because... well, it was Phoenix, and I owed him after last night.

I still couldn't figure out why lasagna had put the fear of God in him, or why he was visibly shaking when I tried to feed him.

I also decided that even if he was mean to me, I was going to keep cooking for him, or, in my case, ordering takeout. Clearly he liked food; he just didn't want to, because he was weird, or maybe he had something against non-organic food? I was going to figure it out if it killed me.

By the time I made it downstairs, I was already running late.

"Bee!" Sergio's voice boomed across the house. "Hurry up!"

"I'm hurrying!" I yelled back as I made my way into the kitchen. Ax, Sergio's brother, was sitting with his wife, Amy, at the breakfast table in deep conversation with Phoenix. Amy was awesome, but the minute she and Ax got married, they'd gotten their own place and had only visited a few times a week.

Then again, they were blissfully happy and married so they deserved that private time.

Phoenix's face was murderous as he glanced at Ax and then at Sergio. His eyes finally found mine, and for a brief moment in time, I thought he was going to smile. I was ready for it, ready for his approval, ready for a silly grin to hit his face, or maybe even one of appreciation. Especially after last night.

Instead?

He glanced, yes, glanced in my direction as if I was as interesting as wallpaper and then looked back down at his green smoothie. Special moment officially nonexistent.

I pushed down the rejection and pasted a smile on my face as I joined everyone and sat down.

"Nope." Sergio pointed at his Rolex. "You're going to be late for your first class if you don't leave now."

"Thanks, Dad," I said tersely, taking a bite out of the dry toast in front of me and reaching for the OJ.

Sergio didn't smile.

Not that I expected him to. He was a lot like Phoenix in that way. They needed a bit of fun in their lives. Good thing I was an expert at entertaining myself; otherwise, I'd probably go insane living with them.

"He's right." Phoenix stood and nodded to Ax. "And thanks for the information. I'll keep a lookout."

"Study hard." Sergio coughed into his hand and smirked in Phoenix's direction.

"Laugh it up, jackass." Phoenix muttered then tucked a pistol into the back of his skinny jeans, pulling his shirt over the back of it.

"Um…" I pointed. "What are you doing?"

"Standing?"

I rolled my eyes. "No way, really? I didn't notice you had two legs poking out of that delish body of yours."

Wow, not even a blush, not a hint of a smirk, just a cold

hard stare. Two could play that game.

"How am I supposed to make friends if you shoot them all?" I crossed my arms.

"Girl has a point," Ax said quietly.

Phoenix moved around the table and grabbed my arm. "We're going to be late, no arguing. I bring the gun, I keep you safe, you make friends, I only shoot them if they do something that pisses me off."

"What? Breathe?"

"Sure." Phoenix nodded. "If they breathe funny, consider them dead. Careful who you choose, little girl."

I hated him all over again. Hated that it was so easy for him to go from cozy little lasagna moment into cold-blooded killer with the need to distance himself from me in any way possible. Then again, he was touching me. As if on cue, though, he released my arm and wiped his hand on his pants — like I was diseased — and opened the back door leading into the garage.

I moved to get into my car but was stopped by Phoenix's hands again.

"What?" I snapped, turning around in his arms. "What could I have possibly done already that has your panties in a bunch?"

He scowled, his blue eyes cold as ice. "No chance in hell are you driving."

"Why not?"

"Because it isn't..." He looked around, his eyes darting from me to the car. "...safe."

"For me or for the pedestrians?"

"For both." Phoenix sighed and pinched the bridge of his nose. "And does everything have to be an argument with you. Who has the gun, Bee?"

"If I said both of us, would you strip search me?"

Phoenix cursed. "No. I'd let Sergio do it. I know how much he enjoys that task."

"Someone's grumpy this morning."

"Probably all that heavy food I ate last night."

"Blame the comfort food all you want... but you liked it."

"This isn't about lasagna. This is about you irritating the hell out of me for your own entertainment. Now, I'm asking nicely, please, get in the car, my car, and I'll drive you to school, where I promise not to point my gun at anyone who doesn't deserve it."

I snorted. "That was you asking nicely?"

"Yup." He crossed his arms in front of his broad chest. "Now what will it be?"

"Like I have a choice," I muttered and brushed past him, attempting to throw him off balance, but it was like a mouse running into a cliff headfirst. It hurt the mouse and made the cliff laugh its ass off.

"About damn time." Phoenix unlocked the doors to his shiny black Mercedes.

I had a really desperate need to scratch my door handle or at least sneeze on the upholstery, but it probably still wouldn't get a reaction from him. I was learning that even the negative reactions were something I craved, because at least it was something. How dysfunctional could I be?

Once we were on the road, Phoenix chose the correct music for our drive. I say correct because, according to him, one didn't start the day listening to hip-hop or anything remotely fun. No. Mr. Rogers had me listening to classical music.

Classical.

Mozart, to be exact.

Not that I wasn't a fan of the arts, but really? It just seemed so against what you would expect from him. He was the bad boy personified; like, if you put his name in the dictionary, right next to it would be *"And mothers warned their daughters to stay away, but the heart wants what the heart wants, and that heart wants that body... bad."*

He was all lean muscle and tight abs.

And I could have sworn he had a dimple, but I'd never actually seen it. Phoenix's dimple was like Bigfoot; I'd seen glimpses in pictures and via rumors, but I had never actually seen it for myself.

One day.

One day I'd catch it and take a mental picture or five. Maybe ten. Needless to say, I knew that if I had one of his smiles, it would be a magical thing.

His hands gripped the steering wheel so hard I had a brief moment of panic thinking he was actually going to rip the thing from the dash and have a breakdown. Sad part? I half-expected it. He wasn't acting normal... well, he was always moody, but this morning he seemed downright suicidal.

"So..." I tried to zone out the instruments assaulting my sanity. "You went to Eagle Elite, right?"

He was quiet for a minute then gave a swift nod.

"Wow, don't talk so fast. I almost didn't get all that."

And crickets. Again.

I cleared my throat. "You graduate?"

"Sort of."

"How do you sort of graduate?"

"Did you bring lunch money?" He asked in a tight voice.

I gaped. "Did you just ask me if I brought lunch money?"

He shrugged.

"You're driving me to school, forcing Mozart on my poor sensitive morning ears, and just asked me if I had money for milk."

"I'm concerned about you eating. Sue me."

"Pretty sure the Nicolasi boss can afford to spare me a few dollars for a sandwich and a can of pop."

"No pop."

"Who died and made you my grandpa? Seriously. I want to know so I can steal your gun and point it at them."

"Nobody touches my gun."

"Which one?" I smirked, hoping he'd find the humor in my sexual innuendo, but who was I kidding? It was Phoenix. He simply grunted, rolled his eyes, and kept driving.

In a moment of pure rebellion, I undid the first two buttons of my white, collared shirt.

"What the hell do you think you're doing?" he asked, his voice calm, his eyes still on the road.

"Wow, you really are like a parent. You can see me even when you aren't looking."

"Button that shit to your chin before I pull this car over."

"Put on Jay-Z, and we'll talk."

More cursing.

I undid another button.

"Son of a bitch, you're annoying."

"Is this our first lovers' spat?"

"Were there drugs in your toast?" He finally glanced at me, his blue eyes chilling me to the bone. "Be serious. I don't want to get called into the dean's office because you're high."

"Do I look like I'm on drugs?"

"Is this a trick question?"

Phoenix turned the steering wheel, and suddenly we were in front of a large wrought-iron gate.

"It's prison." I breathed.

Phoenix swallowed, his eyes slowly gazing up at the giant gate as we were buzzed in. "Yeah, something like that."

"Why are you shaking?"

His right knee looked like something out of Addicts Anonymous, while his fingers clenched around the steering wheel like he had a sudden fear of driving down long driveways lined with trees.

"Not shaking. Are you on drugs?"

"Okay, restless legs." I held up my hands in surrender. "And no, I'm not on drugs, but your concern is noted."

Apparently, that was the end of our conversation. The

next five minutes were spent with me staring between Phoenix's out-of-control right leg and out the window at the huge campus. Trees grew everywhere, scattered about the grounds like cosmic litter. And between the trees sprawled beautiful old brick buildings that looked like something out of a movie.

When the car pulled to a stop in front of a large three-story building with a giant sign that read *WELCOME FRESHMEN,* I almost puked. My hands clasped together, rubbing the clamminess away, I managed a confident smile when really I wanted to beg Phoenix to turn the car around and let me hide under the covers.

I'd never been to a school.

Ever.

Heck, I'd never actually been in public. Forget making friends. How was I going to survive in a crowd?

"Nervous?" Phoenix asked, turning the car off.

"Of course not" I squared my shoulders and lifted my trembling chin as I brazenly compounded that lie with another. "I have you... my only friend... with me."

"Right now your security guard." He sighed. "Not your friend, so don't go assuming I'm going to paint your nails and carry your books."

"But what if my books are heavy?"

"I'll get you a wagon."

"Charmer."

"I try." He opened the car door, and I could have sworn I heard him mumble, "Shit, I hate this place."

Just as I got out of the car, another two cars pulled up, like something out of an actual mafia movie.

Black cars.

Tinted windows.

And the crowds around us grew.

Even more nervous than before, I ran around the car and reached for Phoenix's hand. He was probably too shocked to jerk away like he normally did, because he clenched it tightly within his. Reassurance washed over me. I was going to be okay. Everything was going to be okay.

CHAPTER EIGHT

Flashbacks while walking across campus? Sign me up!

Phoenix

BEE SERIOUSLY MADE ME rethink my decision to stop drinking alcohol, which really wasn't a mark in favor of our new friendship, considering I had to be with her twenty-four-seven. I was going to have to either work out harder, hide a freaking flask in my pocket, or just shoot things when I got home every night.

God help us all if she asked me to help her with homework.

I cringed when her hand touched mine. Not because I was such an ass that she repulsed me — the opposite actually. I had to stay numb to her, unwavering. The way I saw it, if I continued to stay cold, she would eventually find someone to keep her warm. Girls like Bee couldn't help but attract people — attract guys. But the thought of guys approaching her really did have me itching to shoot things or drink, and — look at that — full circle, back to alcoholism.

I wasn't sure how we had timed it so perfect, but Nixon,

Chase, and Tex, the other bosses — bad asses in their own rights — had chosen that exact moment to pull up to the school.

Meaning camera phones everywhere were freezing.

Years ago, The Elect, the four of us, had started Eagle Elite, thinking we were untouchable; there were rumors amongst the students about what we did, about who we were, but we always laughed it off.

Nobody was laughing now.

Because that was another lifetime ago, when we had still been kids playing with guns. Our reality was forced upon us so damn quick we didn't even have time to catch a breath or transition. We all went from made men to bosses within the span of eighteen months.

The minute Nixon Abandonato stepped out of his car… I knew it. I wasn't even looking in his direction, and I knew.

Mouths gaped.

Camera phones were raised.

Girls were fanning themselves.

And Bee's hand clenched mine tighter.

I glanced at the Range Rover just as Chase emerged, earning a girlish squeal from the crowd, and then finally Tex, the Cappo — aka MVP — of the families emerged in his aviators. A gun straight up, strapped inside a leather jacket for all to see. It was hard to miss.

Shit… things just got real.

The squealing stopped.

Talk about an entrance.

It didn't matter if people were trying to upload to YouTube, or if they were posting to Facebook. The security at Elite was controlled by us, because Nixon still owned the freaking school, so yeah… we weren't worried about making CNN, but still, they could have at least *tried* to fly under the radar.

I didn't envy Sergio one bit; he was probably having a

hell of a time shutting down all social media around the campus Ethernet.

Besides, what could the pictures prove? Some rich guys getting out of nice cars? One has a gun but has a license to carry it? He could be a federal agent for all they knew — but the students weren't stupid. Stories of the Elect escapades still ran rampant throughout campus, even though all of us were long gone.

My stomach clenched as my gaze fell on my friends, the three guys that a few years ago, would have taken a bullet for me. I'd hidden everything from them, the sickness of my mind, and the torture from my father. Returning to Elite was a shit idea, but I had no choice.

The girls, or wives as I liked to call them, all filed out of the car. First Mo, Nixon's sister and Tex's wife, her long dark hair pulled into a high ponytail. She waved at me. I didn't wave back. Didn't feel the need to release Bee's hand, and my other arm was busy twitching with the insane need to grab her other. Right, so I was preoccupied.

Trace followed Mo and launched herself into Nixon's arms. I fought a smile. Ever since our little training session, things hadn't been as strained between us. I could almost view her as a friend instead of a victim. But sometimes at night, her face still came to me as a nightmare, and for that reason alone, I kept a healthy amount of space between us.

Mil, my stepsister, performed an elaborate fake gag as she followed Trace and then kissed Chase so aggressively I almost reached for my gun. I kept forgetting they were married, and I still had a hard time when he mauled her in front of me. As usual, his eyes found mine after he kissed her, and a mocking grin spread across his face.

All in all, a great start to the day. Super great shitty start.

Nixon walked slowly toward me. Hands in pockets, check. Aviators, check. Large gun bulging from the holster against his back, check. Pissed off look, check. Damn. It.

"You guys good?" he asked, directing the question more to Bee than myself.

She nodded and moved closer to me, just as Tex approached, his eyes focused in on our clenched hands. When I tried to pull mine away, Bee stomped on my foot. I winced and looked heavenward while Tex choked on his laughter.

"We're awesome!" Bee said a bit too forced, if you asked me. "And Phoenix taught me all about how to make friends last night, so I'm good to go!"

"He did?" Nixon asked dryly. "You're kidding, right?"

"Nope!" Bee just kept on talking even when I communicated with her via telepathy to shut the hell up.

Tex shoved his hands in his pockets and tilted his head in what I could only assume was amusement at my expense. "And what great wisdom did Phoenix impose on you, little sis?"

"Well…" Her grin was evil.

Please God, let the drugs or whatever mood she'd woken up in be out of her system. Mute. Let her be mute. Amen.

"When I want to get a guy's attention, all I have to do is smile and wave."

I drew a cautious breath. *So far, so good.*

"And if that doesn't work, I unbutton a few buttons and wink!"

Tex growled. Out loud. Like a dog. His cold gaze flickered from the blouse to me, the threat evident in his icy, dark blue eyes.

"Oh, and he also said that if someone offers me a drink, I should always take it and drink the whole thing so I don't offend them."

I closed my eyes, willing an asteroid to hit the earth.

"He also said a lot of stuff about shaking my ass and jumping on tables, but I kind of tuned out after he turned on the stripper music. I mean, I think we were both pretty distracted by that point, hmm, Phoenix?"

I opened one eye then the other.

Tex looked ready to rip my body in half… at least three times for good measure, and Nixon looked like he was only too willing to help just in case Tex had a problem pulling my skin from my bones.

"And when that didn't work…" Bee huffed. "…he said to look up *Mr. Rogers' Neighborhood.*"

Both Tex and Nixon burst out laughing.

I didn't.

I'd been serious! In my opinion, there was nothing better than watching Daniel the Tiger tell a little kid how to make a friend and not be shy. But whatever; her loss. That shit had gotten me through elementary school when I was too small to beat anyone up… when I was too small to defend myself against my dad's wrath.

Bee finally dropped my hand. "I'll be fine, brother. You worry too much. And Nixon, stop frowning. You look possessed."

"He is." Tex coughed the words into his hand.

"Hilarious." Nixon elbowed him. "You sure you're going to be okay? I know things haven't been easy."

"I have Phoenix," Bee said simply, making me feel about two feet tall because I wasn't prideful enough to think that would be enough to get her through. I would never be enough.

The guys fell silent for a minute.

Bee challenged them all with a look, sticking up for me and making me feel like I'd been castrated all at the same time.

"You're right," Nixon said finally, nodding. "Just keep him close."

I could have really done without that last part.

Closeness wasn't going to help the situation. Distance. That was what I needed.

"And call us…" Tex added. "…if anything happens, like you get scared or… something." He shifted on his feet awkwardly.

Bee slapped him on the shoulder. "I promise that if the big bad bullies chase me down the hall and call me stupid, I'll text you to pick me up, but Phoenix brought his gun, so I think we're good."

"You do know that's illegal, right?" Tex asked.

I released Bee's hand and crossed my arms. "You do know that's your sister… right?"

"And that's our cue." Nixon's eyebrows shot up as he pulled Tex away from us. "Have fun, Bee, and remember the girls are all upperclassmen, but you can always hang with them in between classes."

Bee saluted them as they made their way back to Chase and the rest of the girls.

Ten minutes later, and I was stuck with four women.

So basically, if Hell decided to come to earth, I was in the middle of it, surrounded by perfume and sharp nails.

"So…" Bee reached for my hand again. "Shall we go experience college?"

I let out a groan, pushing her hand away.

Suddenly clammy, I let my wooden legs carry me through campus, biting my tongue, tasting blood in my mouth. I freaking hated this place. Everywhere I looked memories assaulted me.

The first day Trace came to Elite.

Nixon's warnings.

I looked toward the registrar building, knowing that the building next to it — the Elect headquarters at the time — would be staring back at me. I'd taken Trace in there.

My chest hurt so bad it felt like it was going to crack.

"It's okay, Phoenix." Trace spoke up for the first time, nudging me in the side. "We won't let them hurt you."

A few girls walked by and waved in my direction.

"Ah, she has jokes." I managed a tight smile before realizing I was doing it.

Bee let out a loud gasp.

I stopped walking. "What?"

"N-nothing." Her cheeks blushed bright red. "I just… nothing."

"Nervous?"

"Yeah." She nodded enthusiastically. "That's it."

"Well, let's get it over with then." I pulled her away from the girls and waved goodbye."Your first class is this way."

"Right."

I leaned over and peered into her bright eyes. "You sure you aren't on drugs?"

"Ha ha." Her voice was breathless. "More walking, less talking."

"Read my mind, little girl."

CHAPTER NINE

His smile was like the sun.

Bee

PEOPLE WERE STARING AT me, and they didn't even try to hide it. Phoenix kept a safe distance behind me — and it made me feel even more lonely than before. It was like he was trying to show everyone who saw me that he wanted nothing to do with me. At all.

When I tried to slow down, he slowed down. When I sped up, he only went fast enough to keep up with me.

I passed my classroom on purpose.

Phoenix cleared his throat.

I rolled my eyes, backtracked, and went through the door. Twenty-something pairs of eyes all landed on me; everyone went completely silent. My heart started beating so fast that it was the only thing I could hear as blood surged toward my face. Everyone was already seated. Holy crap, I really was late.

With a nervous smile, I opened my mouth to say something when Phoenix smoothly walked by me and approached the professor. He smiled, freaking smiled, the same way he had with Trace. I knew it! I knew I wasn't losing my mind. Dimple, right cheek, deep, so deep, and sexy. I bit down hard on my lower lip to keep from sighing out loud.

The professor laughed at something Phoenix said, which immediately hurt my feelings. Why couldn't he laugh with me? Joke with me? Was I that annoying? That must be it. I was annoying. Like the little sister he never wanted but was stuck with.

Who fed him lasagna at two a.m. and wouldn't shut up even when he asked me nicely. But it wasn't like I could just turn off my sparkling personality; he just brought out the need for me to get in a good verbal sparring. Again, it was better than nothing.

"Miss Campisi?" The professor addressed me, tilting his head to the side. "Please take a seat in the back."

I tucked my hair behind my ear and quickly made my way to the back of the class. Just as I was about to make it to the empty table, a guy's foot shot out, nearly tripping me.

With a quick sidestep, I managed to avoid the collision then leaned over, as if I needed to fix my pant leg, and whispered, "Try that again, and I'm asking the brother to order a hit on you. Better yet, I'll complete it myself. I may be new to school, but you're in *my* world. And in my world, we don't put up with bullies. We shoot them." I paused as I stood up. "Didn't catch your name?" My voice held a slight tremble, but he didn't seem to notice it. I tended to lash out when I was scared, and in that moment with all those kids, in a school, I was terrified, which meant he was going to be on the receiving end of my wrath. Lucky him.

The guy paled, his skin matching his blond hair. He opened his mouth then closed it.

"Problem?" Phoenix asked, coming up behind me; his hands touched my shoulders briefly before pushing me forward toward the desk.

I turned and shrugged. "Nothing I couldn't handle."

Phoenix stayed put while I took my seat. With a smirk — not a sexy one, but one that had me wanting to back up and lift my hands in surrender — he took the seat next to me and leaned forward, whispering in hushed tones, "Didn't catch your name?"

My breath caught. He'd repeated my words.

"B-brian," the guy whispered.

"Listen... Brian." Phoenix sneered a bit.

The professor, clearly unaware of what was taking place in the back of his classroom, continued talking about expectations and rules.

But Phoenix was laying out his own rules and expectations. "I see you look at her in a way that personally offends me... I cut your finger off then mail it to your parents as a reminder to teach their son some manners. I trust you'll be able to keep all negativity to yourself. After all, we want your college experience to be a positive one, don't we? Granted, you have to live that long first."

The guy started visibly shaking. "Sorry... er, Mr. um..."

"Phoenix—" His teeth snapped. "—De Lange."

"Shit," the guy muttered before he jolted from his seat and ran out the door.

The professor looked back at both of us with a query in his eyes.

Phoenix merely offered an innocent shrug and nodded as if to say, *Do continue with that fascinating lesson on not cheating.*

He'd scared the guy shitless.

And I kind of loved him for it.

"You didn't have to do that," I whispered a few minutes later as papers were getting passed back to us.

"I did." Phoenix handed me the piece of paper, his hand lingering. "And I always will."

I gulped, pulling the paper from his hand. "But he could

have been a friend."

His lips twitched. *Come on, one small smile?* "Friends don't let friends make friends with jackasses."

"More wisdom." I nodded, tapping my temple. "Stored right up here."

"Along with name brands and selfies?"

"Along with dimples and smiles," I said before I could stop myself.

His lips parted as his eyes fell to my mouth.

"Any questions about the assignment?" the professor asked in a booming voice, jolting me out of my daydream about what Phoenix's mouth would feel like pressed against mine.

I raised my hand.

"Yes, Miss Campisi?"

"I'm sorry. What was the assignment again?"

The entire class let out a groan.

I squinted and fired Phoenix a *what did I do?* look.

He shook his head, but I saw a ghost of a smile, and I knew whatever I'd done, I wanted to do it again. One day I'd get a full smile, and I'd deserve it.

ALL IN ALL MY classes weren't completely horrible, but if Phoenix didn't stop asking me to pick a major and get it over with, I was going to stuff my fist down his throat, or maybe just my tongue. It was a toss-up, and I was grumpy because Sergio had rushed me through breakfast.

"Lunch." Phoenix nodded toward a huge two-story brick building. A tasteful black sign with the word *Commons* stamped on it in gold. The Eagle mascot was right below it in red. "Aren't you hungry?"

"Starving!" I started to head for the door but was jerked backward by my backpack. Pouting, I crossed my arms and turned. "You clotheslined me."

"That wasn't clotheslining." Phoenix rolled his eyes. "And I asked if you were hungry."

"And I said I'm *star-ving*." I said the word slower this time like he was a two year old. "So can we go in?"

"Where?"

"There." I pointed back at the building. "Isn't that were lunch is?"

"Not for you."

"Oh." I looked down at the pavement. "Do I have to eat alone or something?"

The thought had me feeling insecure all over again. Yeah, my classes had been fine, but all the students had looked at me like I was a total nut job. The only girl who had been nice to me was the one who'd kindly pointed out that I was about to go into the guys' restroom. And I think she only did it because she was worried I was going to see her boyfriend's parts. He emerged minutes later and attacked her with his tongue — in a totally horrifying way that had me wanting to take a shower.

"Bee…" Phoenix's voice was tired. "…you can't eat with them because they'll just stare at you."

"Because I'm a freak," I mumbled.

Phoenix let out a snort of laughter. "Is that what you think?"

I nodded, still staring at the pavement.

"It's because of who your brother is… it's because of who your family is." Phoenix's voice was grim but all business. "They're afraid of you, and when people are afraid, they do really stupid shit, believe me."

I wasn't convinced. If anything, it made me feel that the situation was that much more hopeless.

"Come on… I'll spot you some lunch money." His voice was back to being light, teasing.

I jerked my head up. "Did you just tease me?"

"Will that make you feel better?"

I gave a weak nod.

"Then yeah, I teased you. Surprise."

Examining my nails, I gave a noncommittal shrug. "You can do better."

"I'm not a monkey. I'm not dancing for you."

"Drop it like it's hot, and it will make my week."

"No."

I pouted, jutting out my lower lip. "Please?"

"Try again." He coughed, shifting from one foot to the other. "And keep in mind we should get going since you only have an hour before your lab."

Scrunching up my nose, I thought about it. "Okay, no teasing... I don't need teasing. Just one smile. One smile. For me."

"That's worse than dancing."

"A smile?" I gasped. "So dance. Lesser of two evils."

"I can't believe I'm negotiating with a terrorist right now."

"Aw..." I fluttered my eyelashes. "Aren't you sweet. Now dance."

"I changed my mind. Stay in a crappy mood." Phoenix's lips did that twitch thing, and then a miracle occurred. A smile, a large smile formed across those gorgeous lips, framing perfect white teeth. And that dimple? Even better this close up. Swear, I felt my entire body heat from that one smile.

"You should do that more often," I croaked.

"I may... if it gets that reaction where your eyes go all crazy, and that trap you like to call your mouth finds the sudden urge to mute itself."

"Happy moment destroyed," I grumbled.

"Let's go." Phoenix nodded toward a building next to the Commons. "Lunch. Let's go feed you."

"I eat, you eat. That's the deal." I rushed to keep up with him.

"I smiled. You're the one officially in my debt."

"I love the sound of owing the great Phoenix De Lange a favor. Please, please let it be sexual," I pleaded.

Phoenix shook his head as if he was totally unfazed by my comment. "Barking up the wrong tree there, little girl."

"I'm not a little girl!" I huffed, barely keeping myself form pushing him into the tree, like a little girl at recess.

"Oh look! Lunch, friends to make, people to talk to..." Phoenix pointed to the door. "Go ahead."

"By myself?"

"Prove you're not a little girl," Phoenix challenged. "Go into lunch by yourself, tons of professors around, cameras everywhere. I'll wait out here on the steps... eat a protein bar, make some calls."

"Fine, Grandpa." I lifted my nose in the air. "But when I come out with tons of friends and forget your name, don't get all moody on me."

"I'll try to restrain myself." He'd already turned around and was moving toward the far side of the stairs.

Nervous, I fought the urge to run after him, wrap my arms around him, and sob into his chest.

But I wanted to prove I could do it. So I turned on my heel and made my way into the building.

The minute I opened the door, the smell of food hit me square in the face. My stomach decided that, yes, going through the door was the best idea I'd had in years. That was until I opened the second door and came face-to-face with a group of twelve students, all sitting around a lunch table and eating. A few other tables were scattered around, one or two students sitting at them on their computers, not paying attention to anything and typing furiously like the world was going to end if they stopped.

The table with the most kids all stopped eating — at the same time, as if they'd planned it.

"Um..." I tucked my hair behind my ear. "I must have the wrong room."

"Hey, you're Bee!" A tall guy with sandy brown hair stood and walked toward me, smile wide, hand outstretched. "Come on in."

I took his hand, shook it, and tried to paste a confident smile on my face as the rest of the students around the table looked at me anxiously.

"How do you know my name?" I asked, taking the only empty seat next to him.

"Student Body President." He shrugged. "It's my job." His eyes narrowed. "You're Tex's sister, right?"

"Right."

"And your bodyguard? Does he eat?"

"Phoenix?" I asked, surprised he knew so much. "No, he prefers protein bars to people food."

"Ah…" The guy was good-looking, clean cut… but not Phoenix. Then again, nobody compared to Phoenix, and when you hung around the guys I did, everyone pretty much paled in comparison to their hotness. My brother excluded, for obvious reasons.

"I'm Pike." He tossed me a menu. "I hope you don't mind, but you were kind of late, and I didn't want you having to wait to eat, so I ordered you a burger and fries."

I sighed in relief, though it was a bit weird that he was expecting me. "Sounds amazing."

A plate of food was set in front of me as I glanced around the room. It looked like a really nice dining room. But it only had space for a few students, and Eagle Elite had over five thousand… I was still trying to figure it out when the girl to my right elbowed me.

I glanced up.

"Name's Hartley." She grinned, her green eyes sparkling like she knew some crazy secret I wasn't a part of. "Are the rumors true?"

"Rumors?" I repeated, stealing a glance at Pike.

"A little rude, don't you think, Hart?" Pike interrupted.

RACHEL VAN DYKEN

"Let her at least eat before you start asking questions."

"Sorry." Hartley tucked a piece of hair behind her ear. "I'm just really curious…" She looked around the table. "I mean I can't be the only one who's curious."

"Hart," Pike warned.

"What!" Hart held up her hands. "I'm sorry. I'm not trying to be offensive, but The Elect leave our school, rumors spread about all these killings, *mafia* is like this revered word around here, and then she shows up at school with a bodyguard, and not just any bodyguard, but one of the original elect who used to freaking run this school with an iron fist. And I'm supposed to keep silent and not ask questions?"

The rest of the people around the table were looking at me like I was supposed to answer them, like I knew the answers.

"Sorry," I managed. "I don't really know who The Elect are."

Everyone burst out laughing.

"She's good," Hart said. "They taught her well. She's a good liar."

"No!" My eyebrows knit together in confusion. "I seriously don't know who they are… and why does my background even matter?"

The room was silent again.

I ate a fry, but it was soggy.

"Because," Pike finally said. "Rumor has it you're not the only implant at the school this year."

"Implant?"

Pike sighed. "Don't worry about it. Rumors are just that… rumors, you know?"

"Petrov," said a female voice from behind me.

I turned and smiled as Mil made her way toward our table. Mo and Trace followed close behind.

If I thought the room was silent before, it was like death now.

"Emiliana…" Pike's smile didn't reach his face. "How goes the business?"

"Business?" Mil tilted her head. "Silly boy, this mouth is for eating, not talking… especially to you."

"Touché." His eyes lit up in what I could only assume was respect.

Mo's fingers brushed my shoulder. "Why don't you come eat with us for a bit? We should catch up."

I felt trapped between making new friends and talking to old ones.

"Go ahead." Pike nodded. "We can get to know each other better later."

Nodding, I picked up my plate and followed the girls to a corner table. I didn't even realize I'd been holding a breath until we sat down and I exhaled my frustration.

"So…" Mo grinned in my direction, then pulled her silky dark brown hair back into a ponytail. "…you make friends fast."

"It was a direct order from Phoenix… make friends, prove I know how." I rolled my eyes. "Though to be fair, all I had to do was walk in here, and suddenly I had a plate of food in front of me, and I was being asked about The Elect."

Mo's fingers paused while her eyes flickered to Mil and Trace.

I sighed. "Spill. Who are The Elect?"

Trace spoke up. "Tex hasn't talked to you about it? Or Phoenix?"

"Tex is holed up having sex with this one." I jutted my finger at Mo. "And Phoenix thinks I'm better seen and not heard."

Mil snorted. "Phoenix needs an attitude adjustment."

"Yeah, well." I played with a fry, dipping it into the ketchup before bringing it to my mouth. "His idea of fun is running ten miles a day then eating things that look like regurgitated baby food, so unless one of us just starts feeding him chocolate intravenously, I highly doubt that attitude adjustment is going to happen."

"It's been a… rough year." Trace and Mo shared a gaze while Mil cleared her throat and looked down at her plate. "For all of us."

"What am I missing?" I lifted a fry to my mouth, waiting for an explanation. "You guys do realize I'm new to all of this?"

Mil shrugged. "Sometimes things are better left… not discussed. All you really need to focus on is school and getting homework done. Let us take care of the rest."

"So play dumb and be ignorant just like my father expected me to?" My voice rose. "Is that what you're asking?"

I was angry, and I had no idea why; it just seemed like I was the little kid at the playground who wanted so badly to play with everyone else only to be told she wasn't old enough to go down the slide.

I wanted to go down the slide.

I wanted to prove I could.

But how could I prove myself if nobody ever gave me a chance to climb the ladder?

"Fine." I licked my lips then pushed my plate away. "I'm not hungry anymore."

"Bee." Mil reached across the table like she was trying to find my hand. "It's not that, it's just… a lot of shit went down, and really we just want to move past it. I mean, we finally get a chance at normal, don't you want that?"

I looked around the room. "You realize we're at one of the most expensive schools in the universe, and it's owned by mob bosses, right? Normal went out the window a long time ago."

"Normal for us," Trace clarified.

"Which is… secrets and more secrets?"

Nobody said anything.

"The Elect? Who are they? Who were they?"

Finally Mil spoke up. "It's best to ask one of the members rather than any of us. Ask Phoenix if you want to know but be prepared for the shit storm that's gonna come when or if he decides to answer. Things are still raw with my brother, and that's all I'm going to say."

"Fine." I pushed my chair in.

"Bee." Trace stood and reached for my arm. "Don't go."

"It's fine. I made friends, right?" I looked over my shoulder. The last table I'd been at had gone dead silent. Okay, so they probably weren't going to take a bullet for me anytime soon, but I had Phoenix.

My shoulders slumped.

Right. I had Phoenix, and again I was reminded that I didn't really have a friend. I had no one. And I seriously didn't even know what real friends did. Could I base my assumption off movies and books? Because as far as those definitions went, that meant Trace would be gossiping with me about Nixon. Mil would be painting my nails and Mo would be complaining about Tex. Instead, Mo was thumbing a knife under the table. Trace was checking her phone, face pale, and Mil was watching every person in the room like a hawk — like they all had guns aimed at her.

Swallowing, I bobbed my head in an automatic I–could-not-care-less fashion and grabbed my books. "I gotta run guys. Thanks for letting me sit with you." I pushed down the swell of emotion fighting to scream its way out of my throat and marched out of the room.

CHAPTER TEN

Even prisoners got time off, right? Or at least a break?

Phoenix

I STARED AT THE phone in my hands and tapped the shiny glass surface... I didn't want to make the call.

I never wanted to make the call.

Maybe in my past life, when I'd still been a horrible excuse for a human being, I'd wanted that type of power, but now it tasted bitter in my mouth, like I was playing God. I had no business saying who lived and who died — I was the least likely of people. I couldn't see past the fact that it was like Satan deciding who should go to heaven. Unfortunately, the decision was made for me when the phone vibrated in my hands.

"Yeah?" I barked.

"Boss..."

I rolled my eyes and took a deep breath. "Yeah, Nick?" Ever since getting the Nicolasi family thrown in my lap, he'd been my right-hand man, from communicating with the men to helping me wade through all of the drama being a boss brought. Luca trusted him; therefore, I had no choice but to do the same.

"We're ready for the meeting, but I gotta warn ya… a few of the men are a bit… upset."

"Define upset."

"They don't wanna come. Said they won't report in."

"Is that a nice way of saying they've gone AWOL?"

Nick cursed. "It isn't like that, boss. They just… they need time."

"Do I look like a damn clock?"

"No, sir."

My palms sweated against the phone, making it slide along my ear. "Listen up and listen carefully. You call the guys who are giving trouble and tell them this."

The phone cracked.

"Tell them—"I reached into myself and let a bit of the resentment free, a bit of the anger I knew I still harbored. *"Che peccato,"* I murmured. "What a shame that they'll never see their families again. Forget their families. They have one sunrise to change their minds. Then I'm putting them on ice. This isn't a threat to scare them into submission. It's a promise. You haven't even begun to see the terror I will inflict on the Nicolasi family if things aren't done my way. Luca left me in charge because I'm the man for the job. If they can't come to terms with that, then I'll at least offer them the opportunity to name their pallbearers before I mess them up and dig a hole. Tell them that, word for word, and call me with their answer. Or hell, just text me one bullet or five. I'll need to know how many of them to shoot. Don't disappoint me, Nick."

"Sir, that is the last thing on my mind… disappointing you."

"Get it done, Nick, or it's your head."

"I'm partial to my head."

"As you should be."

"Va' fa Napoli!" I snapped then hung up the phone.

"There a reason you just told someone to go to hell?" a flirty voice said from behind me. "Because it's kinda hot, you getting all worked up."

Not only did I have to deal with my role as the boss of the Nicolasi clan, but now I was dealing with her… again. "Didn't I tell you to make friends?" I didn't turn around, didn't trust myself not to drink her in. I was always weak after dealing with transactions, after barking orders. It drained me because I really didn't have much left to deal with emotionally.

"Found a squirrel in the parking lot. Does that count?"

"That depends." I shoved my phone in my pocket. "Did it talk to you? Offer you his nuts?"

Bee burst out laughing. "If he showed me his, will you show me yours?"

"This conversation just passed a really disturbing point of no return."

"Yeah well…" Bee sat down on the stairs next to me, pulling her knees to her chest. "That's me, all kinds of disturbed."

"I'm sorry. Have I given you any indication I'm a shrink, willing to listen to your laundry list of issues?"

"Bad phone call?"

"No. Everything's fine."

Bee bit her bottom lip. "You don't look fine."

"According to you, I look hot all the time, so now who's the liar?"

Bee tilted her head like she was examining me, her damn lip still held captive by her straight white teeth. "Hmm, I'd say you still are. Your veins are all popping out on your forehead, and your jaw's clenched."

"Yeah, I always look like that. Comes with the territory."

"Hmm." Bee looked away. "Can I ask you something?"

"If I say no, does it even matter?" I stood, expecting her to follow me, which she did. I knew how to get to her next class, even though we were going to be a bit early, considering she'd clearly failed in the friendship department.

"Probably not." She twirled a piece of her hair and pulled out her sunglasses, making slow work of dipping the edges in her mouth, sucking on them like they were candy.

I looked away. I had to. Instead, I focused on trees, I focused on grass — hell, I even focused on the tiny squirrel that ran in front of me.

I pointed. "One of your friends?"

"I'll call him Chuck."

Do not laugh. Do not laugh. I kept it in — just barely — and gave her a noncommittal shrug. Damn, it was going to be hard keeping my guard up when she kept trying to scale the walls.

"Who are The Elect?"

I stopped walking, nearly stepping on Chuck. Hell, at this point I wanted to drop kick him and take off running.

"You mean like student council?" I played dumb, even knowing it probably wouldn't work, not with Bee.

"Phoenix." She gripped my arm.

I jerked it free and shoved my hands in my pockets, taking a few steps back. She ignored my need for space and stepped forward, closing the comfortable distance between our bodies. "The friends I tried to make earlier, they said you were one of them… like you ran the school or something, and I just… I'm tired of being left in the dark."

Her eyes fell, focusing in on my chest. I exhaled a long breath. "Do you trust me?"

Her head snapped up. "Yes, why?"

"Do you trust me to protect you? Trust me to provide safety to you here at school? Trust me with your life?"

"You know I do," she whispered, reaching for me.

I stepped out of her way and cursed.

"Phoenix?"

"Then trust me when I say that knowing who we were, what we did…" *What I did.* "…doesn't matter. In the grand scheme of things, that life, the one we lived here at Eagle Elite, it isn't even a blip on the radar compared to the shit we're dealing with now. Right? It's history. The past. It. Doesn't. Matter." I needed her not to know anything about me. Digging meant she'd eventually find out what I did, what I was capable of, and I wasn't so sure I was ready for her to know my darkness.

I didn't even like knowing it.

Sharing it with Bee? Well, to me it was a hell of a lot like dumping her in oil and forcing her to sit and try to scrub it off without using her hands.

"So…" Her eyes narrowed. "They were just messing with me?"

My thoughts regrouped a bit. "They?"

"Yeah, Pike, he's a senior and—"

"Pike?" I repeated, incredulous. "You stay the hell away from that kid. Far. The hell. Away. Got me?"

Her brow furrowed. "He seemed nice."

"So do I." I bit my tongue tasting blood. "So do I."

"No, you don't." She burst out laughing. "Nice in Phoenix World is you opening the door for me without slamming it in my face or you remembering to grunt in my direction."

"Just…" I wanted to scream in her face. "…stay away from him."

"Damn, and here I was going to give him my flower."

I lost it.

Instantly.

There was no preparation for the rage I felt. Without thinking, I gripped her by the shoulders and pushed her up against the tree. Her bookbag fell to the ground as my body encased hers, my nostrils flaring, my teeth snapping. "He gets within fifty feet of you, and I'm beating the shit out of him. He holds your hand? I cut it off. He kisses you, and he's going to wake up without any lips to frame his ugly-as-sin face. If he decides to touch you in any way, I'll cut off his balls and feed them to him then put him out of his misery with a bullet between the eyes. And that's going to be on you, princess. All you. So I'd think twice about giving him anything."

Bee's shocked expression turned murderous as she tried to push against me. "Jealous it won't be you?"

"I don't do virgins," I spat stepping away. *Or anyone.*

"I knew you liked men."

"Bianka! Damnit!" I punched the tree trunk. "Can you please just trust me enough to do my job? Stay away from him, and for the love of God, stop thinking I want anything you have to give."

Her lower lip trembled as she reached for her bag and tossed it over her shoulder. "You really are a bastard, Phoenix."

She stomped off.

"Where the hell are you going?" I almost shouted.

"Class!" She flipped me the bird. "I can take care of myself."

Forget that she literally tripped that very next instant nearly twisting her ankle.

I felt like shit.

I shouldn't have lost it.

I had better control than that, but the thought of that bastard's hands on her had sent me into such hatred that I had to keep myself from calling a hit on him. *Ha, great. Only been boss for what? Two weeks? And already I'm killing students. Fan-freaking-tastic.*

With shaking hands, I watched, waiting until Bee made it safely into the correct building then jerked out my phone.

"This better be good," Sergio said lazily from the other end. "I was hacking Amazon."

"Why?"

He chuckled. "Because I'm bored as hell — because I can."

"You need a job."

"Yeah, well, killing people isn't as fulfilling as it should be."

"You need a girl."

So do you.

"I'm hanging up now."

"Wait!" I ran my hands through my hair. "We have a big problem."

"Listening…"

"Well, actually, it's more of… you have a problem, and I'm knee-deep in the shit it's going to cause."

"I doubt it's any worse than inviting all five families in for a commission. Oh wait, we already did that."

"Ha." I barked out a laugh. "He has jokes. Well great, asshole, because the feds have an implant in our school… and I'm guessing the only reason he isn't behind bars with the rest of his Russian drug-lord family is because he cut a deal."

"Who the hell would have the balls to pull that off? Right in front of us?"

"Guess."

"Humor me."

"Pike… Phillip Petrov."

The phone dropped, cursing ensued, something broke in the background, and then Sergio was back on the phone. "Let me make some calls."

"What about Amazon? Boredom? Ring a bell?"

"Screw you." The phone went dead.

I turned around just in time to see Pike and the rest of his friends leave the lunch building. He put on a pair of sunglasses and looked in my direction. I flipped him the bird.

He clapped and gave a little bow.

"Russian bastard," I mouthed.

"Sicilian whore," he mouthed right back and laughed.

That was it. I was talking to Tex, and we were going to homeschool Bee; no way was I going to let him get to her.

I couldn't care less who he was or who he worked for.

One finger, one breath of air in her direction, and his body was going six feet under.

With pleasure.

CHAPTER ELEVEN

Ah, the young Turks… the new mafia, if we live that long.

Sergio

I THREW MY PHONE against the wall.

Second one I'd broken in two days.

Ha! A trend. Nice.

It didn't break, just cracked the screen, making it so I could still look at the number blinking back at me. Of course they knew I knew…because they knew every damn thing that went on.

"What?" I yelled into the phone. "Didn't think I needed to know that piece of information? If he's your boy. You better make sure he keeps his shit together before one of mine shoots his head off."

"So much anger…" A chuckle wheezed in my ear. "And yes, he's one of ours. Think of it as a way for us to make sure all your dealings with the university are legal. Besides, I thought the family didn't trust you anymore. Something you need to tell me?"

"Are you joking right now? Tell me you're joking and didn't implant a Petrov, of all people. You do realize his entire family would rather burn at the stake than save their own? They have no respect for family, no respect for blood, no respect for anything but money and drugs."

"Money talks… so does a promise of no prison sentence. You said no feds."

"Sure as hell looks like your hand's in the cookie jar."

"It only stays there until we're comfortable with how you're handling things within the family, Sergio. We never promised to go away. We're here, waiting for you to come back when it's time. Think of it as a way of making sure you won't take a misstep."

"We won't."

"Yet," he said in a deadly voice. "Yet."

"I'm done here. Hell, I'm done with you. I quit. I won't do it anymore. I won't help you."

"Fine." He sighed heavily. "So I'll have the boys bring you in around five o clock this afternoon? Pretty sure we can book you that early, though the court date won't be for another few months. I'm sure you'll be just fine in prison. By the way, the Russians would be more than happy to have a nice reunion. Maybe we'll let you start a fight club or something."

"One day…" I vowed, my teeth clenched so tight I thought a tooth would crack. "One day I'll kill you."

"I don't think so, son." He sighed. "Stay in touch. Oh, and that lasagna looked good last night. Tell your girlfriend to try to cook it from scratch next time, she is Siclian after all."

The phone line went dead.

In a rage, I started searching for the hidden cameras. Bastards always seemed to think it was funny spying on me. I only checked once a month, and I'd just checked last week. Actually, my brother, Ax, had checked; security recon on all the houses was part of his job description.

I went to all the usual spots.

I even opened the oven. Then finally just grabbed the jammer and let all hell break loose as the jarring sound of technology breaking singed my ears.

"Bingo." I dropped the jammer onto the table and hung my head. I should go to Nixon; hell, even going to Tex sounded like a good idea. But if they knew what I knew — it wouldn't end well. For me. I'd die. It wouldn't matter that I was family; it wouldn't matter that I was blood. Even Ax wouldn't stand in their way.

To them, I would be dead.

And they'd do me the great honor of sending me into the afterlife without praying for the very soul they punched out of my miserable body.

"Damn it." I hit the granite countertop and leaned forward. I was completely stuck, which meant only one thing.

In order to watch Petrov.

I was going to have to join Phoenix in the shit.

Slowly, I pulled up The Eagle Elite website and started going to work. I searched through my identities and found a resume that worked and then hacked the database.

When I was done... I poured myself a glass of wine and popped my knuckles.

I'd just sent a professor into early retirement and given him a hefty bonus in order to do it.

And I was his replacement.

"Doctor," I said aloud then shrugged. "Has a nice ring to it."

"You talking to yourself again?" Ax came into the room and pulled a bottle water out of the fridge. "I knocked, but apparently you and your computer were having a moment. Hope I'm not interrupting." He took a long swig of water.

"I'm going to teach."

He spit out the water onto the counter and started laughing. "You're going to teach what? How to bury a body in ten different ways without getting framed for murder? How to build a homemade silencer? How to piss off the genius bar at Apple?"

"You done?"

"Just getting started."

"I'm going to teach…" I gulped. "…American History."

Ax's eyebrows drew together slowly. "You're Sicilian."

"We're both American, asshole."

"Yeah, but did you even take history?"

"Ten years ago," I mumbled. "I'm also going to need something from you."

"Oh, no you don't." Ax held up his hands. "I'm married. I work for Nixon, not you. We just bought a house. We have a dog. I'm not burying any bodies so Nixon doesn't find out."

"Calm the hell down." I ran my fingers through my hair and paused. "I need you to…" I shrugged. "You know."

"Read your mind?"

"Shit, I hate you sometimes."

Ax grinned and took a seat. "You were saying?"

"I need you to cut my hair."

"Holy hell." His face turned serious. "You really are teaching history?"

"New identity. Can't look like the old Sergio. Now I'm just… Mathew Smith."

"Could you be any more white and nerdy?"

"Could you be a bigger pain in my ass? Cut the ponytail. I can't watch."

"But—" Ax sighed. "You said you wouldn't cut it until everyone was out of prison."

Ha! Little did he know that we would be going to prison if I didn't do something — fast. "Just do it, or I'll ask your wife."

"She doesn't touch your hair."'

"Then stop being a bitch and do it."

"You in deep, bro?"

"Trying not to be," I answered strategically. "You know I always liked to play hero."

"No, you didn't. I did."

"Well, maybe it's my turn."

He let out a sigh. "I'll grab the scissors."

CHAPTER TWELVE

Life hurts — sometimes I wonder if death is better. More peaceful.

Bee

PAIN SLICED THROUGH MY chest as I made my way to my next class. At least it was an easy class and not something that was going to make me want to cry, because I had no clue what was going on.

That was the other problem.

I swear I had a learning disability. The words always seemed to jumble in front of me when I got tired, and when it came to numbers, I was basically useless. But this was math, basic freshman-level math. I could do entry-level. How hard could it be?

I quickly found my desk and pulled out my notebook, just as Phoenix walked in the door and made a beeline in my direction.

One look to the kid sitting on my right, and suddenly the seat was empty. Well, look at that. I was surprised there wasn't a puddle underneath the chair or at least streaks of sweat in the seat.

"Gonna scare all my friends, asshole?"

Phoenix glared, folding his hands on the desk. He opened his mouth just as the professor walked in and started talking.

An hour and a half of teaching.

I learned nothing.

Because my chest still hurt.

It still felt like knives had taken up permanent residence in my body, slicing through skin and bone every single time Phoenix looked at me with clueless eyes. Like he wasn't aware of how I felt about him. Like I didn't matter, even though sometimes he said I did.

People have it wrong. When you lose someone, when they die, it hurts. It's horrible, don't get me wrong. But the type of pain that stays with you? That never alleviates, that never lessons with time? It's the kind that continues to refresh every single time you see a trigger or reminder of it.

Just being near Phoenix, knowing that I was nothing to him, that he'd protect me with his blood but never kiss me.

Knowing he was present but dead inside.

It killed me.

It was worse than him dying.

Because it was a constant tease, a constant reminder of what I couldn't have. Being with Phoenix was like suffering a death every single second of every single day, and I was powerless to stop it.

Class ended.

Phoenix stood. And like a good little girl, I followed him out the door.

I wasn't really paying attention and almost collided with another student.

"Oh, hey, Bee!" Pike stepped back and winked. "How was class?"

Phoenix growled.

I ignored him, though he made it difficult as he wrapped

his thick muscled arm around my shoulder. I half-expected him to lift his leg.

Shrugging him off, I beamed. "It was great."

Pike nodded. "Hey, a few of us are gonna go get coffee in a few minutes. You wanna come?"

"No," Phoenix answered for me. "She's busy."

"I am?" I turned, tempted to smack him on his perfect face. "What exactly am I busy doing?"

"Homework." He coughed." And she has to go to bed... early."

Embarrassment washed over me as I shook my head and offered Pike an apologetic smile. "Sorry about Grandpa. He didn't take his medicine this morning."

Pike burst out laughing.

Phoenix's face tensed. Nostrils flared. I knew that look; it wasn't a friendly one.

"You guys meeting at Starbucks?"

"Yup." Pike nodded. "Hey, give me your cell number, and I'll text you—"

"Nope." Phoenix pushed his outstretched phone away. "If she needs to get ahold of you, I'll put up a bat signal, superhero. Run along before I shoot you."

"Do it." Pike sneered. "You'd just go to prison. Shitty little De Lange thinks he can power-push on campus? Newsflash, you don't own this school anymore. I do. Hell, I'm surprised you even showed your face here after all the shit you did..."

With a curse, Phoenix gripped Pike by the shirt and slammed him against the wall. "Your're right, asshole. I did so much shit. Shit that would have you screaming like a little bitch and sleeping by your damn nightlight. I kill, and here's *your* little newsflash..." He grinned menacingly. "I enjoy it. So make me an offer I can't refuse... I've always loved a good chase."

Pike's smile fell.

With one last shove, Phoenix slammed his hand above the wall and then ushered me out of the building. Fingers dug into the sensitive flesh above my elbow as I stumbled beside him.

My heart was pounding so fast I could feel it in my throat, threatening to choke the life out of me.

We didn't say anything until we got to his car.

When the door slammed, Phoenix released me and pinched the bridge of his nose whispering, "Remember, little girl, his precious little life is in your frail hands."

"What?" I hissed then glanced around us to make sure nobody could hear "You'd kill him?"

"Doll..." Phoenix barked out a laugh. "You have no idea what I'd do to him — what I'd enjoy doing to him. What I'm capable of." His eyes flashed. "Don't push me over the ledge we both know I'm already teetering on, because I will fall into the darkness embracing every damned part of myself, and it's going to be on you. All you."

He meant it.

I knew he meant it. Phoenix's eyes brimmed with hatred; I could almost see the anger steaming off his body as his chest heaved. What would it be like to help him carry some of it? To be the friend he actually needed.

"Should you really be threatening the Cappo's sister?" Yeah, I just had to poke the bear harder.

With a smirk, Phoenix pushed me against the car, his finger jamming into my chest. "Doll, I don't care if you're dripping in gold and the secret to mankind's future survival. You listen to me or people get hurt. Those are your choices."

"So." I gulped. "You hurt people to prove a point?"

"No," he growled. "I hurt people to keep you safe. I hurt people to make sure you breathe another damn day. I hurt people out of necessity, not out of desire. But one false move and the lines blur, princess. They blur into one. The minute that happens I won't hesitate to blame you every single day for the rest of my life, for waking the beast that should have stayed silent."

"It's a choice," I croaked.

"No." Phoenix backed away. "It's my miserable existence. Now get in the damn car. You have homework." He moved around and opened his own door while my fingers were having difficulty even connecting with the smooth steel.

Finally, the door opened. I got in and crossed my arms. Pissed at him for making me feel stupid. Again. Angry that his opinion really meant that much to me. And lost… yeah, that's what that empty feeling was.

I belonged nowhere.

Was wanted by no one.

And the one guy who invited me to coffee was going to get freaking killed if I as much as sent him an emoji text.

We drove in silence the entire way to the house — if silence counted as Phoenix's heavy breathing and cursing under his breath in Sicilian. The guy still looked like he wanted to run with the bulls and bring a semi-automatic, just in case one of them got feisty.

Phoenix put the car in park.

I didn't move.

I was scared to do anything except look straight out the window. But I wasn't scared of him. He would never hurt me.

Maybe I was scared of me, scared of my reaction to him, scared that when he did nothing but warn me away, I was desperate for more attention and would do anything to get it.

"Bee…" His voice was gruff. "…I need you to understand something."

I exhaled, waiting for another scolding.

Instead, Phoenix's voice was barely above a whisper. "Guys like Pike, guys like me… we aren't the good guys. The ones girls dream about. We don't bring flowers to a first date, we don't wait the allotted few dates for sex or a kiss. We don't imagine a white picket fence, a yard full of kids, and a dog named Spot. That's not our reality, but, princess, it could be yours. Tex wants that for you. I want that for you. So please... just listen to me when I warn you. It's not because I'm a sick controlling bastard who's hell bent on keeping you from having fun and living your life. It's because I'm a controlling bastard who can't imagine a life where even one hair on your head is out of place."

Tears pooled in my eyes. Slowly, I turned, waiting to see the usual anger behind his eyes.

Instead, all I saw was regret.

Regret on Phoenix looked like a gaping black hole just waiting to be filled with something — anything that would make the darkness go away. Hollow. He was so hollow and empty.

I reached out.

He jerked back. "Homework."

"Right, God forbid you and I actually have a moment."

His lips curled as if he was about to smile, and then he coughed in his hand. "Believe me, if we were having a moment, you'd know it."

"Warm fuzzies?"

"I don't do warm fuzzies."

Well, can't win 'em all.

"I do scorching blazes," he muttered under his breath. "That sear you alive."

My heartbeat quickened. "I'm trying to find the romance in that."

"Ha! Try all you want." He nodded. "You'll find no romance in me."

"Is that a challenge?"

"Good God, Bee, just get out of the damn car so I can put it in the garage."

"You better hope you put up a good fight, Phoenix." I stepped out of the car and leaned my head in. "Because I don't give up easily."

His face transformed in that moment from hollow to hopeful, almost as if his own body and soul were screaming for me to keep pursuing, even though his words said something else entirely.

"You're always welcome to try whatever you want in your free time, Bee. But it will never happen. Now, run along, do your homework, pour yourself a glass of milk, and if you're a really good girl, I'll turn on *Cartoon Network.*"

"Go to hell, Phoenix." I rolled my eyes at his grunt then slammed the door in his face and stomped up the stairway into the house.

CHAPTER THIRTEEN

Life is made up of crappy days rolling into more crappy days with maybe one good day in between. Unless you're Phoenix De Lange; then you get no good days. Only bad.

Phoenix

I PULLED INTO THE garage and turned off the car. The desire to chase after Bee had been so strong that my body ached. Everything about her told me to stay away, but her eyes... they were like bread, water, my possible survival. My body craved her, and I hated myself for it.

Which was pretty impressive, considering how much I already loathed my own existence.

She was making everything worse.

And we were... what? We were officially at Day One, and I was ready to do something. Hell, my fingers itched for me to do something irrevocable, something that would put me at odds with my new family and at odds with my old one.

With a curse, I got out of the car and made my way into the house.

Screaming erupted from the kitchen.

Sergio and what sounded like Nixon.

Wow, as far as days went, this one wasn't turning out to be my favorite. I rounded the corner and froze.

"Sergio?" I blinked twice. "What the hell did you do to yourself?"

"Makeover," Bee said from the corner, lifting a can of coke to her lips and watching in rapt fascination. "He cut his hair."

"Why?" I shook my head. "I thought you liked the whole Prince Charming look."

"Yeah." Nixon pushed against Sergio then set his gun on the table and spun it round and round. Ha! Nice, almost like spin the bottle, only the end game is someone getting shot. "We'd all really like to know, Sergio. Why the sudden change of appearance? You thinking of going underground?"

Sergio rolled his eyes, briefly glancing at me then at Nixon. "It's complicated."

"Uncomplicate it..." Nixon seethed. "...before I shoot you."

The gun spun again. Nixon's finger settled on the trigger. Shit. Whoever said that marriage tamed the man had been clearly deranged.

Sergio exhaled a curse then bit down on his lip, damn near drawing blood from the looks of it. "I'm going undercover."

"Why?" Nixon leaned over the gun and pointed it straight for Sergio's heart. "Why now? You've been more than happy tinkering away on your computers."

"Hacking," I said helpfully, reaching for a bottled water from the countertop.

"Well..." Sergio closed his eyes. "...I got a fun little phone call from Phoenix. It seems that the feds have an implant at Elite."

"The hell they do!" Nixon spat.

"Actually…" I swallowed. "They do, but this isn't the place to discuss anything." My eyes fell to Bee.

She was grinning from ear to ear; then she ran her finger along her plump lips as if zipping them. "Come on, guys. I'm like a vault."

"Guarantee I could tap you in three seconds flat." I growled.

Her cheeks went pink.

Both Sergio and Nixon went deathly silent.

Hell-in-a-freaking-handbasket. Not what I meant.

"Not like that guys." I rolled my eyes as if my brain wasn't conjuring up images of said tapping and her soft body beneath mine. The image always ended up horrific, so I pushed it away — far, far away — and popped my knuckles. "We'll talk tonight at the meeting." I shrugged.

Nixon nodded slowly. "Fine, but if shit-for-brains makes a run for it…" He pointed at Sergio. "Shoot him."

Ah, nice.

"Please." Sergio let out a sour chuckle. "Phoenix has been itching to shoot me, way-ta tempt him."

Nixon shrugged. "Not my problem." He picked up his gun. "I'll see you guys tonight…" He paused and almost smiled. "Bee, how was school?"

"Awesome!" She glanced at me and winked. "Phoenix even held my hand the whole way to class."

"Did not," I said in an entirely way-too-defensive voice.

"But he wanted to." She nodded as a smug grin spread over her face. "I could tell by the way he kept looking at my cleavage and licking his lips."

"Dear God, I know I deserve everything I get, but hell, could you just *stop* for *one minute*?"

She grinned. "Nope. I like driving you insane. You like that I like it too. Admit it, and I'll stop."

"Never."

"Kids…" Nixon held up his hands. "…bicker later. And

Phoenix, a word?"

I glared at Bee and followed Nixon out of the house. How I hadn't noticed that his car had been parked in front was just another clue as to why the hell I needed to stay focused on my job and not Bee. I missed details when I focused on her, details I couldn't afford to miss.

"How'd it really go?" He put on his aviators and stuffed his hands in his pockets.

"Oh, you know." I crossed my arms as the winter air bit into my sweater. "As can be expected. I hate that place, Nixon, you know that. Just being there…"

That was the most honest I'd been with any of the guys.

Nixon was the only one I felt like I could let my guard down with. He wouldn't hold it against me, would merely nod his head and pat me on the back.

He was a rock. One I didn't deserve.

"Have you thought of maybe talking to someone about it?"

"Ha!" My smile mocked his sentiment. "And say what exactly? Pretty sure any shrink is going to turn me in for the demons I unleash in his office."

"You have me."

"I have no one," I spat then instantly regretted being an ass. "Look, Nixon, I know you're trying to help, and I know I don't deserve it. Let me just deal with things on my own. I promise it will get better. I just need time. It heals all… right?"

He hung his head. "I wish I believed that."

"Yeah. Me too."

"See you tonight."

"Can't wait," I said sarcastically. "You know, being boss isn't exactly an all-night party with unlimited booze and girls."

Nixon barked out a loud laugh and unlocked his Range Rover. "No shit."

WE MET AT EIGHT that night. To my great dismay, Bee wouldn't let me leave her at the house; she'd said she was afraid of the dark, and frankly, I was so tired of arguing with her I had only been able to only grunt and make sure she wore a seatbelt.

I was exhausted.

Nightmares had a way of stealing all sleep from a person while systematically eating at the soul.

When we got to Nixon's house, Bee opened the door and rushed past the guys and straight into the living room, where I'd told her the girls would be hanging out and watching movies.

"Did I ever have that much energy?" Tex asked, once I joined them at the kitchen table.

"Your sister's on drugs." Chase tilted his head. "Either that or she just really likes movies."

"Yes, to all of the above," I grumbled and reached for a glass of water.

It was our second meeting. All the bosses were present, and since I was new, I had the unfortunate job of having to take notes at the meetings to make sure I didn't take a misstep.

What made it worse was that Luca had been a crazed man when it came to how he ran his network.

All killings were clean.

All transactions so clean it made a man wonder if he was even in the mafia.

All connections? Clean.

He was a relative god, and I had to follow in his footsteps. Right, the dirtiest of dirty had to take over the business. I spent most nights alternating between delegating jobs out to the associates and wondering what the hell I was going to do if any of them decided to rise up against me.

Loyalty wasn't passed down.

It was earned.

And I'd barely been given two weeks to get it.

"So, how was school?" Chase asked, a shit-eating grin spreading across his face.

I itched to punch the ass in the jaw. "I learned so very much." I scowled. "How was babysitting?"

He swore under his breath. "I wasn't babysitting."

"You were," Tex piped up. "Like all day."

"Babysitting means I was watching a kid. Instead, I was watching some punk-ass-associate do his first deed."

"You watched him in the bathroom?" Nixon joked.

Chase flipped him the bird just as Mil, my stepsister, took a seat and huffed out. "How long does this have to be? I need to clean my gun."

"Hot." Tex winked.

Chase growled.

The door opened, and Sergio walked in with Ax.

The entire room fell silent as all eyes watched Sergio take a seat at the table. Ax held up his hands. "Before everyone starts yelling, yes, he cut his hair. Yes, I helped him. It's not a big deal."

Tex stood. "Nobody changes a hair on their head in this business without some pretty damn good reason."

"Sit!" Nixon barked.

Tex's eyes narrowed, but he sat, which was a small miracle, given he outranked Nixon in every freaking way.

"Let's start at the beginning." Nixon held out his hands on the table.

"Like…" Tex sneered. "…why the hell Sergio decided to stop looking like a little girl and cut his hair like a big boy? If you run, I will find you."

"I'm not running." Sergio's voice was gruff, his accent more pronounced. "I have intel from your boy that a Petrov's at Elite."

All eyes fell to me. "Yeah," I croaked. "And, Tex, stop staring at me like that. Bee's fine. I threatened the guy within an inch of his life. But it's Pike. The only reason he'd be at Elite would be because he's an implant... no way would we actually let the bastard in. Whose job is it to look at enrollment anyway?"

All eyes fell to Chase.

Cursing, he shook his head. "Look, if I had seen a Petrov, I would have shot him in the ass before he even stepped foot onto campus. And FYI, it's not like we haven't been busy making sure Tex doesn't kill everyone."

"Valid point," Sergio muttered.

"Oh, screw you!" Tex stood again.

"Tex." Nixon seethed. "Sit."

"Like a good boy." Sergio laughed.

Tex pulled out his gun. "Say it again. Really, I've been wanting to kill you for weeks."

"Pull," Chase whispered under his breath.

I cleared my throat loudly. "Petrov's in the school. I called Sergio first thing for confirmation. The rest is his to tell."

Sergio ran his fingers through his short dark hair. It had a slight wave to it now that it wasn't long, not that I usually paid attention to that sort of thing, but if the idea was to make him look younger than his twenty-eight years, it worked. "I'm going to teach."

"Ways to hack Amazon?" This from Tex.

"Ways to steal social security numbers." Chase nodded. "Awesome."

"History." Ax spoke up, his eyes alight with humor.

And silence. Again.

Followed by howls of laughter.

The only people not laughing were me and Sergio. Then again, I never laughed.

Sergio scowled. "It will keep me close. I can gain intel, help Phoenix out since he's the only other brave soul willing to hang out at Elite."

"I graduated!" Chase all but yelled, as if he was petrified

Nixon was going to make him go back into hell.

Tex nodded his agreement. "We both did."

And I hadn't — the unsaid little jab.

Sergio rolled his eyes. "Whatever. I have two doctorates."

"Thus the teaching." Nixon clasped his hands in front of him. "Fine, gather whatever intel you can. It's possible Petrov is there just to make sure we aren't doing anything… illegal."

"Right, because we're known for following the government's rules." I swore.

Nixon shrugged. "We've survived a commission. We can survive anything. Now, on to the rest of business. Phoenix…"

Why the hell was I in the hot seat?

"…how's the adjustment?"

"Awesome. Someone even sent me flowers yesterday with a thank-you card. How the hell do you think it's been?" I looked away from everyone and stared out the window. "My old family despises me, and my new family would rather see me drown than take over the Nicolasi empire. So, between babysitting the Cappo's sister, making sure she walks in straight lines and doesn't get herself shot — oh, and running a multi-million dollar enterprise, I'm pretty sure I'll never sleep again, not that I ever got much sleep to begin with, but whatever."

Chase slapped me on the back. Yeah, the last thing I wanted was comfort. "Give it time."

If I heard that one more time. I was going to scream. I made brief eye contact with Nixon.

He cleared his throat and started asking Chase questions about the new associate.

Officially out of the line of fire.

My ears tuned out the rest of the conversation as feminine laughter floated in from the living room.

Her laughter.

Bee.

"Phoenix?" Nixon barked.

"Hmm?"

"Does that sound good?"

"Sure," I lied. What the hell were we discussing?

"Really?" Tex's eyebrows drew together. "Well, I guess if he's okay with it, I have to be. Nobody else is going to protect her anyway." He stood, basically meaning the meeting was over, while I stayed glued to my seat, wondering what the hell I'd just agreed to.

The guys and Mil went into the kitchen and grabbed a bottle of wine.

Chase stayed next to me. "You do realize what you just agreed to?"

"Suicide?"

"Sort of." He chuckled. "Look, I still haven't forgiven you. I still don't think you're clean, so you know it's bad if even I feel sorry for you."

"What? Why?"

"Freshman class trip." He nodded, and a smile broke out across his face. "You just agreed to go."

"Class trip?"

"A weekend of fun up in the mountains... the hot springs... bikinis, Tex's sister..." He whistled. "Yeah, have fun with that, monk."

I snorted. "I have self-control."

"Right." Chase leaned in, whispering. "And we both know it's only a matter of time before that thread freaking snaps, and in the end, who do you think's going to cause it?"

As if knowing our entire conversation, Bee waltzed into the room and pinned me with a helpless look. "Math homework? I think I'm stuck, and the girls can't help me."

That made no sense. Couldn't help? They had no problem with math — adding, anyway — when they raided the stores on their mega-shopping trips. I stared at Bee. Had she even asked them?

"Yeah, good luck with that." Chase slapped me on the

back. "I highly doubt Tex is going to give you any sort of blessing for the thoughts running through your head."

"I don't think like that... not anymore."

Bee put her hands on her hips and tilted her head in my direction. Her lips pressed together in what was probably supposed to look like irritation, when really I felt something entirely different.

"Then you really are dead inside. Because that girl looks at you like you just promised to buy her the moon — and you look at her as if you did more than promise it."

He walked away.

Bee hefted her book onto the table. "What was that about?"

"Astronomy," Chase called behind him. "Have fun kids!"

I wiped my face with my hands as she plopped down next to me and pulled her chair as close as humanly possible. Her vanilla-scented essence damn near suffocated me to death.

"I feel stupid." Her shoulders hunched. "I mean, it's Basic Math 101, and I'm confused already."

Math I could do. Just focus on the numbers.

With a deep breath, I pulled out her notebook and snatched the pen. "Alright, let's start at the beginning."

CHAPTER FOURTEEN

Sometimes I just wish he would see me.

Bee

"IT MAKES NO SENSE!" I hunched into myself and slumped against my chair. "I know you're thinking it, you may as well say it." We'd been back at the house for over an hour, and I still wasn't any further than we had been at dinner.

Phoenix's eyebrows drew together in confusion before his scowl was replaced by a softness I'd never seen grace his face before. "Bee, you're not stupid."

"Yeah, I am." Everything about school was hard. I probably wouldn't have even made it into college without my brother's help. "But whatever, it's fine. I've got my looks, right?"

Phoenix slammed the book closed and pulled me to my feet.

"Whoa, I was kidding. You don't have to lock me in the pantry or anything."

We'd gotten home an hour ago. Phoenix had promised to help me finish the rest of my homework, but I was a useless case. Even Sergio threw up his hands and walked off.

Story of my life.

It was nearing midnight, and I still had hours of reading to go through.

Phoenix released my hand then opened the fridge. "How many lasagnas?"

"Um..." The cold air hit me in the face. "One?"

"It's just a lasagna, like those are just numbers. They don't hold any power over you yet. For someone who hasn't experienced real food in a long time? It may as well be like climbing Everest. Every bite, every damn time you chew, it's painful. It's hard even when it shouldn't be because you're the one making it hard. You stop looking at it as food and decipher it as a threat, as just one more step into something that could be your downfall."

He slammed the door shut then ushered me back to the table and pointed at the math homework. "This is your Everest. We all have them. We all struggle. But that doesn't make you any less intelligent. It makes you different. Don't let the thing that terrifies you overcome you so much that you can't even take a bite. So we start slow. We start at the beginning. And eventually, you'll be able to eat the whole plate, or in your case, finish every problem. You helped me with lasagna. I'll help you with this."

I choked back a sob. "Because I fed you?"

"No." Phoenix stood, running his hands through his hair, giving me a view of his six-pack because his dark black shirt had ridden up. "Because you were the only one who even recognized I was hungry."

Stunned, I could only stare at him.

The room buzzed with tension as his eyes met mine, and not just in a way that was indifferent. Something had changed, altered. I wasn't sure if it was me or him.

"Thank you," I whispered, "for making me feel better."

Phoenix's lips twitched. "Nobody's ever thanked me for

making them feel better."

"Good. Then I'm your first."

He shut down. His eyes closed, his lips stopped that sexy twitch, and instead of opening up more, he crossed his arms and shrugged. "Go to bed, and I'll help you with the last two problems in the morning."

Apparently, the conversation was over.

I nodded and turned on my heel, not wanting to tempt fate, knowing that each moment I was given with him was something I should keep for myself and protect with my life.

It was nearing midnight, so I quickly grabbed a shower and went to bed. Only, I couldn't sleep. Story of my life. It was like Phoenix was rubbing off on me, or maybe it was just the fact that I'd been so used to being his captive that having freedom of my own was weird.

"Stop squirming!" he said in a hoarse voice.

"Well! I saw a rat!" I fired back. "And why the hell is my father keeping me in the basement of all places?"

"He's protecting you."

He was lying; this new associate of my father's was lying. And I hated him for it. Hated him almost as much as I hated my own father.

"Screw you!"

He rolled his eyes; I could see the movement even though it was dark.

Something scratched at my leg.

With a squeal, I backed away and landed in the guy's lap.

He shoved me off.

So I took the opportunity to shove him back.

What ensued was him pinning my wrists above my head and nearly head-butting me. "Stay calm before I give you a reason to scream."

"In pleasure?" I teased, trying to gain an advantage even if it was sexual. It was the only thing I had to work with. He had a gun. I had my body.

"You're a child," he spat. "Like you could hold my interest."

I leaned in and whispered against his lips, "I already do."

He backed away like I'd just shot him in the face and swore into the blackness.

"So, what's your name, soldier?" I finally asked when he was done swearing.

"Phoenix."

"Like the bird?"

"Like the ash."

"The bird rises from the ashes…"

"Yeah, too bad the story ends there."

"Huh?"

"What happens after the bird rises?" His voice was hoarse. "I'll let you in on a little secret." He leaned in so close to me I could smell his spicy cologne. "It does everything it can to keep from falling."

"So don't fall."

"Then stop tempting me to jump."

That was it. Our first conversation. After that, Phoenix had given me a wide berth, and I never could decipher what he'd meant. At first I'd thought he was attracted to me, but the more I got to know him, the more I realized that the guy was clearly indifferent to all females. All humanity.

I punched my pillow and turned on my side.

The clock said 1:30 a.m. Great. I was officially going to look like crap in the morning. I had one more day of classes before the freshman class trip. I may have told my brother I was going rather than asked, but whatever. He wanted me to live my life. I was going to live it. And that started with meeting boys who weren't named Phoenix and gaining a kiss from someone who actually liked me.

"Whatever." I scrambled from my bed and made my way down to the kitchen to get a glass of juice. Brilliant light spilled through the doorway, and I entered to find Phoenix sprawled across the table, papers scattered all over the place. It looked like chaos had taken up permanent residence.

I pulled the juice from the fridge, poured myself a glass, and watched Phoenix sleep.

Like a total loser.

He looked so peaceful, like he didn't hate the world or hate his position within it.

I tapped my fingernails against the glass in my hand, tempted to wake him up almost as much as I was tempted to watch his beautiful face. He was breathtaking, the type of hot that girls gossiped about. Strong jaw, full lips, perfect face. Damn, the man looked like he didn't have a scar on him. But I'd seen his back; they were just hidden, expertly so, as if someone had beaten him every day of his life only to make sure nobody ever found out.

I cleared my throat.

He didn't move.

Setting the glass down, I walked over to him and poked him in the shoulder with one of the pens lying on the table.

He jerked awake.

And instead of yelling at me or cursing, he simply pointed a gun at my head.

I jolted back.

"Bee?" He set the gun down. "Damn it, don't sneak up on me."

"Then don't moan my name in your sleep!"

His face paled. "I was saying your name?"

I grinned as a surge of triumph washed over me. "Guess you'll never know. By the way, we have school tomorrow, so you should probably go to bed."

"Sleep." He pushed away from the table and stood, his body cracking as if he was ancient rather than in his early twenties. "Right."

"I could always keep you company," I offered. "Like we used to—"

"Hell, no!" He stomped right past me, nearly knocking me against the granite countertop. "Go to sleep, Bee."

"Right." I swallowed, all excitement from his earlier reaction flew out the window. "Night, Phoenix."

The only sound left was that of his footsteps banging on the stairway and the slow drip from the faucet.

I sank onto the chair he'd just vacated and glanced at the paperwork in front of me.

It looked like gibberish. Lots of numbers, names, contacts, off-shore accounts. Really, none of my business.

I pushed some of the pictures around; my fingers hovered over one of a girl who'd been badly beaten.

She looked familiar.

After a quick glance at the doorway to make sure Phoenix wasn't coming back, I picked up the picture.

Trace Rooks, now Trace Abandonato.

She looked horrific.

I put the picture down and picked up the next one. Bruises lined her ribcage.

Was this what Phoenix was protecting me from? Some sick bastard getting his hands on me or using me against my own brother?

With a shudder, I picked up the final picture; a sticky note was attached to it. *"Fingerprint match with Phoenix De Lange — watch list."*

Gasping, I dropped the picture back onto the table.

"So," a hoarse voice said from the doorway. "Now you know... Those invitations you keep throwing out may as well be labeled monster. I highly doubt you want that anywhere near your bed. Sleep, Bee."

Phoenix grabbed a bottle of water from the table and left the room.

He did that?

To Trace?

But why? Why would he hurt a girl? A woman? And how did Nixon let him live? A tremor of unease wracked my body.

I lay down knowing full well sleep would elude me, not because I wasn't tired. I was exhausted. But images of Phoenix hurting Trace seemed to be the only thing my brain would focus on.

By the time I woke up the next morning, I couldn't even bring myself to be chatty. I grabbed a granola bar and went to the car where Phoenix was waiting.

The drive to school was painfully silent.

Finally, I couldn't take it anymore. "Can I at least ask why?"

"Why?" He turned off the ignition. A muscle popped in his jaw. He knew damn well what I was asking him.

"Why did you beat her up?" My voice sounded so foreign and small; long gone was the teasing of yesterday.

He snorted. "I didn't just beat her up. I damn near raped her. Is that what you wanted to hear, Bee? That I'm the monster that goes bump in the night and steals girls' virginity?" He shook his head and slammed his hand against the steering wheel. "The sooner you stop looking at me like I'm your hero the better off we'll both be."

I swallowed, desperate to get rid of the giant lump in my throat. "And how am I supposed to look at you?"

He turned slowly, his eyes meeting mine. "Exactly how you are right now. Like I'm a monster. Because I am. Now get out of the car before you're late for class."

I scrambled out of the car, more out of irritation and anger than fear. He'd almost raped her, and, no matter how many times I tried to come up with a reason for him doing something so horrific, all I could decide was that he wasn't the man I thought he was.

The Phoenix I knew, while scary, didn't seem capable of doing those things to Trace, to his best friend's wife.

The Phoenix I knew had stood in front of me when the first gunshot had rung out, when my father had returned from one of his drinking binges and pointed the gun at my forehead, a regular occurrence, since, according to him, I resembled my cursed brother too much.

Phoenix was a protector not a monster.

To me? Never a monster.

But the evidence was there, in pictures — graphic pictures. I should stop asking questions, stop wanting to claw at the truth.

His answer hadn't made me less curious.

Or less hesitant to want to find out what made him tick.

If anything, it had fanned the flame. Yes, I was disgusted and fearful, but there was more to the story; otherwise, he would be dead.

My own brother trusted him.

So by default — I trusted him.

I just wished I knew, after seeing all that, why I still did.

And why I still wanted to.

CHAPTER FIFTEEN
Back to where it all began…

Sergio

I STRAIGHTENED THE PAPERS on my desk and watched the clock like it was a damn grenade. Each tick may as well have been someone chanting *pull… pull… pull.*

Students shuffled in the classroom, most of them looking more innocent than what I expected from an Eagle Elite freshman. I suddenly felt extremely ancient, like I was one unfortunate sneeze away from having to replace my hip and go on blood thinners.

"Yo." A kid nodded at me.

Shit, did I look like his homie?

"You new?"

No. Old. So. Very. Old.

"Find your seat." I barely restrained myself from barking at him then pulling out a gun just to see if the kid would really shit his pants. Then again, it would probably just solidify that whole homie statement.

Groaning, I pinched the bridge of my nose and waited for

the rest of the students — kids, young ones with less chest hair than my aunt — find their seats and wait for me, their new teacher to open his mouth.

A few girls giggled.

I hated giggles; it was as bad as having to watch Tex and Mo hump one another during family dinner. The giggles continued — okay, so it was almost as bad.

I checked my watch one last time and cleared my throat. "I'm Mr. Thomas. I'll be your professor for US History this semester."

Blank stares.

Yeah, this was going to be absolute torture. I started handing out the syllabus and waited for the inevitable, a hand to pop up.

I had already calculated who it would be.

The girl or guy who had something to prove, teacher's pet, not a hair out of place, and probably still a virgin. Yay me.

One, two, three, four — ah, and there it is, ladies and gentleman. A hand popped up from the back of the class.

I kept my smile to myself and barely managed to keep a mocking laugh in. The hand belonged to a girl, but I couldn't see her face; she was too small, hidden behind a kid who looked like he was once a defensive lineman.

"Yes?" I tilted my head. "Please stand while you ask your question, Miss…?"

"Oh!" She popped out of her seat, knocking a book to the floor and nearly tripping over her own feet. So maybe I was wrong after all.

She blinked overly large brown eyes in my direction as if she was confused as to where she was and tucked a piece of white-blond hair behind her ear. She looked like she belonged in the elf kingdom of *Lord of The Rings*. Her features were seamless, perfect, from her petite bow-shaped lips to her little button nose.

Beautiful.

"Yes?" I said hoarsely. "Your name and question?"

"Andi," she said slowly. "And I was wondering if you would be keeping track of attendance. It doesn't say on the syllabus and—"

"Planning on skipping class, Andi?"

"No, but—"

"Is your education not important? Tell me, how much money does it cost to sit in one of these chairs over the course of twenty-four hours?"

Another hand shot up.

"Yes?"

"Eight-hundred-and-seventy dollars a day, sir."

"Bingo." I didn't take my eyes away from Andi; couldn't if I tried. "So you tell me, Andi, would it be in your best interest to throw away that type of money?"

"No." Her lower lip trembled. "No, sir."

"Good answer," I said in a low tone. "Now, any more questions about the syllabus?"

"But..." Andi raised her hand again, still standing; the rest of the class groaned.

Surprised, I arched my eyebrows as I stared at her. "But what?"

"Um..." She twisted her hands in front of her. "I, um, I have a condition, and sometimes I need to skip class because of it."

Her cheeks turned a dull shade of red.

The class burst out into hushed laughter while I continued to stare her down. "Condition?"

She nodded.

"See me after class, Andi."

With a quick nod, she finally took her seat, and I was free to discuss expectations to the rest of the class. While I talked and they listened, or pretended to listen, I did a mental checklist of each individual: none of them posed a threat, but two of the guys sitting in the front row liked to hang around

Pike and his friends, which meant they were officially on my radar, a place nobody should want to be, if they wanted to live to see graduation day.

An hour later, I was dismissing class, and Andi was making her way toward my desk. I studied her movements: the light airy way she walked, the sway of her hips, and the closed-off expression on her face. Her eyes really were huge; a guy could get lost in those eyes.

A guy much younger.

Much more available and not currently pretending to be a teacher in order to possibly order a hit on a drug family.

"Sir…" Andi stopped walking and crossed her arms. "I'm sorry for interrupting your class and asking silly questions. It's just my condition."

"Yes." I gave a curt nod. "Your condition? Do you have a doctor's note?"

"Well, the doctor doesn't know I'm a vampire, and that may be weird so…"

"Huh?" I blinked.

She grinned. "I was kidding… making a joke."

"Ha," I said dryly. "Now, your condition?"

Andi heaved out a sigh. "Sometimes I get sick and can't make it to class. I've already spoken to the campus nurse. I'll be sure to get you a note explaining the details."

"Why don't you explain the details?"

"Talking about your own death is kind of a mood killer for the second day of school." She shrugged. "But if you're asking about my terminal condition…"

"No." I held up my hand, feeling sick to my stomach. What kind of monster had I turned into that I couldn't be sensitive to something so serious? "Don't worry about a thing."

"You don't have to do that," she whispered.

"Do what?" I stood and started packing the extra pieces of paper into my briefcase.

"Pity me," she said softly. "I get that enough from my dad. Pity just makes it worse... but feel free to be grumpy like you were before. Makes me feel more normal."

Chink. Was that the sound of my armor breaking?

With a gulp, I turned to face her again. "So you want normal treatment?"

Her shoulders sagged with relief.

I fought a smile. "Then get the hell out of my class. I have more important things to do."

Her grin damn near brought me to my knees. "Thanks, sir."

"Anytime," I croaked and stared as she bounced out the door. I continued staring at that same door for at least five minutes and tried to figure out why I suddenly felt off-balance, like the world was tilting and I was standing still.

Low blood sugar.

Not interest.

And definitely not attraction.

After all, she was as good as dead.

And so was I.

CHAPTER SIXTEEN

Squirrels piss Phoenix off — note to self.

Bee

THE ONLY BRIGHT SPOT in my day was when Chuck, the woodland creature I'd befriended, followed me to class or at least tried to until Phoenix told it to screw off.

He didn't just rain on parades; he freaking hurricaned them, and then when that didn't work, he stomped around and made obscene gestures with his gun. It seemed no matter what I did that morning, it pissed him off.

I tried giving him a granola bar as a peace offering, and he threw it in the trash.

When I tripped over my own feet, trying to get into the building on time for my morning classes, he told me to watch where I was walking, and that if I tripped again, he was going to put me in a wheelchair and push me down a hill.

My last class of the day was a human anatomy and physiology lab that had me ready to puke into my brand new boots and take off running in the other direction.

But it was a Gen-Ed, so if I wanted to please my brother

and not make Phoenix want to strangle me, I had to walk into the classroom.

My feet froze as I stepped through the doorway.

"It's just another class, Bee." Phoenix sighed. "A few more steps and you can find your seat. A few more steps after that and you can sit down."

"I don't like blood," I whispered, feeling my face go pale just thinking about it. Would I have to dissect things? Holy crap, was the room swaying? And why in the heck were there pictures of parts on the wall? Human parts. A pair of lungs, a stomach, a heart. Dear God, I was going to lose my breakfast, lunch, and possibly not be able to eat dinner.

I swayed again.

Phoenix gripped my arm in his hand and walked me over to an empty desk.

"Bee?" He cupped my face with his hands, his blue eyes laced with concern. "Bee, are you okay?"

"I don't like blood."

"You said that."

"It should stay inside the body."

"For the most part, it does." His smile was small, inviting.

I leaned in until my forehead touched his chest.

He tensed but didn't push me away; instead he patted my back awkwardly. "You think you can handle sitting in here for forty-five minutes? I have it on good authority you won't be cutting anything up today."

I jerked back and covered my mouth with my hands.

He let out a low chuckle. "Okay, so no mention of parts or blood."

I shook my head no, which only made the room spin faster. Right, I talked a big game about being violent and taking care of myself, but I was pretty confident that if I had to actually follow through, I'd be more traumatized than I was willing to admit.

"Blood isn't all bad, Bee."

"Not helping," I said through my hands.

"Blood…" Phoenix leaned in. "…pumps through your body, keeps you alive." He reached out and grabbed one of my hands then turned it around, his fingers tracing the inside of my forearm. "Look at the blue lines… the lines that carry your blood, the miracle that's life. Here's the thing, Bee. You should never be afraid of something that gives you life, purpose, meaning. This blood—" He tapped my skin with his fingertips. "—holds every part of you, and look, it's on the inside, where it belongs. Nothing to fear."

"Nothing to fear," I repeated in a wobbly voice.

"Right." He pulled back and popped his fingers then flexed his hands a few times before scooting his chair away.

"Phoenix?"

"What?" He didn't turn to look at me.

The professor walked in and turned down the lights as the PowerPoint presentation started.

"What are you afraid of?"

He cursed under his breath, still not meeting my eyes. "That's one secret I think I'll keep to myself."

"Bees?"

He pressed his lips together, but a smile escaped. "Yeah, I'm scared of getting stung."

I smiled back, even though he wasn't looking at me, and whispered so only he could hear. "Well, the good news is I don't sting."

He sighed. "But you do. You just don't realize you're doing it."

Phoenix scooted his chair away.

And that was the end of the conversation. I wondered if I'd made it up, the little moment we shared.

But, at the end of class, he was different, not as distant, not as… sad.

"Bee!" Pike rushed toward me. "Hey, you going to Freshman Retreat this weekend?"

"Yup." I took a step closer to Phoenix. "Wouldn't miss it."

Pike eyed me up and down. "Can't wait."

Phoenix coughed.

Pike rolled his eyes. "Well, I guess I'll see you tomorrow morning. Or are you not taking the bus?"

"I'm taking her," Phoenix barked.

"Easy." Pike held up his hands. "Geez, Bee, think you could tell your guard dog to lay off a bit? At least give him a treat or something."

Phoenix lunged toward him.

Pike stumbled backward and laughed. "Easy dude. Bee, seriously, put him on a leash."

In a flash, Phoenix was reaching for his gun.

I moved to stand in front of him and forced a laugh. "See ya later, Pike, we have a thing we have to get to."

"Right." He nodded then walked off.

Phoenix's breath was hot on the back of my neck. "Don't you ever do that again."

"What?" I didn't move.

"Stand between my gun and my target."

"You can't just kill people because they piss you off, Phoenix."

"Says who?" he asked in a dark voice. "I mean it, Bee."

"So do I." I quickly turned around and poked him in the chest. "You want me to make friends? Then you can't get pissed every time someone comes up and talks to me. Would it be different if it was a girl?"

His jaw cracked. "Of course it would! A girl wouldn't be trying to get into your damn pants!"

"Really?" I placed my hands on my hips. "Who's to say a girl wouldn't want this too?"

"You're impossible." He scowled, throwing his hands into the air.

"You almost pulled a gun on a student and *I'm* the

difficult one?" I tilted my head. "You can't control everything all the time, Phoenix, and you sure as hell can't control me!"

"You think?" he snarled, his hands reaching for my shoulders. Fingertips dug into my skin; his lips were inches from mine. "I only let you see what I want you to see, Bee, and that's the truth. If I wanted to control you, I'd control you — and you'd like it, believe me."

"Try me."

With a growl, he released me and reached for his keys. "You aren't worth the effort."

The words were like the final blow to the miniscule amount of self-esteem I'd managed to build up over the last few days. My body physically reacted, slumping into itself and disabling the armored blanket I'd once been able to wrap around my heart.

Bruised.

Broken.

Battered.

"Bee—"

"No." I said in a hollow voice. "You're right. Funny, I remember my dad saying the exact same thing to me before he died."

"Bee—"

"Let's go home." I marched past him and didn't look at him again, not when he started the car, not when he turned on Jay-Z, or even when he stopped at Starbucks and ordered my favorite drink.

I was silent.

Because he'd finally gotten his wish — he'd broken me. How many times can a girl face rejection before the only way to find comfort is to close herself off from the very world that rejected her in the first place?

Freshman Retreat.

I'd focus on that.

I'd forget about Phoenix.

I'd flirt with whomever I wanted.

I'd make friends.

And in the end, I'd be okay. I had to be okay. Because if all else failed, what did I really have to look forward to in life?

CHAPTER SEVENTEEN

Never let them see you cry.

Phoenix

"YOU SURE YOU'RE READY for this?" Nixon asked. I'd told him I needed him to come. He said if he came, so did Mil, Chase, and Tex.

All five bosses.

Together again.

Only they were there to show their support, rather than fight.

I wasn't myself. Hell, when had I actually been myself over the past few weeks? I was still pissed at losing control with Bee, at hurting her feelings. I knew what her triggers were, and I'd blatantly played with them until I'd gotten the result I wanted.

Her hurt.

So why did I feel so bad?

She hadn't talked to me the entire ride home, even when I'd bought her coffee, something that I had been convinced would do the trick.

When I'd knocked on her door that night to tell her I was leaving and that Sergio was staying behind if she needed anything, I'd been greeted with silence.

Panicking, I'd broken down the door only to find her listening to music and doing homework — in nothing but a sports bra and a pair of tiny shorts.

She looked up, unfazed, and gave me the finger.

"It'll be fine," Mil said, regaining my attention as she squeezed my hand with hers. "Remember, you're their boss."

I nodded and took a deep breath. It was one of the first official meetings I'd called, with Nick's help.

I had no trouble running the business with the Nicolasis; hell, it practically ran itself. What I did have trouble with? Its men and their loyalty. It was time to prove a point, time to be boss.

"When all else fails—" Tex slapped me on the back. "— shoot first."

"Oh, great advice," Chase muttered. "Because that's always been the answer to world peace. Shooting things."

"Just saying." Tex shrugged.

I walked through the doorway and looked around. We were meeting at one of the restaurants the Abandonatos owned, a Chinese place close to the lake that looked more like a warehouse than anything. It was popular with the locals and had soundproof rooms.

Two bonuses.

No one to hear the screams.

But enough people to cover for us if it was necessary.

The men were all piled into the back room, eating a dinner I'd specifically set out for them. If there was one thing I knew, food always made people less angry. I should know; I was freaking angry most the day, and I was pretty sure it had to do with the fact that I was still drinking protein shakes instead of eating Bee's lasagna.

Forcing her out of my head, I made my way into the

room.

Absolute silence greeted me as the men looked up from their plates. All in all, I had thirty of them who were close to me; the rest were simply foot soldiers, not needed in one of these meetings.

"So..." Nick stood. "...if we'd known we would be entertaining the Cappo, we might have had a parade."

"Ha." Tex clapped his hands once. "You're cute. Tell me your name so I can remember to say a prayer on your behalf before I shoot you between the eyes."

Nick's eyebrows shot halfway up his forehead as a smile curved across his lips. "Phoenix, if this is the company you keep, we may be in for an interesting few years."

"It is," I said in a tense voice. "And, by the way, he will follow through on that promise, so I'd watch it."

"Noted." Nick chuckled.

The men around the table were still inspecting us; most of them had been at the commission, but a few had still been in Sicily when Tex had taken control of the five families, the day Luca had died.

When he'd left me with his legacy to keep up.

Damn it.

"Find your seats," I said in a low voice.

Nixon, Chase, Tex, and Mil all went to sit on the left side of the table where a few seats were empty.

The door opened and then closed behind me.

I didn't need to turn to know who it was.

"Frank, you're late."

"Sorry." He chuckled then laid a hand on my back.

Slowly, I turned to face him. Luca's brother and, at the end of his life, his best friend. It still hurt to look at Frank because he reminded me of Luca, of what he was to me, of what he'd done for me. I saw his eyes in Frank's. I saw his strength, and it killed me inside that I might never live up to the legacy that he'd left behind.

"Blessings…" Frank took my face between his hands and kissed both cheeks. "…to the new boss of Nicolasi."

"*Salud!*" Nick lifted his wine, and the rest of the men followed.

"He would be proud." Frank nodded and slapped my cheek with his right hand. "So proud to see you here standing in front of your men."

I swallowed the lump in my throat because Frank knew the truth. I'd done nothing in my life that had garnered that word. Pride. I was the exact opposite, and the faith he had in me did nothing but make the weight heavier on my shoulders.

Frank released me and walked over to his seat.

"First order of business." I pulled out my gun and fired two shots at the man sitting directly in front of me. The one who, after lots of digging, Nick had discovered was talking to the feds about our family. At least we knew where the leak had come from.

He slumped against his chair as blood splattered across the wall behind him.

"That," I said in a cold voice, "is what happens when you go to the feds. That is what happens when you choose the government over our own blood. I spill yours. *Capiche?*"

The men nodded with murmurs of agreement.

"And the second order of business…" I looked around the room and finally, finally felt a rightness settle over me as I was about to do something that Luca had been fighting for ever since he had been forced to leave the US, forced to leave his brother and the love of his life that he'd never reunited with. "We're staying."

"Staying?" Nick repeated, his accent thick.

"In the states." I nodded. "It will be as it was before. The five families in Chicago, working together. We stay."

Nobody said a word. It was a quiet moment, not tense, just quiet, as if each man was trying to figure out if my word could be trusted.

I walked over to the table, grabbed an empty glass, and poured some red wine into it. When I lifted it into the air, it was with purpose, a purpose for some reason that Luca had thought I was ready for.

"To keeping his legacy alive." I lifted the glass. "To keeping the family safe. To blood... to Luca Alfero Nicolasi. May he rest in peace."

The rest of the men stood and lifted their glasses.

"And to the new boss." Nick centered his gaze on me. "May he find meaning in the Nicolasi blood."

"All is not lost," I said back.

"All is ours," the men repeated.

"Salud." I took a drink and everyone followed.

Luca trusted me, which meant he saw something that even I couldn't see. He saw a sliver of potential, a sliver of good. He saw what my father had failed to see for my entire existence.

A need to belong.

A thirst.

He saw potential, but most of all...

He saw hope.

THE REST OF THE meeting passed by in a blur. I made sure I debriefed the men on the potential threat at Eagle Elite and also named my second in command — Nick. He was thirty-two, bloodthirsty, and trustworthy.

By the time the meeting ended, it was around midnight. I'd had crap sleep the night before, so I hoped that at least getting the meeting out of the way would make it so I could sleep nightmare-free; then again, I'd just disposed of a body, so I wasn't confident in my ability to fall asleep without watching that same body sink through the rough waters of Lake Michigan.

When I got back to the house, all the lights were off.

I stripped out of my clothes without bothering to turn on the light and quickly jumped into bed. It smelled like vanilla, just like Bee.

"Damn it," I muttered, scooting over to the side. My hand flopped over the covers and came into contact with something warm.

A body.

Holy shit.

I froze.

A feminine moan escaped and then a curse. "Phoenix?"

"You have exactly three seconds to explain why you're sleeping in my bed."

"I didn't mean to."

"So you accidentally wandered into my room, took off your clothes, jumped into my bed, and fell asleep? Are you drunk?"

"No." Bee's voice was small. "I couldn't sleep. I got scared and came in here…"

I couldn't see her face, but it sounded like the truth. "And fell asleep?"

"Why is it so hard to believe I fell asleep?"

"Why the hell didn't you go get Sergio if you were so afraid?"

"He was in his room, but the door was locked. I heard a noise, and I ran into your room with my Kindle. End of story."

I sighed heavily. "Well, now I'm here, things are clearly fine. Go to bed."

She didn't move.

"Bee, you have to be up in a few hours for your freshman class trip. I have to be up in a few hours to make sure you don't walk into any walls. Do us both a favor and get the hell out."

Nothing.

Had she left? Had I imagined the whole thing? I reached

across and found her body — still clothed, thank God — huddled into a tiny ball as if she was trying to turn into herself.

Panicked, I rose to my knees. "Bee? What else is wrong? Did someone hurt you?"

"Y-yes, I mean no," she choked out. "I'm sorry I'll leave."

I knew it was wrong — to ask her to stay — but I was so weak in that moment I would have done anything to keep her from crying.

"It's fine," I said in a rough voice. "Just… try not to touch me."

"You mean it?"

"Yes, I mean it. Don't touch me."

"No, you mean I can stay?"

"Just for tonight…"

"Like old times."

"Yeah," I croaked, turning on my side, "exactly like old times."

Except in the old times I'd practiced restraint, because not practicing it meant that I would give up my secret identity to her father.

Not practicing restraint now meant I'd either get shot by Tex or do the honors myself, on account of tainting her purity.

"Thanks, Phoenix." She sighed happily, and her deep breathing soon followed.

I was going to get no sleep, and I had nobody to blame but myself — well, myself and my inability to say no to the one girl I really needed to be saying no to.

CHAPTER EIGHTEEN

Falling asleep with a nightmare, waking up to a dream

Bee

HOW PATHETIC COULD A girl get? I heard a noise, one small noise, and next thing I knew I was in Phoenix's room. His smell was so familiar, so comforting, despite his jack-assery, that I lay down on his bed and started reading, fully planning on leaving in an hour or so, once I'd calmed down.

Instead? I fell asleep.

And woke up with him freaking out because he'd found me there. But he'd said I could stay... and here I was waking up again. Next to his warmth.

Not just touching his perfect body or staring at his naked chest, but straight up tangled in his legs, in his arms, my head resting in the crook of his neck.

It felt right.

So right that I was afraid I was dreaming, afraid he was going to wake up and yell at me for doing the one thing I promised I wouldn't do — touch him.

He was a wall of solid muscle and warmth. I could lay in

bed with him, just touching his smooth skin forever.

Slowly my gaze slide down his torso to where the V of his muscles dipped beneath the blankets.

I knew the minute he woke up, because the very muscles I was currently salivating over, tensed so extremely that it seemed like he was trying to do a sit up without actually moving.

"Bee." His voice was gruff. "What are you doing?"

Staring, lusting, imagining— Really, take your pick. "Taking advantage of you with my eyes. What's it look like I'm doing?"

"Whatever it is, it's creepy. Stop it."

I smiled and took my chances by looking at him.

Bad choice.

His hair had started to grow out a bit more since he shaved it so close to his head; pieces of light blond peeked out from some of the dark, and, to my amazement, it had a slight curl to it. Not reaching out and touching it was killing me inside. It seemed Phoenix could use more of that — touching.

"You look surprised," he said, eyes narrowing. "The open-mouthed look isn't so hot on you, Bee."

"I'm touching you."

"You are."

"In your space."

"Right again."

"And you aren't yelling."

With a sigh, he gently pushed me away. "I think I can manage not to be an ass first thing in the morning."

"Weird, since usually I imagine you spend your mornings kicking puppies and shooting birds that chirp." I smiled.

"Hilarious." He raised his hands above his head.

My body hummed with want. The man was gorgeous, so gorgeous it was impossible not to stare at every single inch of him. "I... um, owe you an... apology."

"What was that?" Holy crap, I really was dreaming. I'd fallen asleep in the monster's bed and woken up to find a prince.

Phoenix's face tensed. "An apology."

"Say it with a smile, and maybe I'll believe you."

"So that's what she wants in the morning…"

"Amongst other things." I reached for the blanket and covered up the lower half of his body.

He hissed.

"Hey, don't kill a girl for trying."

"Let's make a deal."

"Wow!" I moved to my knees and let out a laugh. "First, you don't wake up yelling. Second, you apologize, and now… you want to make a deal? Did you fall into a radioactive tub of Prozac last night or something?"

His lips twitched.

"Aw, it's okay to smile." I leaned in and whispered, "I won't tell."

His eyes darted to my lips and stayed there, as if he was waging a war within his mind as to whether or not he wanted to taste. I leaned forward; he met me halfway.

My body buzzed with warmth. Was this really happening?

He stopped moving and cupped my face with both of his hands. "I'm an ass… but everything I do has a purpose." He released a soft sigh. "But when that purpose ends up hurting you more than helping, then I apologize. So, I'm sorry for what I said yesterday. You are… and always will be… worth the effort, just not from a guy like me. But someone better." He tilted his head. "Yes."

"But—"

He placed his fingers against my lips. "Don't ruin the moment by talking."

I puffed out a frustrated breath.

"So this deal…"

His fingers were still pressed against me; it took every ounce of willpower I had not to either lick them or take a small bite and savor his taste.

"...if I smile and play nice, will you please return the favor this weekend? No running off with Pike, no late-night make-out sessions, no going out of my sight, and, for the love of God, no more YouTube videos of turtles." He removed his hand and crossed his arms.

"You smile, and you have to eat a normal breakfast."

"I smile, and I eat a protein bar."

"And you take me to Starbucks."

"Ah, the terrorist negotiates."

"Only when the jailkeeper corners me." I smiled.

"Fine." He cleared his throat and looked away. With a deep exhale, he made eye contact again and smiled.

A devastating, heart-stopping, knee-knocking, movie-star smile that had my entire body going limp.

The dimple went deep.

The teeth were straight and white.

His eyes no longer looked haunted.

And I, seriously, felt my heart skip a beat in my chest.

"Now," he said softly, "get the hell out of my bed."

"Aw, and we were so close with that moment. It was like friendship-carpet time."

"Feel free to shoot me if we ever — and I do mean ever — have a moment that includes the words friendship, carpet, and magic."

"Ha, didn't say magic!"

"Out." He pointed to the door, the blanket going lower across his muscled body.

Just a little farther, and I'd be able to see what all the fuss was about.

"Bee." There it was, the warning tone I was so used to.

With a huff, I jumped off the bed and walked to the door.

"What?" Phoenix asked when I didn't step all the way

through. "What's wrong now?"

"Thank you...." I didn't turn around. "...for not yelling at me."

He swore under his breath. "The very fact that you have to thank me for that tells you the type of man I am, Bee, a piece of shit."

"No." I exhaled my frustration. "Just scared of being stung, right?" I looked over my shoulder, expecting to see an irritated expression; instead, I saw nothing but hunger, and I was pretty sure I knew who it was directed toward. With a shudder, he turned away.

Another moment gone.

Maybe if I kept piling them up, they'd be more permanent. I could use permanent, or maybe I could just use Phoenix.

CHAPTER NINETEEN

The secrets: we keep. The truth: we find.

Sergio

THE INFORMATION MADE NO sense. Pike was working for the feds, but I saw nothing about a deal or about his family getting out of prison for his participation, so what could he possibly have to gain by helping them?

I researched until my eyes went crossed.

Finally, I was about ready to shut my computer down and pour some more morning coffee when my thoughts went to Andi.

I quickly found her in the database then did a background search on her. I expected it to be mildly tame, easily accessible.

But the minute I clicked on her name...

The entire screen froze.

What the hell?

I opened up another screen and did a similar search, this time plugging in all the right keystrokes in order to gain access into her file.

And again, I was locked out.

The only reason the system would lock me out would be because it was top-secret information, but I'd helped design the damn system, which meant either it had a virus or somehow the girl had gone above even my head to make sure that her file was secure.

The only other person who had access was sitting in a nice comfy seat downtown.

Calling him would look suspicious.

I'd rather just hack my way in.

But why the sudden obsession? I wasn't sure; maybe it was the fact that I knew my own time was already up and I wasn't doing a good job of dealing with it, yet she seemed happy almost chipper about her impending death. How the hell did someone face that every day with a smile?

I groaned and ran my hands over my face just as Phoenix made his way into the kitchen looking less haunted than usual.

"I take it things went well last night?"

He dropped the coffee cup in his hand. It shattered against the granite and spilt across the counter.

"Or it went horrible and you want to commit suicide via slicing your wrists open with your own morning cup of coffee?"

Phoenix pressed his hands against the counter. "Sorry, I was… squeezing too hard."

"Well then, better be careful when you take a piss this morning."

"Ha!" He rolled his eyes and reached for another mug. "And yeah, it went well last night. The Nicolasi family is here to stay."

"Surprise, surprise." I closed my computer, just in case he walked around behind me, and rose from my seat.

"They thought so."

"They don't trust anyone or anything. Of course, they

thought they were going back to Sicily. That's where we sent them in the first place." I never did ask why the family was sent away, figured it wasn't any of my business, but the very fact that they were staying meant bad news for everyone; they just didn't realize it. Hell, they had no clue the shit storm that was coming their way. I could only stop it if I was alive, and I knew that it was only a matter of time before I, the last remaining loose end, was going to get killed.

I had a feeling, a suspicion, of who my replacement was.

And it made me sick to my stomach, but all I had was speculation and a funny feeling that things weren't going to end well for me, not if Nixon found out, not if Tex found out. Hell, if any of them found out... I was a dead man.

Then again, I was already dead.

"Boys." Bee skipped into the room and stole the coffee from Phoenix's hand. I expected him to yell, but instead he moved away from her so fast you'd think she just offered to rub him down with poison ivy.

"Bee..." I crossed my arms. "...how was your night?"

"Uneventful," Phoenix answered for her. "Are you packed, Bee?"

Their exchange was different than usual; she stood a good distance away from him. Normally she was all over him, taunting like a puppy with a chew toy.

She nodded. "Yup."

Phoenix grabbed another cup, poured some coffee, and took a large sip.

"I even packed condoms just in case."

Coffee spewed out of his mouth and onto the counter.

"Hmm... whatever did I say?" She shrugged, her eyes dancing with laughter.

"Bee..." Phoenix set his coffee down and wiped his face with a nearby towel. "Stop screwing around. Remember what we discussed."

"You mean last night?" She tilted her head again.

And shit just got interesting. "Last night?" I repeated.

"In bed." Bee winked in my direction.

"Before bed," Phoenix corrected.

"Or was it after?" Bee added with a wink.

"You just can't help yourself, can you?" Phoenix asked, his voice low. "You have to push and push and push until—"

"Boom." Bee's eyes widened. "Until you break, yes, yes I do."

"Sorry to disappoint you, Bee." I cleared my throat. "This one's already broken, been that way for quite some time."

"I'm good with a hammer." She winked. "Phoenix, you good with nailing things?"

"Shit…" I whistled under my breath. "Bee, take it easy on him, I hate the guy, and even I feel sorry for him if this is what he puts up with every day. Your brother's going to murder him before the year's out if you keep it up."

"Maybe that's her plan." Phoenix looked heavenward. "Have her brother kill me so I don't have to fall on my own knife and all that."

"Don't be dramatic." Bee sighed. "I was kidding… at least about the condoms. Lighten up, boys!" She floated out of the room, carrying her laughter with her.

"Damn." I whistled. "She's getting worse."

"Day Four." Phoenix braced himself against the counter. "I'm on Day Four."

"Killing never looked so easy, am I right?" I teased.

Phoenix returned my smile with one of his own. "Too right. Hold the fort down while we're gone this weekend. I'll take my cell and make sure to tail Pike for anything suspicious."

"Good."

Phoenix was just about to step out of earshot when I yelled, "Hey, can you look out for a girl named Andi too? You know, just in case."

Phoenix would be wise not to read into that. He simply

paused and then asked, "Last name?"

"Smith."

"Typical."

"My thoughts exactly."

"Any reason I'm tailing a freshman girl?"

"Let's call it a feeling…"

"Yeah, I don't know what those are." Phoenix barked out a laugh. "But I'll take your word for it."

"Do that."

He left.

I sat and felt more relaxed than I had all evening. I might not like Phoenix, but I trusted him to get the job done; he'd do whatever it took to protect family, and I counted on him for that. So did everyone else.

CHAPTER TWENTY

Watching Phoenix drink hot coffee? Nothing sexier.

Bee

"HOW'S THE STARBUCKS, PHOENIX? Is it everything you ever dreamed and more? Do you want to take a dive into the danger zone and dedicate your body to coffee when you die?"

"I'm curious." He set his latte down in the cup holder. "Do you come up with this stuff on the spot? Or is it hours of deciding the best way to push my buttons."

"I like buttons."

"Bee..."

"And pushing."

"No shit." He rolled his eyes. "Drink your coffee, play nice, remember the deal."

"Yeah, yeah." I sighed and took a sip of my macchiato. "Are we there yet?"

"I could always drug you."

"I took a no-drugs pledge when I was six. Thanks anyway."

"Could have fooled me."

"Ha!" I slapped my knee. "Someone's got jokes this morning. I think you're chipper because you woke up on the right side of the bed... with me on the left. That's what I think."

"And you're delusional." He sighed and took a left. The sign above the road said *Starving Creek Rock*, and right next to it a white banner fluttered with the words *Welcome Elite Freshman* scrawled across it in electric blue.

"They're going to make us do icebreakers, aren't they?"

"Oh, yeah." Phoenix let out a low chuckle. "Make sure you have your favorite color and pizza ready at any given time... oh, and it helps to know your potential major and who your parents are."

My stomach sank.

"If they ask just say you spontaneously burst onto the scene via a miracle and leave it at that." He reached his hand across the console and tapped my leg then jerked it back as though it were on fire.

"Were you just trying to comfort me?" I asked boldly, taking in his rigid profile. The dark long-sleeved shirt hugged his body so well that it should have been illegal. It didn't help that his jeans were tight or that he wore aviators like they were created for him.

"Did it work?"

"People show more affection to their cats, and I have it on good authority that cats have attitude."

"Good authority?" Phoenix squinted. "You've never had a cat?"

I gave a wry shake of my head.

"Dog then?"

Another headshake.

"Any pet?"

"I had an imagination," I said with a sigh and looked out the window, recalling the one time I'd asked my dad for a furry friend.

"Why do you need this?" he yelled. "Are the gifts and presents not enough?"

No. I wanted to scream. I just wanted something to hug. I wasn't allowed teddy bears or anything comforting. The one doll he had given me was glass — cold, just like him.

"I just... isn't it good for kids? To have responsibility?"

He barked out a laugh. "You see this?" He aimed a sweeping gesture around our large mansion. "This is your responsibility. You keep your room clean and try not to mess anything up and then, when you are older, you marry a man of my choosing. That is final."

"I'm twelve. I—"

His slap came fast and hard, nearly toppling me over the couch. "You will not disrespect me in my own home. Go to your room. No dinner."

I ran to my room and slammed the door then grabbed one of my picture books, the last one he'd failed to remove from my bedroom, and glanced at a picture of a little puppy named Spot.

I traced Spot with my finger and prayed that one day I'd find someone who would love me as much as Spot.

Which was sad.

Pathetic.

Because Spot wasn't real.

But in my heart, in my head, he was, and one day, I was going to be able to escape my prison long enough to find a puppy to hug.

One day, I swore, I'd be loveable.

"Hey..." Phoenix pulled the car to a stop. "We don't have to stay for this, you know. I'm sure I could come up with an excuse for Tex. I mean, if you want to go home."

"I have no home." The words escaped my mouth before I could stop them. I closed my eyes and groaned, ready for Phoenix to jump down my throat just like my dad would have.

Instead he sighed and said, "Me either."

We sat in complete silence while students filed out of the large bus with their weekend bags.

It was the one time we didn't have to wear uniforms. I

pulled at my simple jersey T-shirt and smoothed down my ripped jeans.

"You look beautiful," Phoenix whispered.

My hands froze on my thighs, and I turned to look at him. I was sure my eyes looked as wide as they felt. "Th-thank you."

"But..." He nodded toward the building. "In order for others to notice, you gotta get out of the damn car, little girl."

"Right." I exhaled. "Okay."

"And if anyone looks at you funny, I'll shoot them. Sound good?"

"At least we have options on where to bury the body," I muttered.

"Who buries bodies?" Phoenix shrugged. "Throw 'em in the lake, that's what I always say..."

"Oddly enough this conversation isn't helping my nerves, Phoenix."

He offered me a small smile; it was enough for me to want to lean across the console and kiss him — hard. "I'd be concerned if it did. Now, out of the car. Baby steps."

Reluctantly, I got out of the car and went around to grab my bag, but Phoenix beat me to it.

"Go." He nodded toward the lodge. "Check in."

I rubbed my hands together and slowly made my way past the groups of freshman already starting to whisper as if my entrance was more important than theirs. I was nothing, a nobody, yet I was somebody to them, something interesting, something dangerous.

I was mafia.

A criminal.

The bad guy.

Yet, they had no proof of it.

None at all, except rumors and associations.

By the time I made it inside the large lobby, I was sweating. I could feel Phoenix behind me, and that was the only reason I had enough strength to go to the desk and mumble my name.

"Oh, Bianka Campisi!" the lady said loudly. "I have you with Andi Smith for the weekend. You'll just love her. She's—"

"Right here!" A petite girl with bright blond, almost-white hair popped out in front of me and held out her hand. "Hi."

I took her hand and shook it. "Hi, I'm—"

"Bee," she finished with a wink. "I know. Well, no offense, but everyone knows. Then again, it's college, almost like high school, yet Elite is turning out to be worse."

I smiled, a real smile. "You're telling me."

"Come on." She shrugged. "I'll show you our room, and then we can go to lunch. They have some activities planned after that."

"Okay." I didn't budge.

She tilted her head then looked behind me. "Uh, he can come if he… wants?"

"Oh." I turned to see Phoenix watching Andi with interest, an interest I wasn't at all comfortable with. "No, he's… um, fine. He's staying. Stay, Phoenix."

"At least give him his treat." Pike said, sauntering up to the table with his hands up. "I'd say it's only fair for his good behavior."

"Bite me," Phoenix mumbled then strangely dropped my bag next to my feet and walked off.

"Huh." Pike shrugged. "Looks like the Ghost of Elite Past has decided to give you a break for the afternoon. What should we do first?"

His friends had started crowding around us, each of them eyeing me with interest.

"Well, I was going to go see my room with Andi."

"Andi?" He looked around then down. "Holy shit, you're tiny."

"Fun-sized." She winked. "And we were just going to the

room. You guys are more than welcome to join."

"I'd never say no to an invitation like that," Pike said in a gruff voice. "Let's go!"

CHAPTER TWENTY-ONE
Out of my element — completely.

Phoenix

IF I HAD ANY HOPE of gaining useful info, I had to let Bee hang out with him, and hopefully she'd be able to leak information to me without even knowing it. As a plan, it sucked, but it was all I had. Besides, I figured it was the only way to actually get real intel without just ripping the guy's fingernails off, one by one, until he shit his pants and told me his dirty secrets.

I pulled out my phone and dialed Nixon's number.

"Prodigal, how goes it?"

"Ha!" I laughed. "Stop hanging out with Chase, he's rubbing off on you."

"So very true."

"I'm at the retreat. I just wanted to make sure I was on the right frequency for the listening devices."

We ran through a few more of the steps as I set up another camera in Bee's room, one I knew she wouldn't find, even if she was looking for something suspicious.

When I hung up from Nixon, I called Tex to check in, not

because I had to, but because I was pretty sure that had I not, he would drive up here and ruin everything. He was getting more protective of Bee by the day. The second day of school, I'd had to snap a picture of her eating so he knew she was getting enough protein. It was beyond ridiculous.

I was just exiting her room when Andi came around the corner, nearly colliding with me. Her hands pushed against my chest. She backed up and smiled.

Something about her was familiar, but I couldn't quite place it, almost like a memory that I'd purposefully forgotten.

"Sorry." She shrugged. "I wasn't watching where I was going."

"What did you say your name was again?" I knew her name; I just wanted to see how comfortable she was with using it. If she hesitated or forced it in a cheerful tone, I'd know she was lying — at least about her identity. Smith, my ass.

"Andi," she said slowly, her eyes narrowing. "You think it's a stupid name, don't you? It's okay. My dad came up with it. He had a thing for the name Andrew and surprise! Out came a girl."

She blushed.

That I could work with.

Not that I wanted to, but I really had no other choice. With a seductive smile, I slowly reached out and cupped her face. "I kind of like it. Fits you."

"Th-thanks." Her blush deepened.

"What's your dad do?"

"Huh?" Her eyes glazed over.

"Your father?"

"Oh." She shrugged. "He died when I was young."

"I'm sorry to hear that." I mentally stored that tidbit and pushed further, making sure her body was stuck against the wall while I leaned almost completely against her. "That must have been so difficult for you."

My body reacted as if I'd just drunk poison. I hated playing the part, and that was why I kept Bee away. Because women made me want to hate; they made me want to hurt. I could act with the best of them, but being this close to her made me want to do something horrible, like puke or run in the other direction — then puke.

"Yeah, it was." Her shoulders slumped a bit. "But, you know what they say. Life goes on." She licked her lips; it was a nervous gesture. Her eyes flashed, and then the innocent look was back. Someone wasn't who she said she was.

"It does."

She swallowed, her gaze falling to my lips.

"Andi? Phoenix?" Shit, I knew that voice. It was Bee, and our current predicament looked like I was just about ready to pounce on her new friend — her only friend.

"Nice meeting you, Andi." I stepped back and winked at Bee, hoping it would put her at ease.

Instead, her entire face fell; she looked down at the floor and moved out of the way while I stepped beside her.

It was one of the first times she didn't try to touch me.

And I hated it.

The next hour passed in a blur. I basically sat in a corner drinking coffee while the freshmen played games, ate dinner, and laughed way too loud. Had I ever been that stupid? They were so careless so... inexperienced. By that age I'd already killed several times.

Life wasn't really fair, was it?

I'd never be able to experience the type of freedom they had, and they took it all for granted.

It was a pity.

And it was also making me wish my coffee was whiskey. With a wince, I rose to my knees and looked around the large rec room for Bee.

Nowhere to be seen.

Well shit, that's where daydreaming got me.

I quickly scanned the room again. When I didn't find her, I went to her bedroom. Empty.

"Shit!" I pounded my hand against the wall and ran outside. There were so many trails, so many possibilities it would take forever to find her. I quickly turned on my app so I could track her and saw the little red light blink about a quarter of a mile behind the lodge.

I ran like hell.

A bonfire blazed in the distance. I knew she was probably there, probably safe, probably acting like all teenagers should act their freshman year of college, but I had to see that to know for certain.

When I got closer, I ducked behind the trees and waited.

The first thing I saw…

Beer.

The second thing…

Pike holding Bee's hand.

The third thing? Absolute red.

I stomped into the circle took one look around and already knew. Half of them were drunk; the other half were on their way. And by the looks of Bee, she was already too far gone.

"Bee," I barked, halting a few feet away. "It's time for bed."

"Ooo, hear that?" She cupped a hand around her ear. "You want to take me to bed."

Some nearby girls fell into fits of laughter.

"Bee," I growled, conscious that I sounded like a rabid animal. "Get up."

Pike held out a beer. "Hey, sit down. Stay awhile. The party's just getting started."

"It's ending. Now," I said in a voice I didn't recognize. "Bee, say goodnight to your new friends."

"Damn, he's bossy," said a girl to my right as she eyed me up and down. "I could use bossy."

"He's not yours!" Bee shouted in a horrifyingly loud voice. Holy shit, was she jealous?

I didn't see Andi anywhere, which didn't surprise me, as she didn't seem the partying type, and I knew Pike's only interest was in Bee.

"Where's your roommate?" I asked.

"Wouldn't you like to know!" Bee yelled in a sharp voice. "What, you wanna kiss her again? Have sex with her under the stars or something!" She threw her hands into the air, nearly sending herself off Pike's lap.

"That's it." I scooped her up into my arms and hoisted her over my shoulder.

"Put me down!" Her tiny fists hit my back, then my shoulder, but I barely felt them.

I rolled my eyes and kept walking.

"I said put me down," she just about screeched.

"Like you could even walk."

"I *can* walk!"

"Fine." I dropped her to her feet and waited while she gained her bearings. "Then march."

"Ugh." She pushed against my body but did a pretty good job of making straight lines toward the lodge. "You're so stupid! I'm stupid too!"

"Why are you insulting your own intelligence?"

"Big word, intelligence."

"Remember that pledge about drugs? If I was you, I'd take it for beer too, just to be safe."

"Ugh! There you go again!" She threw her hands into the air, stopped walking, and turned around. "You're so bossy! So hot and cold! One minute you're so nice I want to cry, and the next minute you're so mean... well... I guess that causes tears too."

"So, no matter what, I make you cry?" My patience was gone, absolutely gone. Mosquitos were biting me in the ass, and the most beautiful girl in the world was off limits, and I made her cry — by breathing.

"Yeah! And you like my roommate!"

"What?"

"She's pretty." Bee glowered, kicking the dirt with her boots. "Prettier than me, huh? Because she's blonde."

"Do I give you the impression I like blondes?"

"You almost kissed her."

"You're drunk."

"I have eyes, Phoenix!" Bee stumbled into my arms and pounded my chest. "I know you wanted to, just say it!"

The pounding continued against my chest.

I sighed and steadied her on her feet, willing her to calm down. Finally, she slumped against my chest and whispered, "Why won't you kiss me?"

Oh, hell.

"Bee, we need to get you some water, maybe some bread."

"I don't want bread. I'm gluten-free."

I bit my lip to keep from laughing.

"And I hate water."

"You do not hate water."

"Do too, and to prove it, I refuse to shower for the entire year! Mark my swords!"

"Swords?"

"Words." Her eyebrows pinched together. "Phoenix?"

"Yeah, little girl?"

"Am I pretty?"

I sighed and leaned my forehead against hers, only allowing myself that much contact. "You're gorgeous, Bee. Absolutely breathtaking."

She nodded.

I thought the conversation was over.

I thought wrong.

In all the scenarios I'd gone through in my head, this was one I hadn't even entertained, because there was no possible way to figure Bee out.

With a crazy amount of strength, she wrapped her arms around my neck and kissed me.

Full on the mouth.

I was too shocked to do anything.

So many feelings roared to the surface of my mind that I thought I was going to black out. The kiss reminded me of too many I'd shared in anger, in hate, in misuse, mistrust.

But her moan.

The sound of her innocence brought me back to reality, and that reality was... Bee. The innocent Bee was kissing me. A killer.

And she wasn't crying.

I sighed in relief that I wasn't tempted to hurt her then gently tried to push her away. It was a mistake, that one movement, because she hoisted herself into my arms and wrapped her legs around my waist.

And. I. Was. Gone.

With a surge of lust, I pushed her against the tree and opened my mouth, tasting her and only her. Want poured through my limbs, pounded through my veins until I was dizzy with it. Her mouth was so soft, so perfect, so tempting.

My hands moved to her sides, running up and down, and then I froze.

I couldn't.

She was drunk.

It was wrong.

All wrong.

Images flashed before my eyes.

I released her in absolute horror.

She blinked up at me, her swollen lips more tempting than anything I'd ever seen in my entire life. "I liked that."

"You won't remember it in the morning." *Thank God for that.*

"I'm going to pray I do." She leaned toward me. I backed

away and grabbed her hand.

"It's time for bed, little girl."

"You called me pretty."

"I called you gorgeous."

"You kissed me."

"You kissed me, and I almost suffocated to death. Don't read too much into it Bee, you'll only get hurt."

She laughed and then put her head on my shoulder. "I liked it a lot."

"Yeah well, we all like playing with bombs — until they go off."

"Are you a bomb?"

"What do you think?"

"I think..." Her eyes were clearer than I'd seen them all day as we walked into the lodge. "...that you're full of shit."

"Ha, *that*, I hope you remember tomorrow."

"I will!" she shouted triumphantly then almost walked into a wall trying to get into her room.

"You were saying?" I crossed my arms.

"Screw you. I'm tired." She yawned and slammed the door behind her while I just stood there, horrified.

I pulled out my cell to call Tex.

And dialed Chase instead.

"Problem." My voice was hollow. "Big problem."

"Oh shit," Chase mumbled. "Did you kill someone?"

"No."

"The feds are there?"

"No."

"Dude, I don't see a problem."

"Bee got drunk."

Chase whistled.

"And attacked me with her mouth."

He let out a low curse then started laughing hysterically. "And you wanted to gossip about it or what?"

"Asshole. Do I call Tex?"

"That depends. Do you want him to cut off every toe but one, paint them, and then mail them to you, just so you can see what they look like unattached to your feet?"

I groaned. "She got drunk, and I tried to make sure she got back to her room safe. It was nothing. You know..." My voice cracked. "...you know I can't... ever since."

Chase muttered a curse. "I know, man. I know. I mean, I don't know the hell that goes through that brain of yours, but I can imagine it isn't pretty, and I can imagine that touching a girl after... well, after all that shit isn't the easiest thing... are you... okay?"

For some reason, my throat felt thick. Why the hell had I called Chase of all people? "No. I don't think so."

"You still get anxiety attacks?"

"Daily."

"Okay, so tonight might be worse than normal. Make sure you take something to help you sleep, and I'll monitor the cameras and watch Bee sleep. Which, by the way, sounds like the worst idea I've ever had since my wife just gave me bedroom eyes, but I'll do it. Just go to sleep and maybe take a shot of whiskey."

"No whiskey, but sleep sounds good."

"I got you."

That damn lump in my throat reappeared. "Thanks, Chase."

"Don't mention it."

I laughed.

"No, seriously, don't. Sometimes Tex scares the shit out of me, and if you go down, you go down alone."

"Understood."

"Night."

"Good night." I shoved my phone back in my pocket and made my way to the room I was staying in — by myself.

I took a sleeping pill and closed my eyes.

As expected, images of the girls I'd raped, images of

Trace flooded my vision until I spent half the night puking in the bathroom.

Funny, a part of me had expected her kiss to save me.

Instead, it just reminded me of my past, and of my future — if I ever gave into it again.

CHAPTER TWENTY-TWO

Regret always comes in the morning… always.

Bee

LAUGHTER WOKE ME FROM my amazing dream about Phoenix. He'd tasted like cinnamon. And I'd always been a huge fan of anything spicy.

I tried to swallow, but my throat was so dry it was like my body had stopped producing saliva. Slowly, I rose from the bed and winced. My head was pounding like crazy too. What had I done last night?

I shook my head. It only made the pounding worse.

"Beer." Andi stood to my right, holding out a bottle of water and two Tylenol. "I said no to drinking. You stayed."

"You're a wiser person than me."

She grinned. "I know, but it wasn't because I didn't want to have fun. I just can't mix drugs with alcohol."

"Drugs?" I repeated. "You're on drugs?"

"The doctor kind." She winked. "Oh, and by the way you should probably wash your face and put on two tubes of ChapStick before you go downstairs."

"That bad, huh?"

She nodded. "Afraid so, but, on a brighter note, it looks like someone kissed the ever loving crap out of you last night."

My hand moved to my mouth. My lips were tender to the touch, and the skin around it felt numb. "Holy crap! Who did I kiss?"

"Hey, you could have just run into a tree or something," Andi offered with a solid nod. "Wouldn't be the first time."

"That a freshman made out with a tree after getting drunk?"

"Sure, why not?"

I groaned and put the pillow over my face, willing my body to remember something — anything! — about the night before. Pike had asked me if I wanted to go to the bonfire, then he'd given me beer, that I remembered. I also remembered being pissed that Phoenix had hit on the one girl who I actually liked.

So I'd drunk.

And I thought I saw where things had gone south. I'd drunk, even though it tasted horrible, and when Pike had given me more — I'd taken it.

How did I get home?

I vaguely remembered almost falling off Pike's lap and then Phoenix yelling at me, carrying me. My shame knew no bounds. I continued to cringe as small images started to trickle back into my brain.

I'd stumbled, poked him in the chest. He had yelled again.

Gorgeous, he'd called me.

I'd asked him if I was pretty. *Kill me now.*

And then… I gasped aloud and moaned.

"What?" Andi was at my side in a heartbeat. "What's wrong?"

"Oh, no." I said into the pillow. "Oh, no, no, no!" I jumped out of bed, despite my headache, washed my face, brushed my teeth, and threw on a pair of clothes with a beanie.

"You gonna fill me in?" Andi asked from the door. She took in my outfit and winced. "Shabby chic?"

"Ah! I need to find Phoenix."

"The hot bodyguard?"

"Yes, my hot bodyguard." I added the *my* in there just in case she didn't get the picture.

She held her hands up into the air. "Got it. He's yours."

I stomped from the room, louder than necessary, and turned just in time to collide with Phoenix's chest.

"We're sure chipper this morning," he said in a monotone voice.

I reared back and stared into his eyes, my own narrowing in suspicion. "You, you, you…"

"Is she still drunk?" he asked over my head, apparently directing the question to Andi, even though the *she* to whom he was referring was standing right in front of him.

"Don't think so, but she did just scream into a pillow three times."

"Well, that explains it." Phoenix sighed. "Andi, why don't you go to breakfast, and I'll take care of Bee."

"I'm sure you will," she said in a saucy voice.

I wasn't sure how to act. Wasn't sure if I should apologize for attacking him or thank him for not laughing in my face. Embarrassed and irritated that he was most likely going to ignore whatever it was between us even if it killed him, I stared hard at the cement floor.

"How are you feeling, little girl?"

"I'm not little."

"You want me to call you fat?"

"No." I lifted my head. "Call me gorgeous like you did last night."

"Well, shit." Phoenix ran his hands over his face then grabbed my arm and dragged me down the hall into a darkened corner. "You remember?"

"You kissed me."

"Prove it."

"What's wrong with you?" I pushed against his chest. "You like me! Admit it!"

Phoenix made a face. "You were drunk, launched yourself at me, and I caught you. Did we kiss?" His eyes went completely black. "Yeah, we did, but it meant nothing."

"Really?"

"Really." He hissed out a breath through his teeth.

"Prove it."

"What?"

I pushed him against the wall. "*Prove it* meant nothing. Let me kiss you now, and if it meant nothing it will be like… what? Kissing your sister."

"I've sworn off women."

"So this should be an easy test then, right?"

"Bee…" Phoenix's face was pained, as if I was holding a gun to his head rather than offering to kiss him. Was the idea so abhorrent? "Please…" His voice had a pleading tone I'd never heard before. "Don't do this."

"One. Little. Test." I rose up on my tip toes and kissed him full on the mouth.

His lips refused to move against mine.

I wrapped my arms around his neck.

He stiffened even more.

Irritated, I bit his lower lip. He gasped, and I slid my tongue inside his mouth. He pushed me away with a curse then wiped his lips. "Done. Your little test is done. I didn't respond. Happy now?"

His eyes were furious; the blue flashed like lightning against his skin. His fingertips shook as he made a fist.

"You like me."

"Bee…" Phoenix pinched the bridge of his nose with his fingertips. "…find someone your own age, someone who's interested in you in the way you deserve, alright?" His tone was gentle, and maybe that was what hurt the most.

It was like he was letting me down slowly, hoping I didn't break.

But the joke was on him.

Because I was already broken.

I didn't want boys my age — I wanted him.

"You're a good liar." My eyes narrowed. "And you're lucky I'm patient."

"Lucky?" He sputtered out a laugh. "That you like toying with me?"

"No, lucky that even though you constantly push me away...I keep coming back for more. But, Phoenix... everyone's time eventually runs out."

"Go to breakfast, Bee."

"Go to Hell, Phoenix."

I stomped off, leaving him to his thoughts, and made my way into the dining room. Andi was already sitting next to Pike. I grabbed a plate, filled it with meat, and slammed it down onto the table.

"Uh, could you not slam things?" Pike winced. "Still got a headache over here."

"Oh." I stabbed the eggs with my fork. "Sorry."

"How'd it go last night after your knight in shining armor rescued you from my dangerous grasp?" He smirked and leaned forward.

Something about Pike was seriously off; maybe it was the way he stared at me, as if I was naked, or maybe it was just his presence. He seemed too old to be in college — too old and too knowledgeable about everything.

"Oh, you know, we had wild monkey sex in the woods, and then I woke up with a pinecone attached to my ass." I grinned then shoved the eggs into my mouth and chewed.

"Classy." Pike whistled.

"Always."

"Students!" The new dean, whose name I couldn't remember, walked to the front of the room and clapped his hands. "Make sure to check your itinerary for the day. We have you split up into eight teams for the day's activities. Enjoy!"

"Yay." I twirled my fork into the air.

My lack of enthusiasm got worse when I was paired on Pike's team, and we continued to lose every single activity, including beach volleyball.

Apparently, he was competitive.

And because I had no idea how to play any sport of any kind, I was the reason we kept losing. I apologized, but it did nothing to calm that stupid vein that kept twitching near his temple.

The next day passed by in a blur.

Phoenix rarely spoke to me, and when he did, it was only to bark orders and make sure I was always — and I do mean *always* — where I was supposed to be. If I didn't check in on an hourly basis, he hunted me down.

The fun was officially gone. I just wanted to go home. But I had no home to go to, not really.

I had no place I felt comfortable.

Except in his arms, or maybe in his room.

But now there was this giant chasm between us, one I couldn't jump across, because he didn't want me to even try.

I was the job. Nothing more.

CHAPTER TWENTY-THREE
Working for Tex officially sucks.

Phoenix

THANK GOD IT WAS the final day. I wasn't sure how much more I could take of Bee prancing around in her bikini while attempting to play beach volleyball. It was like the girl had the athleticism of a two year old, and what made it worse was that her body was that of a woman, so even when she missed the ball, things still... bounced.

And I still watched.

Like every other male within her vicinity.

I wrote down the worst offenders, mentally begging them to do something stupid so I could have the chance to shoot them.

We were leaving in an hour, and I still needed to get the final camera from Bee's room.

The door was closed. I knocked twice.

Bee answered and rolled her eyes. "What do you want?"

"Just checking in," I said smoothly, my eyes locating the camera immediately. I'd have to come back when she was in the bathroom or something.

"Well…" Bee turned around and lifted her hands into the air. "…care to strip search me, or are we done here?"

I let out a sigh and sat on the bed. "Am I going to have to deal with this happy attitude the entire drive home?"

Bee put her hair up into a tight ponytail, her movements jerky. "Probably. Is that going to be an issue?"

"Not at all. I can wear headphones."

"I'll scream."

"Try me."

"I'll hit you so we run off a cliff."

"You hate heights."

"Agh!" She stomped her foot. "How can you always be so calm?"

"You think I'm calm?" The idea was laughable, completely ridiculous. If she even knew how close I was to snapping — all the damn time.

"I bet if I punched you in the face, you'd grunt, maybe shrug."

"Well, there's only one way to find out."

"You're like a freaking robot!"

Ignoring her, I stood and grabbed her duffel bag. "This all packed?"

"Yeah," she said in a broken voice. "Oh wait." She ran into the bathroom then ran out and stuffed her bikini into one of the side pockets.

It was yellow.

And I was obsessed with it.

Not that I'd ever say it out loud, lest I lost the last of the control I possessed.

"Hold on," a voice whispered on the other side of the door. "Yeah, I'm alone." It was Pike.

I gave my head a shake.

Bee didn't move.

"No, nothing. Do you think I'm stupid? No, I understand.

I'll get it done, I just need more time. I can't just—" He swore under his breath. "I said I'd get the job done, and I mean it. Just keep your end of the deal."

Something slammed against the door, possibly his hand.

"I don't give two shits! We made a deal. I expect you to follow through on it. I'm giving you two heads. You damn well better give me one."

Bee's cell phone chose that moment to buzz off the nearby desk and onto the hard wood floor.

In three seconds, Pike was going to come barreling into a quiet room and know we'd heard.

So I did the only logical thing I could think of. I tugged Bee against my chest and kissed her like I'd always wanted to.

Hoping...

Praying...

She'd respond like her life depended on it — because it probably did.

With a moan, she wrapped her arms around my neck.

I ripped at her shirt, purposefully trying to make it look worse than it really was so that Pike would get the idea that we were more than just making out — ready to take it to the next level.

The door burst open, but I pretended that I didn't hear. I slammed Bee into the nearest wall, causing a mirror to shatter against the floor. Her body was so tight beneath mine that I almost forgot we had an audience, almost forgot what the hell I was doing. And then the images, the ones I tried so hard to fight, pushed forward.

I pulled back from Bee just as Pike swore under his breath. "Sorry, guys. Didn't mean to... um... interrupt." The door closed behind him.

And I lunged away from Bee like I'd just been stung — repeatedly.

She didn't say anything; instead, she stared at me, her eyes searching, and, I hoped to God, not finding out why I was the way I was.

We needed to leave.

I needed to leave.

Instead, she grabbed my hand and, because I was so damn weak, I went to her. Because I wanted to taste her again, I fell into her embrace and kissed her again, this time softly, like she deserved.

The images tried to flash, but I concentrated on her taste instead of the evil, her lips, instead of the monster I was. I told myself to go slow. I told myself this was the last taste.

I lied.

Because I kept tasting.

It was like I couldn't stop.

Just as I predicted, anything good, even food, would eventually cause me to stumble, and I was lost, tumbling down the rabbit hole and taking the most precious thing in the world with me.

Bee reached for my shirt and tried to pull it over my head.

I let her.

I was so tired of fighting.

So tired of saying no when all I wanted to do was say yes.

Another image flashed, and I took a step back from her.

"Stay with me," she whispered across my mouth. "Just like this."

I focused on her voice and deepened the kiss.

My phone rang in my pocket.

I ignored it, paying attention to her neck instead, licking my way down her ear. My body soared at the fact that I was able to touch her and not feel pain.

From the floor, Bee's phone rang.

She ignored it too.

When my phone rang a second time, I knew it was important. Reluctantly, I stepped back, almost feeling like I'd been drugged, and answered with a gruff. "What?"

"Well, you're in some deep shit," Chase said in a low voice. "That's what."

"Chase... not now."

"Yes, now, you ass. I just saw you, and unfortunately Tex chose that inopportune moment to look over my shoulder."

"What the hell are you talking about?"

"Camera, in her room. I was monitoring her, checking in like I do every morning to help you out."

"Shit." I glanced back at the camera. "Oh, shit!"

"Yeah." Chase sighed. "Drive straight here. Best to just let him shoot you then make it fun for him by running."

"Right." I would have laughed, but it was anything but funny. The one time I'd done the wrong thing, taken one misstep in the past few months, and I just happened to do it right in front of the Cappo — with his little sister.

I hung up and slid the phone back into my pocket.

Bee reached for me.

I backed up. "Tex...."

"So what? He doesn't have to know."

"Ha!" I licked my lips and threw on my shirt. "Too late, he already does."

"What do you..."

Without a word I went behind the desk and pulled the tiny camera from the drawer.

"You son of a bitch!" She lunged for me. "You were spying on me?"'

"How else can I watch you while you sleep and make sure nobody breaks into your bedroom, Bee?" I yelled right back at her.

"I don't know! Maybe by actually admitting you have feelings for me, growing a pair of balls and sleeping in my room!"

"You think I don't sleep in your room because I can't admit I have feelings?"

She nodded, her lower lip quivering.

"I have too many of them, that's the damn problem. I feel hatred, anger, sadness, guilt... every single second of the day, and then you come barreling into my life making me remember the reason I feel all those things... I'm evil. I raped girls, did you know that? I raped them, Bee. I tortured them, all for family, all for blood. I almost killed my best friend's wife because I couldn't help myself! Is that what you want to hear? That I have those types of feelings? Well newsflash, I'm able to admit it all day long, I'll scream it if you want me to, but don't for one second think I'm running from things you have no business even knowing about! I hurt people. I hurt girls. I'll eventually hurt you. Better you know that now, than later, when it actually happens." I stormed toward the door and pulled it open just as Bee spoke.

"You would never hurt me."

"The sick part, Bee..." I didn't turn around. "Is as much as I wish that were true..." I hung my head in shame. "I can't promise you that. I just...can't."

CHAPTER TWENTY-FOUR
Murder and Mayhem. Just don't kill my only friend.

Bee

THE DRIVE TO TEX'S house wasn't a happy one. Phoenix was pale and silent. And I had a sinking feeling it was because my brother was about to shoot his head off, all for touching me.

I tried not to think about what Phoenix said. Raping girls? Hurting them? I couldn't imagine him doing it, not that I didn't think him capable, I just... the man I knew now, didn't seem the type to be able to carry it out without having a serious problem with it.

But the issue that made me sick to my stomach.

Was I really the type of girl that would look past that type of darkness? All because I wanted to believe the lie? I was at war within myself, wanting to believe the best in him, yet sick that it was completely possible I didn't know him at all, and never had.

The man he was, the man he used to be, had carried it out... and from the sound of it, he'd been far too good at his job.

"Let me do the talking." Phoenix said gruffly as he turned off the car and slowly made his way into Tex's compound.

It was only a few miles from Nixon's but had security like something you'd see around the White House. Men were everywhere, guarding, constantly watching.

It was an old style colonial brick home that had been completely redone on the inside; it should look inviting. Instead, each step was like walking toward certain death.

The large oak door opened. Chase shook his head from side to side, then reached out and took Phoenix's hand. "It doesn't look good. He nearly destroyed the entire kitchen. Mo's pissed because it was her wedding china." He released a breath then looked at me. "Hey, Bee, long time no see."

"Apparently not." I crossed my arms while he winced. I used to think Chase was gorgeous, like a painting, but now, comparing him to Phoenix... he failed in so many ways. Where Chase was pretty, Phoenix was rough; everything about him spoke of a harshness that Chase didn't possess.

With a sigh, Chase opened the door wider. "Everyone's inside."

"Everyone?" I gulped.

"Yeah." Chase nodded. "The wives and us."

"Great."

"Think of it as a family dinner." Chase said in a much too hopeful voice. "Only this time someone *will* get shot."

Phoenix let out a curse as we walked into the living room.

Tex was pacing back and forth across the carpet, itching the back of his neck with a gun. Not a good sign.

Nixon was calmly sitting down with his hands folded across his thighs and Trace was standing next to him, rubbing his neck.

Mil was drinking a glass of wine by the fireplace.

And Mo was trying to get Tex to calm down, which clearly wasn't working. She reached for his hand but he jerked away, continuing on with his pacing as if that would solve the problem altogether.

Chase cleared his throat, announcing our arrival.

Tex paused, his coppery brown hair brushing his forehead as he jerked up and glared at us. In an instant his gun was in the air.

Phoenix pushed me out of the way just as the gun went off...aiming for his chest.

He fell to his knees with a grunt and swore.

I screamed, or at least I think I did, before I saw blood start to pour from a wound on the right side of his chest near his shoulder.

Another gun shot rang out.

Are you freaking kidding me?

Everything happened in slow motion, Phoenix's eyes were shuttered, completely closed off from the rest of the world as he blinked, and then with a wince touched another wound on the same shoulder. Two bullet holes, two shots that went directly through him.

Blood rapidly poured through the wounds staining the white T-shirt I'd been admiring while he was driving.

Strong arms wrapped around me and pulled me back from his bloody body. I tried to puke but couldn't even find the strength to do that. He needed me, didn't gun shots kill people?

My brother stood over Phoenix, the gun aimed for his head. "No!" I shouted elbowing whoever had me in their arms with all the strength I had. "Tex, stop!"

Tex tilted his head, and pressed the gun against Phoenix's temple.

"Tex!" I sobbed, unable to even see the scene anymore because my tears were making it impossible to see anything other than the dark gun against Phoenix's pale skin. "Stop now!"

The arms holding me, released. I slumped to the ground

and watched in slow motion as Nixon charged Tex and slammed him against the wall, punching him in the jaw and then in the stomach.

Tex fought back, screaming at the top of his lungs.

Nixon cursed, kneeing him in the stomach again and again.

Tex knocked his head against Nixon's.

And then Chase was in the mix pushing both of them apart. A sucker punch to his face must have pissed him off, he roared "bastard" in Italian and kneed Tex in the balls.

With a cry, Tex fell to the ground.

Nixon slumped down next to him, and Chase bent over, heaving.

Phoenix was still bleeding; I reached for him but didn't make it as blackness overtook me.

"BACK OFF!" THE VOICE grumbled.

"The hell I will!" I think it was Phoenix's voice. "You're a bastard, you know that?"

"Oh, I'm the bastard?" Tex said, though his voice sounded fuzzy. "You were kissing—"

"Guys, arguing isn't helping," Nixon said in a calm voice.

"I will kill you," Tex said in a hateful tone. "Maybe not today, not tomorrow, but soon I will end your pathetic excuse for a life for even thinking you could touch her and—"

"Son of a bitch!" Chase roared. "Tex, Cappo or not, I will seriously shoot you in the face if you keep yelling that loud."

That was definitely Mil.

I blinked my eyes open. The room was blurry. I saw blood again, a black T-shirt, and Phoenix's stained white T-shirt. I reached for him before I reached for anyone else.

He took my hand.

My brother's jaw clenched so tight I heard a pop before

he swore under his breath.

"Phoenix is alive?" I croaked out.

"Unfortunately," Tex answered with a bur to his voice. "You gave us quite a scare, little sis."

"I hate you," I mumbled.

"Me?" Tex's eyebrows knit together. "What the hell did I do?"

"Wow, sounds like he wants a list," Nixon said from the other side of me. "I don't know. Shot her friend in front of her?"

"Bee and Phoenix aren't friends," Tex said in a confident tone. "She's his job. There's a difference."

Tears threatened again as I looked at my brother, like really looked at him. He didn't know me at all; he was going about this whole family business wrong, all wrong.

"I have one friend," I whispered in a hoarse voice. "And you shot him. Twice."

"One friend?" Tex repeated.

Phoenix simply stared at me, his gaze concerned. His blue eyes didn't reveal anything except for something I was beginning to think was admiration. His shoulder was wrapped in white gauze, and he was pale, but, other than that, he looked alive, breathing, not six feet under or attached to some cement object that was going to be thrown into the lake.

Everyone fell quiet.

"She's scared of blood," Phoenix finally said, gripping my hand and pulling me up to a sitting position. "Which you would know if you took your head out of your ass long enough to actually get to know your sister."

"He's seriously asking to be shot again," Chase mumbled under his breath.

"Oh, bite me," Phoenix snapped. "Nixon shot Tex in the shoulder for kissing his own sister. I'm surprised I still have all my teeth."

"A dental exam can be arranged." Tex's chest puffed up.

"Oh yeah? Try me, Cappo!" Phoenix shoved my brother hard enough to send him stumbling backward a few steps.

"That's it!" Tex threw down a towel he was holding against his face and lunged for Phoenix.

Another gun went off.

I turned.

It was Nixon; he'd just shot at Tex's feet.

"What the hell, man? In my own home?" Tex roared.

"Next time, I shoot your hand." Nixon's voice was low, gravelly, his eyes were dark as he approached the group, gun still raised. "You're bosses. For the love of God, act like it. This is not how we do business."

"Pot." Tex seethed at him.

"Kettle," Nixon said right back with a smirk.

"Son of a—" Tex slammed his hand on the wall and paced in front of me, his steps most likely making permanent marks into the hardwood floors. "Fine, why the hell were you kissing my sister?"

"Which time?" Phoenix asked in a calm voice.

Tex clenched his teeth and closed his eyes then took a deep breath and swore. "The first, asshole."

"Pike," I said in a quiet voice. "He was outside, talking to someone. It sounded… bad, and then my cell phone went off, so we needed him to think we hadn't heard him."

Tex scratched the back of his neck and mumbled under his breath. "Fine, so the first excuse flies, and the second kiss?"

Phoenix opened his mouth.

"I begged him!" I said in a rush. "I've been begging him for weeks, months."

Phoenix's eyes narrowed.

"And…" I swallowed the dryness in my throat. "I just… the first kiss was so nice. I'd never actually had a kiss, a real kiss before, so I begged him, and then I just… it was me, I attacked him, I'm nineteen. I have hormones… and needs." I choked out the last part while Tex's face flushed a bright red.

Chase looked down at the ground, his smile nearly breaking his face while Nixon rolled his eyes and let out a chuckle.

"This isn't funny," Tex growled.

"Pretty damn funny, if you ask me." Nixon put his gun away. "Looks like you shot him twice… for no reason."

"He still touched her," Tex pointed out.

"He was just following orders," Chase piped up. "…from the Cappo's sister, which, if we're going to be real legal about shit, outranks any one of us. Right, Bee?"

"R-right." I nodded my head and glared at Tex. "He was just listening to me."

"Well, maybe he should stop listening to you."

"And maybe you should stop being such a-a-a big bully!"

Nixon and Chase burst out laughing.

Tex crossed then uncrossed his arms. "I'm not a bully, I'm just… protecting you…"

"By killing my only friend," I said in a sad voice.

"Make new friends, Bee!" He threw his hands into the air. "When I assigned Phoenix to you, it wasn't so that you could paint each other's nails and braid hair, damn it! He's to protect you, never touch you, and make sure you have enough to eat during the day."

"Don't forget drive her to school," Chase interjected with a chuckle.

"Or go to class," Nixon added, grinning.

Tex lifted his eyes toward the ceiling. "I'm not equipped to handle girls. I'm really not."

"Pray for sons." Nixon patted him on the back.

"Bee…" Tex reached for my hands and shoved Phoenix out of the way. "Next to Mo, you are my life. I can't…" His eyes filled with tears. "Phoenix is with you because he's the best."

I glanced sideways at Phoenix. His expression reflected the surprised I felt.

"But he's..." Tex let out a sigh. "...he's—"

"Damaged." Phoenix said it for him. "Completely and totally damaged, used goods, dark, evil, Satan himself." With a terse nod, Phoenix kept talking. "I'm no good, Bee. You're brother's right, and the sooner you learn that, the better off we'll all be."

"I don't believe it," I whispered through the searing pain in my heart.

The guys were silent. Even Nixon and Chase looked uncomfortable as Tex and Phoenix shared a look.

"I'll talk to her," Phoenix said quietly. "Just give us a minute."

"No kissing." Tex released my hands and shoved past Phoenix.

When we were alone, I reached for him, but he didn't put his hands out, didn't return the affection. In fact, he stepped away, putting visible distance between us.

"Bee..." Phoenix licked his lips, and his eyes held that same haunted look I'd grown to hate, as the black circles beneath them seemed to pulse with each second that went by. "Thank you for defending me."

I opened my mouth, but he reached out and pressed his fingertips against my lips.

"Let me finish." He cleared his throat. "Thank you for protecting me, for taking the blame, but it wasn't yours to take. Your brother's right, so damn right, to shoot me for touching you, for even thinking that it was okay for one second to expose you to the person I am. It's wrong. It's so damn wrong that I wish he would have killed me."

Tears filled my eyes.

"You are everything." His full lips trembled as he spoke. "You are everything that's beautiful and pure in this world, and you deserve so much better than this life, than what any of us have to offer. Than what *I* have to offer."

My heart sank to my knees; it wasn't just rejection I was

feeling, but complete loss, like he'd taken my heart out, broken it into tiny pieces and scattered them into the wind.

"I can't believe that about you. I won't, Phoenix."

"Damn it, Bee!" Phoenix gripped my shoulders. "How much do you want me to tell you? Do I have to show you every ugly thing I've ever done in order to scare you away? Clearly you aren't getting the picture."

"You aren't like that anymore."

Phoenix's fingers dug into my arms. "Bee, you don't know what goes through my head, the nightmares, the images. Hell, I can't freaking eat a hot meal without feeling guilty at the pleasure it brings me. I can't experience good, because every time I do, it pushes me closer to the edge, closer to the breaking point, and, Bee, you are that final push. It would be too easy." His voice broke. "Too damn easy to allow it... and in the end..." His eyes turned completely black. "...I would destroy you."

"So confident in your own darkness," I whispered, cupping his face. "But what about the light, the good?"

He pulled my hands away from his face and took another step back. "It died the minute I flat-lined two months ago, Bee. I may be alive, but I'm not living."

Tears streamed down my face. "What if you just tried?"

"You think I don't try?" he spat. "You think I don't want more?"

"I think you punish yourself."

He slammed his hand on the table next to me. "Because I deserve to be punished, Bee! Don't you get it? I'm the murderer on death row that gets no appeals. I'm alive to do a job. I don't get a second chance."

"Says who?"

He swallowed and removed his hand from the table, turning his body so I couldn't see his face anymore, only the muscular build I'd become so obsessed with.

"Do you want me to ask Tex to assign someone else to

you?" he asked, voice hollow.

"What?" Panic rose in my chest. "No, no you can't!"

"Fine." Phoenix nodded, his body still turned from me. "But from here on out, Bee… no kissing, no touching, no taunting or teasing. Leave me alone, because I can only handle so much temptation before I take that bite, before I allow you to push me, and I'll hate myself forever for destroying what you are."

"I can't make any promises."

"Then I'll tell Tex to give you someone else."

"Phoenix, wait!" I jumped off the table I'd been sitting on and gripped him from behind. Instantly, I started melting from the inside out; his body was so warm pressed against mine. He went rigid in my embrace. "Fine. I — I promise. Just don't leave me."

"Bee…" He hung his head and slowly unwrapped my warms from his torso. "I couldn't leave you even if I wanted to. You're a part of me, always will be."

"If I told you I loved you, would it change things?"

He heaved a choked sigh. "Everyone loves a bit of darkness — until it consumes them."

Phoenix walked down the hall, opened the front door, and slammed it behind him. The sound of the car starting was my only cue that the conversation was finally over.

And that Phoenix De Lange was officially walking out of my life.

CHAPTER TWENTY-FIVE

Even his sister doesn't believe in him. What does that even mean?

Bee

"YOU OKAY?" MIL TOOK a seat next to me on the couch, coffee mug in hand. "I'm not really great at girl talk, but if you want me to kick your brother's ass, I can hire it out."

I suppressed a laugh and shrugged.

"Tough cookie." She sighed and leaned back. "I used to be tough like that. Don't let people see the hurt, the pain, the complete and total fear I felt at just waking up and breathing every day."

"And now?" I croaked, my eyes trained straight ahead at whatever was on the TV.

"Now," Mil said calmly, "I have someone to lean on, makes things easier."

"Chase?"

"No, my Glock, but Chase helps too."

I laughed and turned to face her.

"Kidding." She winked. Mil had just cut her hair to her

chin; it was a silky black. She had strong features just like Phoenix. Even though they were step-siblings, she resembled him in a way; maybe it was the harshness she always carried with her. Mil used it as armor; Phoenix used it to hide.

"I don't have a gun."

"Ask Tex for one."

"Yeah." I snorted. "Because he's been so generous lately."

"You don't get it do you?" she said in a harsh tone.

I reared back, a bit shocked she'd react like that. "Get what?"

"This is war." Mil's eyes flashed. "We've spent the last two years getting shot at, fought against at every turn, conspired against. Hell, we shouldn't even be alive. Your brother is doing the best he can to keep you alive. There are people who would stop at nothing to get to you — in order to get to him."

"And here I thought he was just being overprotective." I swallowed down the fear and wrung my hands together. "I guess I never thought of it that way."

"Yeah well…" Mil shrugged. "…maybe you should. This isn't a game. Every day we're given is a gift. And Phoenix? He's been dealt a rough hand. How much do you know about his past? About The Elect?"

I chewed my lower lip. "Enough to give me nightmares."

"Good." She patted my leg. "Maybe you should stop fighting us and listen to what everyone's been telling you all along. My brother." She looked down at the carpet. "He's not the same as he used to be, which is a good thing, in a way… but he can't be both at once."

"I'm confused."

Mil tried again. "He doesn't know how to balance it. The killing, the darkness, and dirty side of the mafia and real life. He lost the ability to do that a long time ago. It's not something he's ever been really good at anyway. He's either all good or all bad; there is no in between for him. He doesn't know how to do it, can't function in that way. Tex... hell, the guy can rip toenails then kiss his wife afterward and give a high five to a toddler. Nixon freaking smiles when he shoots people, and Chase?" She shuddered. "He tortures people and eats takeout while doing it. I guess what I'm saying is Phoenix isn't like them, so don't think that this is going to end the same way it has for all of us. The best thing you can do is let him do his job and love him from afar."

"But I want to love him close." I choked on the words. "I want to save him. I can do it. I know I can, if he just tried—"

"It slices me open to say this, Bee, but Phoenix—" Her eyes filled with tears. "He's beyond saving."

CHAPTER TWENTY-SIX

Rip my soul out and feed it to the birds.

Phoenix

I STARED AT THE glass of whiskey in my hand like it was poison — as if it would bite me in the ass if I touched it.

Two hours had passed since I'd poured the glass.

And I was still staring at it. Each time I'd brought it to my lips, I'd set it back down, hands shaking, unable to take one simple drink.

An image of a girl screaming flashed through my mind; she was faceless. They all were. After all, what type of sick bastard remembers their faces? But their eyes... I never forgot their eyes. When people say they're the window to a person's soul — it's absolute truth.

Eyes reveal too much. They show pain, fear, excitement— Every damn emotion is visible through the eyes.

Her eyes were fearful.

I'm sure mine were as well; after all, when a monster acts out of necessity, it's usually fear that's the driving force. I was afraid of losing everything, afraid of the person I was becoming, afraid of turning into my father.

And by feeding that fear…

I became exactly what I'd been trying to run away from.

My fingers tapped against the glass as I stared at the amber liquid. Another image came and then another, until I squeezed my eyes shut, forcing them away, forcing away the screams of terror, the way the girls' nails had felt against my skin as they'd fought for their very lives.

And the taste of their fear as I'd taken and taken until they'd had nothing more to give, until I'd had it all.

When I was five, I'd wanted to be a superhero.

Batman, to be exact.

When I told my dad, he'd said that heroes were weak; it was the villains who had real strength — because they were the only ones willing to do whatever it took to survive.

The hell with that. I just wanted a cape and cool gadgets; I wanted people to adore me, to applaud me. I wanted approval, and maybe that's what had driven me to become the villain.

Being the hero had gotten me nowhere.

But being the villain? For a while? Got me everything.

It sated me, for a brief moment.

Until I needed more.

Until I stopped recognizing the man I'd become.

With a forceful exhale, I pushed away from the kitchen table and reached for my glass. My hands shook as I dumped the contents into the sink and eyed the fridge.

"Just lasagna," I whispered, opening up the door and examining the food. I reached for my usual green apple, and my hand brushed up against Greek yogurt.

It was blue.

Son of a bitch, was I actually afraid of blue now too?

Would eating something that actually tasted good… something other than fruit or vegetables… actually kill me? Probably not, but it would make me crave. It was like an alcoholic's first taste of the finest whiskey; it's so good, why not pour a little more? In the grand scheme of things, one drink is almost like having two, if you go really slow. A person can justify absolutely anything.

Tasting Bee wasn't enough.

Holding her wasn't enough.

Feeling her — would never be enough.

I craved her in a way that was bordering on obsessive because I'd taken that leap, and now I didn't know how to get back on the damn ledge. Just being around her was going to be difficult; smelling her, knowing that she was actually willing to touch me, black as I was?

Absolute Hell.

Out of all the people in my life, my sister included, Bee was the only person who actually saw past the bad and tried to reach for the good.

To everyone else I was a lost cause.

To her? I was someone worth fighting for.

But somewhere along the way, I'd stopped fighting for the most important thing in my life.

Myself.

"Hungry?" Bee said from behind me.

I damn near collided with the fridge as I jumped back and closed it. "I didn't hear anyone drop you off."

She smiled sadly. "Yeah well, I didn't exactly stomp through the house like you're known to do."

I returned her smile. "I don't stomp."

"You do." She nodded. "Daily. And if you aren't stomping, you're grunting."

"Well, I sound like a complete joy to be around. Thanks for that."

Bee lifted her hand and touched my shoulder. "How's it feel?"

"Like I got shot."

"Put ice on it?" She scrunched up her nose. "Sorry, I

didn't exactly enroll in any gunshot wound classes at Elite."

"Ice." I nodded. "I'll... uh, see if that helps."

"Okay, well... I'm going to go to bed." Bee's mouth opened and closed like she wanted to say something else but decided not to. She turned and walked out of the kitchen then stopped. She wrung her hands together in front of her and turned on her heel, making a beeline for me again. "One more thing."

"What?" I leaned against the fridge.

"This may not make sense, and you may laugh at me for saying it... and I know I'm just a girl, and—"

"Bee."

"—I believe in you," she blurted, tears in her eyes. "I just... I want you to know that despite everything... I believe in you. That's all."

She nodded her head and stumbled backward, nearly colliding with the kitchen counter, then practically ran out of the room.

I stared at the space she'd just escaped for a good five minutes, my head pounding.

The last person who had said that to me was Luca Nicolasi.

Chills erupted across my skin. I gripped the handle to the fridge and jerked it open.

Without a second thought, I pulled out the blueberry yogurt.

CHAPTER TWENTY-SEVEN

Change was coming — and I wasn't ready, not by a long shot.

Sergio

I WOKE UP EARLY so I could be home by the time Bee and Phoenix got up for breakfast. I threw on my running gear and took off.

The sun wasn't up yet. The road was quiet, eerie almost. I hated being alone with my thoughts, hated exercise in general, but running, for some reason, helped me cope.

Right, the killer needs help coping. Hilarious.

My feet hit the pavement in a steady rhythm. When I reached the field, I pretended that I needed to stretch just as another runner stopped.

"You got what I need?" I asked, not bothering to look at her.

She reached into her hoodie and pulled out an envelope. "It's all here."

"You know they could kill you for this." I took the envelope and shoved it into my pocket, still refusing to look her directly in the eyes.

"I'm already dead," she said in a confident tone. "My cover was blown ages ago. They only keep me around to toy with me."

I finally looked at her; she was young, probably my age, dark brown hair in a ponytail, face makeup-free, not gorgeous but pretty, youthful. A pity that she wasn't going to live long enough to enjoy life.

"If I don't see you later..." I gave a curt nod.

"I knew the terms when I signed up, Sergio, so did you."

I licked my lips in irritation. "We had completely different reasons, I'm sure."

She smiled sadly. "Yeah well, dead girl walking." Her smile was sad, her eyes unfocused.

I knew what I had to do. "What's your name?"

She squinted and tilted her head. "Um, why?"

I offered a comforting smile "Just tell me."

"Sarah."

"I like it. It's pretty." And probably fake.

She snorted. "Well, when you see the name Sarah in the obits this coming week, don't feel sorry for me. Then again, they'd have to recognize the body."

"For what it's worth, thank you for getting this information for me."

"Like I said... dead girl walking." She offered a wave.

Brave. She was facing her own death in a way that was braver than me; so in that moment, I decided to extend mercy, a mercy I knew would never be extended in my direction — ever.

"Hey, Sarah?" I called.

She turned around.

I pulled out my gun and fired two shots directly into her chest. Her expression went from surprised to peaceful in seconds.

She slumped to the cold hard ground. "Th-thank you."

"May God have mercy on your soul," I whispered, firing

a third shot and kissing her across the forehead as her head hit the gravel road. I pulled her lifeless body to the side, covered her up with some brush, and continued on my run.

When I reached the next mile marker, I cleaned my gun and forced thoughts of the girl's death behind me. She'd been brave.

And I wanted to honor that bravery. After all, I knew firsthand what they would do to her once they needed to tie up a loose end.

What I'd done ? Was a kindness.

I patted the heavy envelope in my pocket and ran like hell the rest of the way home. When I rounded the corner into the kitchen, Bee and Phoenix were already sitting at the table eating.

"Have a good run?" Phoenix asked, not looking up from the newspaper.

"It was…" I shrugged and poured myself a glass of orange juice. "…interesting."

Bee smiled at me.

I returned it.

And shoved my free hand into my pocket so she wouldn't see the shake… the shake that always happened when I took a life, the adrenaline that surged, and the absolute loss I felt as another piece of my soul was taken away.

CHAPTER TWENTY-EIGHT

Sometimes I missed her arguing... sometimes.

Phoenix

BEE DIDN'T ARGUE WITH me when I told her we were going to be late for her classes. Nor did she roll her eyes when I handed her a granola bar, just in case she got hungry.

When I turned on Mozart, she sighed and looked out the window as if she was content with the world. Meanwhile, a freaking storm was stirring inside my chest at the sight of her short skirt and tight blouse.

I cleared my throat, forcing my eyes away as I pulled the car up to the Elite campus and parked in our usual spot.

"Don't forget about your—"

"Pop quiz," she finished, opening her door, not waiting for me to run around and get it for her. "I'm all over it."

"Great." I grabbed her book bag and handed it to her.

"Bee!" Andi charged toward us. "I was worried you weren't going to come today. Do you always run this late?"

"Usually." Bee shrugged and offered me a pathetic smile, one that still had my entire body as tight as a drum and ready to attack her without a second thought. "But he's trying to keep me in check."

Andi's eyebrows rose. "Yeah about that…"

"What?" Bee looked from me back to Andi.

"Pike's been saying some stuff…" Andi fumbled with her backpack. "Look, it's probably nothing, but he's saying that you're screwing your bodyguard."

Shit.

My fault.

I hadn't gotten that far in our plan, far enough to threaten Pike within an inch of his life that he needed to shut the hell up and keep Bee out of the school gossip, which meant I was going to have to go talk to him and try not to shoot him when my finger was feeling trigger happy.

"Oh," Bee said in a calm tone. "Well, I guess that's not so bad. It's just a rumor right? It will die down."

Andi exhaled a whistle. "If you say so. Ready for class?"

"Yup!" They linked arms and trotted off.

I followed at a safe distance, and when I saw them enter the building and the right classroom, I excused myself and went in search of Pike.

He was easy to find, mainly because I had his schedule memorized. Lucky for me, he was in Sergio's class.

Toying with him would be the highlight of my day.

I knocked on the door twice then let myself in.

"Phoenix…" Sergio stood, his eyes questioning. "Did you need something? We just started class."

"I need someone," I said loudly. "Pike? He in this class right now?" I knew he was, but I wanted the kid to squirm.

"Absolutely." Sergio's face was expressionless, but I was pretty confident that he was doing a little cheer on the inside on my behalf; none of us liked the little shit, and I was getting to do the honors for the first time. Lucky me. "Pike, a moment please."

Slowly, Pike stood to his full height, his shit-eating grin

making me want to take his life more than my next breath. "Problem?"

"No." I placed my hand on his shoulder. "At least not yet. I need to talk with you."

"No offense." Pike shrugged away from me. "But you're a private bodyguard to another student. You can't take me anywhere."

Sergio grinned. "Pike... of course he can. Don't you know who this is?"

"Do you?" Pike sputtered. "Because I have it on good authority that he's bad news and can't make me do shit."

"Well..." Sergio clasped his hands together. "...I should get back to teaching. Have fun, boys."

"But—"

"I'm going to enjoy this." I grabbed Pike and shoved him toward the door then shut it behind us. The hall was completely empty.

Pike didn't move, simply snorted. "You can't make me do anything. You're a has-been. You're not even a real student! A paid bitch, that's what you are."

"Keep talking." I popped my fingers. "Really, it just gives me more time to plan what I'm going to do with you in excruciating detail."

Pike paled. "You can't touch me."

"Oh, I can..." I nodded. "...I will..." I kicked him in the shin then grabbed him by the neck and whispered. "...because I'm not just some girl's private security detail. I'm the head of security at Eagle Elite. I'm also the boss of the Nicolasi family." I paused long enough to eye him up and down. "Then again, you already knew that, didn't you? I'm the judge, jury, executioner... and for the next five minutes, I'm your only hope of walking on two legs for the rest of your life, so I'd cooperate, before I get tired of hearing your pathetic voice and rip your throat out." I tightened my grip. *"Capiche?"*

Pike tried to jerk away from me. I found an empty

classroom and tossed him into it, slamming the door behind us.

"Y-you can't hurt me!" Pike yelled. "Do you know who I am?"

I chuckled. "Why? Are you having an identity crisis, little guy?"

Roaring like a caged lion, he lunged for me. I moved out of the way and kicked him in the ass then slammed his body against the brick wall.

"Try that one more time. I dare you."

"If I die, they'll know you did it. You'll start another war — do you really want that?"

"I live for war." I slammed him again, blood spewed from his mouth. "Or weren't you listening. I'm Nicolasi. I cut my teeth on violence. Now, stop fighting like a bitch and have a seat, before I get really pissed off."

He stopped fighting against me, so I pushed him into an empty chair and stood in front of him. "Stay away from Bee."

"Is that what this is about?" He laughed. "Some girl? What, you can't keep her interest?" Realization crossed his features. "Oh I get it. She's disgusted because she knows what you did... classic. Tell me, do her screams get you off?"

A litany of graphic curses spewed from my mouth as I punched him in the jaw. When I gripped him by the shirt, blood trickled from my knuckles onto his white buttons. "Listen, you little prick. Whatever business goes down between all of us is our business — you leave Bee out of it. She deserves normal at this school, and I'm trying to give her that. Spread one more rumor, and I'll cut off your dick and mail it to Russia with love."

Pike gulped. "You're bluffing."

"Think long and hard, Pike." I grinned menacingly. "You know my last name. You know what I'm capable of. I don't have feelings — hell, I don't even have a conscience. Your choice. The rumors stop... or you lose an appendage." With a snarl of disgust, I released him and waited.

His eyes blazed with fury. "Fine. No more rumors. But I can't — I'm not going to stay away from her, not if she wants to hang out. Some of us need friends to survive. We aren't all cold-blooded killers."

"I'll be sure to tell that to your pops next time I visit federal prison."

Pike pushed away from the chair and muttered, "Whatever," under his breath. "We done here."

"For now." I nodded. "Oh, and clean up. You look like hell."

He gave me the finger and left the room.

And I felt better than I had in months, which was probably a bad sign, considering what had made me feel better was torturing someone under the age of twenty and toying with the idea of cutting up his body nice and pretty for school pictures.

I straightened my shirt, wiped my knuckles with some tissue from the professor's desk, and sauntered out into the hall.

CHAPTER TWENTY-NINE

Violence isn't always the answer, but it does make you feel better... sometimes.

Bee

"WHOA!" I STOPPED DEAD in my tracks as Pike's swollen face came into view. "What happened to you?"

"Ran into a wall?" he offered with a smirk. "Don't worry about me. I'm more concerned about you right now."

Andi elbowed me. "Sorry, kids, gotta go. I don't want to be late for my ride!" She ran off, leaving me alone with Pike.

"Me?" I shrugged. "Why would you be worried about me?"

Pike smiled. It was nice, his smile. I knew that, according to Phoenix, he was bad news, but he was a good-looking guy, and he was giving me attention. Talking to him wouldn't kill me, and if it did, we had way bigger problems.

"Walk with me?" He stepped aside.

I glanced around for Phoenix, but he was nowhere I could see, so I followed.

"If you're looking for the bodyguard, you can always send him a text so he doesn't freak."

I laughed. "He'll be fine."

"You're safe with me." Pike elbowed me in the side. "Promise."

"So, you're worried?"

Pike nodded, his sandy brown hair falling across his forehead. "Yeah, I mean, I know everyone thinks I started those rumors, but the truth is I've been trying to stop them. Kids here can be really cruel and… well, your bodyguard is a De Lange. Not only that, but he used to take advantage of girls, you know that, right?"

My stomach dropped. "Yes."

"He raped them. Everyone knows it… and, well, some of the kids are saying that you like it rough."

My stomach heaved. "But he would never, I mean, we never…" I shook my head back and forth.

Pike pulled me into his arms. "Hey, hey, don't cry. Let's go grab a coffee, okay? That'll make you feel better."

Numb, I nodded.

Never had the idea crossed my mind that others would know about Phoenix's past or associate me with it. I felt dirty, even though I had done nothing wrong, and then I felt guilty for feeling that way, knowing Phoenix was probably horrified at the prospect.

But I had kissed him.

And he had warned me.

"You know he pays prostitutes, right?" Pike said in a soft voice. "That's the only way he can keep the edge off. Pays them… killed a few back in the day too."

"How do you even know this?" I stopped walking. "It's not like it's public information."

"I have my ways." Pike shrugged. "Look, the campus coffee shop is just up ahead."

I glanced at the building. Orange cones lined the grass

and sidewalk, and a large yellow and black sign warned *UNDER CONSTRUCTION.*

"The sidewalk's closed off."

"We'll go around." He shrugged and led me back around the building by the trees. When he released my hand, I looked up just in time to see a large burly man approaching with a black sack. I stumbled back.

Searing pain hit my neck.

Everything went black.

CHAPTER THIRTY

Paranoia… it was my life now.

Sergio

CLASSES FINALLY ENDED, AND I was free to look through the packet that Sarah had given me that morning.

I locked my door and dumped the contents on the desk.

A flash drive fell out as well as a few pictures. The pictures I was familiar with; they were of the Petrov family, greedy drug-pushing bastards. Most were rotting in prison — all except our friend, Pike.

It could be nothing.

Except, why would the agency implant Pike in the school?

To keep an eye on us?

To keep an eye on me?

To tie up loose ends?

Nothing was making sense, and I figured it was probably because I was daydreaming about one of my students with bright blond hair and an easy smile.

She haunted me.

And I hated her for it. Freaking took it out on her in class today, nearly yelling at her for not having her pencil.

Great, asshole of the year award goes to... yours truly.

With a curse, I shoved the flash drive into my laptop and double-clicked on its icon.

More pictures that bored me to tears.

And then documents.

Contracts, to be exact. Contracts with the Petrov name on them... which, honestly, wasn't all that surprising, considering they used to own a large amount of shipping companies. Huge shock there; they shipped their drugs from other countries into ours.

I clicked through the files, not finding what I was wanting and still not sure what I was looking for.

A few phone conversations popped up. I clicked on the text and read.

Petrov: *Two heads are better than one.*

Agency: *Infiltrate, and two members go free.*

Petrov: *Infiltrate the family?*

Agency: *By way of the sister — figure out a way in. Marry her, kill her, do what you need to do, but we need control of at least one of the arms.*

Petrov: *Rumor has it Nicolasi named a new boss.*

Agency: *So kill him, throw a wrench in their plans. We need in, by any means necessary.*

Petrov: *I do this, and they go free.*

Agency: *You do this, and the US Government helps you disappear.*

Petrov: *Deal.*

I read over the script a few more times, my stomach plummeting. So that was his plan? Kill Phoenix? Or hurt Bee? Either way, it would be traced back to Petrov, not the feds. He was just a means to an end.

My stomach kept clenching into together knots as realization dawned...

"We'll find a way in, Sergio. It's just a matter of time." He clicked his tongue and sucked harder on the cigar. "So, you either offer us the information we need, or we take it by force."

"You take it by force. You start a war, you won't win," I said in a confident voice.

"You're good at what you do, Sergio, you really are. But I'm starting to wonder if you're usefulness has come to an end."

"What? So you simply kill me? Make it look like an accident?"

"Gentlemen." The booming voice was the only thing keeping me from launching myself across the table and beating the shit out of him. "Let's keep things friendly."

I rolled my eyes.

The voice was coming from my superior, someone I'd never seen before in person. The conference call was supposed to be a debriefing.

"Gentlemen." The voice coughed. "It seems we are at an impasse. Sergio, you are no longer needed. Stay in hiding until you're activated again, and stay out of our business. We'll find a way in without you."

"But—"

"Sergio." The man sighed into the speaker, the whoosh of air sounding like static over the phone. "You've done us proud, son, you really have, but you know, when it comes down to it, we can't ask you to betray your own blood."

"But I'd do it..." I choked. "You know I would. For you. I would."

"I wouldn't ask it of you. You are nameless, faceless, nothing to us, officially deactivated immediately."

I rubbed my face with my hands. Could this be the way in? My fault from the beginning? Regardless, I needed to call Phoenix. The last thing we wanted was Bee alone with Pike. He'd stop at nothing to use her to his advantage, and I knew that Tex would rather start a war with the entire country than see his sister hurt.

CHAPTER THIRTY-ONE

The heart doesn't know what it's missing until it's too late.

Phoenix

"WHAT?" I BARKED INTO the phone while my eyes frantically searched the area for Bee. She was supposed to meet me after class, and I'd already warned her not to wander off with friends. It was one of our rules: *Always stay put until I find you, and then I'll take you home.* No other option.

Sergio cursed on the other end. "I think... Pike's going to come after you."

"No shit." I rolled my eyes. Where the hell was she?

"I think he's going to use Bee."

"Sergio, no offense, but cut the shit. I'm currently searching for the lost princess, and I don't have time for your theories right now."

"You can't find her?"

"No." I started walking toward the student center. "It's like she just disappeared or something. Damn that girl. She's probably with Andi, who, by the way, I'm not entirely sure is a good influence on her."

"Did you check the bathrooms?"

"Yes." I grit my teeth. All ten of them.

"What about her tracking device?"

I stopped walking. "Do you think her missing has something to do with Pike? What aren't you telling me right now?"

A vision of Sergio's black folder rushed to the surface of my memory. I hadn't looked at it. Luca had left specific instructions to look at the folders only if absolutely necessary.

"Look, don't panic, everything's probably fine, but it looks like Pike really is working for the feds and… they want in… into the family, by any means possible."

"Well, that's stupid. We don't let outsiders in."

"I never said anything about letting them do shit… but by force? Negotiations? They can do whatever the hell they want."

"Fine, I'll check the tracking device. Hold on." I turned on the app and glanced at the screen, waiting for it to load.

Her red dot was nowhere near campus.

It was moving… directly out of town.

"Shit!" I roared into the phone. "Call Tex. Now."

"What happened? Where is she?"

"Tell him I've got this… don't send anyone. It could be a trap, alright? Just tell him… to stay put."

"Right." Sergio swore. "That sounds like a great plan."

"Do it."

I hung up the phone and ran toward my car, nearly dropping my phone when I typed in her coordinates.

Blood surged through my body as I hit the accelerator and sped off campus.

I fought to keep the monster in.

I tried everything from deepening my breathing to focusing on the positive, on the good. I'd find Bee, and I'd save her.

But what if I couldn't?

What if she was hurt?

What if?

My heart twisted in my chest. Could I really live without her? Did I want to? My thoughts haunted me the entire drive to my destination.

When the beeping stopped, it was in front of an old building right next to the lake.

Petrov Enterprises.

The building was worn down. Paint was chipping off the sides, and what used to be an incredible empire now looked like something from the Great Depression.

I got out of my car, pulled my gun, and crept with caution toward the door.

When no gunshots rang out, I pushed it open.

And came face to face with Nick, my right hand man, the man I trusted, the man Luca had trusted.

"What the—?"

His gun was at my temple before I could finish my sentence. Without saying a word, he smirked and pushed me forward into the darkness.

"Wow, some cavalry," Pike said, stepping into the light. "Tell me, was your plan to just shoot whoever came at you first then search in vain for Bee?"

"If you hurt her, I will kill you," I spat.

"Please, like I'd hurt someone so pretty," Petrov scoffed then snapped his fingers.

Bee was brought forward into the light, and she was dressed like a whore.

A red corset that looked too tight for her body was wrapped around her middle, cutting into the tender skin of her breasts as they ballooned above the garment. Black lace underwear peaked from beneath it; black garters attached to sheer stockings. Tall, shiny black boots with spike heels completed the ensemble. Her mouth was bound with masking tape, and a pair of ruby red lips had been drawn across the tape.

Her eyes were blurred with tears as she tried to cover herself. But her hands were tied in front of her, and her gesture was useless.

"Now it's a party." Pike chuckled. "Alright, let's get down to business." He pulled out a nearby chair and sat. "I give you Bee, the Cappo's sister, who we all know you're secretly in love with, and you turn over the Nicolasi family to me."

I swallowed a snort. "You want me to hand over a multimillion-dollar organization... to you? A twenty-year-old kid? For what purpose? Daddy ran out of money?"

Pike tilted his head. "My employer thinks it would be... prudent to know the inner workings of the family. But with you in the way... it's... difficult."

"And Nick?" I turned to glare at the man I'd named my right hand. "What about him?"

"He works for me." Pike puffed up his chest. "And my employer. He's been in deep with Nicolasi going on five years."

"Too bad we don't give out trophies," I said through clenched teeth.

"What do you think yours would say?" Pike taunted. "Son of a murdered boss, unloved by everyone he comes into contact with? Murderer? Thief? Rapist? My, my, I don't think all those words will fit in such a tiny space."

"So what? This is your plan then? This is all you have?" I spread out my arms and turned around in a circle. "Kid, you have another think coming if you think I'm going to bend to your demands just because you dress up the Cappo's sister like a whore."

Bee flinched.

I ignored it. I had to.

"You mean, you don't care about her?"

"How can a dog care about its fleas? They're a nuisance, nothing more."

"Hmm." Pike stood. "You're good at lying, Phoenix, always have been, but I know something you don't know."

I pretended to look bored when really my heart was racing so hard I thought he would hear it.

"Shrinks found you fascinating, and I have to admit... I do too. The case studies about your psyche..." He shuddered. "It wasn't at all hard to find that information. You know, you really should have Sergio do a better job. Tell me, do you still black out and then forget what you've done? Do you still have that monster inside of you?"

I clenched my hands into tight balls.

He grinned then walked over to Bee and pulled out a knife. "Does the violence still set you off, Phoenix? Does it make you... want?"

With a chuckle, he sliced part of Bee's garter, causing it to fall over her boot, then he sliced the other.

The knife hovered around the strings tying her underwear to her body.

"Sweetheart," he whispered in her ear. "I think it's time to unleash the beast. After all, once he starts, he won't stop, and we can't have someone that unstable leading the Nicolasi family."

My breaths came out in gasps as the room faded around me. I tried to focus in on Bee and nothing else.

"Now..." Pike motioned to Nick. "...eventually, you'll snap, and all Nick needs to do is show it to the rest of the family. You do realize that the Nicolasis have been without stain for over forty years? Most of them don't trust you. The other half are afraid of you. Imagine the response the elders will have when they see your deranged behavior." He chuckled and pointed up. "Cameras, everywhere... Have fun, kids."

I was still trying to figure out what the hell he was doing, when the lights turned off then flashed back on.

Screams.

That was the first thing I heard.

Then I heard my father's voice. "Do it son. Just do it. You must do the hard thing."

"No!" I begged. "I can't. Please don't make me."

"Do it! Or I will!"

My father was three times her age. Just the thought had made me want to vomit.

The girl's soft cries played in the background.

And then to my utter horror, the wall lit up with pictures.

Of every single girl I'd ever raped.

Every girl I'd hurt.

With an ugly red number next to it.

One hundred and seventy-five.

I'd never counted.

Always suspected.

I fell to my knees as the screams got louder.

My eyes locked with Bee.

And I heard a faint whisper from Pike as the door closed behind him. "Now you see him for what he really is. See if he spares you, the way he didn't spare them."

CHAPTER THIRTY-TWO

He was broken, maybe too broken to fix.

Bee

I'D NEVER UNDERSTOOD THE concept of breaking someone — until I saw Phoenix on his hands and knees and then in the fetal position.

I wasn't sure if going to him would help or if I should just remain standing under the blinking light. The screams seemed to get louder and louder, each of them female.

My lower lip trembled as tears poured down my face... tears for them and then tears for him, their tormentor, a man absolutely broken, a man torn, a man who was clearly not in his right mind and could potentially return to that state so easily.

He'd warned me.

He'd told me over and over again what kind of monster he was.

And I'd refused to listen.

I wasn't going to listen now.

Even when I had proof. Even when I saw the numbers,

the pictures. I couldn't allow myself to believe he was the same person; for some reason it felt like if I did, all would be lost.

Including the last of what made Phoenix human.

He whimpered and then slowly lifted his head. His eyes locked with mine. I offered a sad smile.

He didn't return it.

A heaviness blanketed the room. I shivered. He didn't blink, not once, just continued to stare at me.

I licked my lips.

He groaned.

"Ph-phoenix?"

His eyes squeezed shut. "Please…"

"Please? What do you need, Phoenix? Anything, just tell me." It wasn't lost on me that I was the one in the awful position, wearing basically nothing, defenseless, yet he felt more like a victim than I did. In that moment, I may as well have been wearing armor for how vulnerable Phoenix looked on his knees, as if the agony of taking his next breath was too much to contemplate.

My hands were still tied together. I frantically looked around for something sharp so I could cut the masking tape. In the frenzy, I didn't see Phoenix approach me until it was too late.

One minute he was on his knees — the next he was in front of me.

Eyes black, expression grim.

He shoved his gun into my clasped hands.

I staggered back. "Phoenix?"

"Please," he whispered, pushing the cold gun harder into my flesh. "Just do it."

I dropped the gun onto the ground, but he picked it up and forced it back into my hands. My wrists were tied together, making it awkward to hang onto anything.

He stepped into the gun and held me tight against him.

"Pull."

"No!" I tried to drop the gun, but his hold was too strong. "Phoenix, stop!"

"Bee…" Tears filled his eyes. "I thought I could… I thought I could, but I can't… I just can't. Please, please…" Tears dripped down his face onto his full lips. "…please, I can't live like this, with this in my head." He started to full on sob. "I'm broken, can't you see? I'm broken, Bee, so fix me! Just fix me!" His forehead touched mine as he pulled the gun harder against his stomach.

"I can't… I can't do what you're asking me to do."

"You're better off," he said hoarsely. "Everyone is, I shouldn't be alive… he should be alive. Luca should be here, not me. I don't deserve it. Look around you, Bee! This is my legacy!" He stumbled back and turned in a circle, lifting his hands into the air. His legs shook, like any second he was going to crumple to the floor again. "The great Phoenix De Lange, remembered for this." He shook his head. "One hundred and seventy-five daughters, sisters, potential mothers… *friends*." His voice cracked. "I. Am. Undone." Chest heaving, he stumbled toward me again. "Please, Bee, save what humanity I have left."

The gun slid between my fingers. I nodded. "Okay, Phoenix. Okay."

His shoulders sagged as he closed his eyes.

It broke my heart, absolutely shattered every part of me, that the only time I'd seen him truly at peace was in that moment — when he was asking for his own death.

I leaned forward then threw the gun to the side and kissed him as hard as I could on the mouth.

It was the only way to show I trusted him, despite the pictures around us, despite the screams.

The only option of saving him wasn't killing him, but reminding him who he was in the first place.

Just a man.

A man who had been given a second chance.

A man who was doing better — a man who was worth living for.

And a man I was completely in love with.

I tasted his tears, licked them away from his lips, and then kissed him harder. Slowly, his arms came around me, and he tugged me toward his body. He ripped the tape from my wrists. Pain sliced through my skin, but it was nothing in comparison to the fire burning in my soul at his touch.

"You aren't him," I whispered across his lips. "Now tell me who you are." I pulled back.

He shook his head. Tears pooled in his eyes, glazing them over.

"Who are you?" I pushed against him. "Damn it, Phoenix, who are you?"

"I don't know..." He licked his lips.

"Yes, you do." I gripped his shirt. "You're mine... my family, my protector, you're my friend. You aren't *this*." I shook my head. "You're better."

"I'm not."

"You are."

His eyes burned into mine. "Bee."

"I love you," I blurted.

He stumbled back away from me. "What did you say?"

"I love you," I screamed. "I love you!"

"How?" His voice cracked.

"You love a person for who they are, embracing what they've been and hoping for what they'll become. I make my judgments based on what you did for me when my father tried to attack me in my room... for what you did every night when I had nightmares before going to sleep. For the moments you held my hand when you didn't really want to. For feeding me when my father tried to starve me to death because I refused to let one of his men rape me. That's the man I love — that's the man you are."

The door to the warehouse burst open.

Tex and Nixon ran through first, followed by Chase and Frank.

"I'll kill him!" Tex roared. "You hear me, Petrov? You're mine!"

His voice echoed across the empty room.

"It could be a trap!" I held up my hands.

"It's not." Sergio said, entering the same door they just did. He seemed calm, too calm. "Believe me, it would be in their best interest to keep us all alive."

"What the hell happened?" Tex turned and glared at Phoenix. "What did you do?"

Phoenix didn't defend himself; he was making a bad habit of that; instead, he simply stared at Tex with a blank expression.

And didn't even lift his hands when Tex punched him so hard the back of his head fell with a crack against the cement.

"Phoenix!" I screamed.

"A little much." Nixon cursed, kneeling down next to his body. "You could have killed him."

"If he touched her…"

"He saved me!" I shouted at the top of my lungs, absolutely sick of everyone thinking the worst of the one man who was willing to die in order that I would live.

I forgot all about the screams that were being blasted through the sound system, all about the images, the numbers. So, when Tex stumbled back and shook his head, his face going completely white, I knew it was over. Whatever relationship Phoenix and I could have had was gone… because no brother, regardless of how sorry the guy was, would let his sister within a hundred-mile radius of someone with that red number marring his past.

"Holy shit." Chase covered his mouth.

"Turn it off." Nixon's eyes were frantic as they glanced from side to side, taking in every picture, the number. With a roar, he slammed his hand against one of the cement poles.

Sergio frantically ran around the room, just as a picture of Trace filled the next slide.

"I said turn it off!" Nixon yelled so loud it hurt my ears. He fell to his knees just as the power cut.

The screams stopped.

But not before we were all witness to the horror that was Trace's attack and Phoenix's expression while doing it.

CHAPTER THIRTY-THREE

Back to the chair… of course.

Phoenix

OF ALL THE SCENARIOS I'D played out — this wasn't even close to being on my list.

I was freaking tied to a chair.

In The Space.

The exact same spot I'd been tied to when Nixon had freed me last year, when I'd gotten shot, when I'd agreed to help Luca and Nixon trick Anthony.

History was a bitch.

So much for redemption and all that shit. I try to do better, and the solution — the problem — always equals my torture.

My fault.

It was all my fault.

And I knew that. I'd known that the whole time. Didn't stop me from wishing things were different.

It wasn't enough that I kept trying to earn penance for my sins; they just kept coming back to haunt me.

My back hurt, my neck was sore, and my lips still tasted like her. Every time I closed my eyes, I heard her voice.

"I love you."

Her eyes had been so earnest, so pure, that in that moment, I'd believed her, even though I knew I didn't deserve it. I held onto those words and let them seep deep into my soul.

And for the first time since I could remember, it felt like I could breathe again… until I got sucker-punched by her brother and ended up with a concussion on the cement floor.

And now, trapped.

Waiting for whoever the hell was going to come in and torture me.

Story of my life.

I survived, only to die right when there was a piece of happiness within my reach.

At least, I'd had a few moments with her. At least I'd gotten to experience love — once in my life.

God knew, I would have chosen a different path, a different life. Maybe I would have actually gone to college, played football, married a beautiful woman like Bee and had kids.

Laughable, how opposite my life was to the American dream.

And ridiculous that I was jealous of boring.

I was jealous of men who worked forty-hour weeks and came home to pot roast. I was freaking jealous of everything about their lives that I would never ever have.

I kicked the heels of my boots against the metal chair and swore as tears of rage pooled in my eyes.

She loved me.

She loved me, and I had nothing, absolutely nothing to give back to her — no love, no heart, no soul. All I could do was stare at her in absolute shock that she was willing to waste such precious words on someone like me.

Swallowing the bile rising up in my throat at the pictures, images, screams, the past that was brought up and thrown into my face, I prayed.

I could care less if my own death was swift — just that I could die in her place.

Maybe God did care. Maybe the only way to set things back into balance was to sacrifice myself so the girl could live, the one girl I hadn't soiled with my hands, with my body.

"Just take me…" I whispered under my breath. "…but leave the girl." My lips trembled. "God, just leave the girl. I can't—" A choked sob escaped. How many girls had I refused to spare? Why the hell would God spare Bee? Did a sinner's prayer… a sinner's plea… even make it to heaven?

The door to The Space burst open.

Nixon walked in.

And déjà vu started taking over my consciousness.

Only this time, I wasn't talking shit back to him. I was broken. Threats wouldn't work, because really? What did I have to live for other than the girl that smelled like vanilla and fought me with every breath in her body?

"So…" Nixon popped his knuckles, pulled up a chair and sat in front of me. He was wearing a white T-shirt and jeans, stupid, since they'd both be a bloody mess by the time he was finished with me.

"So," I repeated.

"…you okay?" He licked his lips and leaned back, crossing his arms slowly.

"Am I okay?" I let out a humorless laugh. "No, man, no, I'm not okay. Would you be okay? Would you freaking be okay if every single sin you'd ever committed, every single shameful thing of your past was broadcasted for everyone to see? And not just strangers but your friends and family? Would you be okay with facing your monster knowing full well you created it? Would you be okay with loving someone so much, wanting to protect them from the evil, and finally realizing that in the end… You. Failed?"

Nixon's jaw clenched.

"So, no." Voice hoarse, I hung my head. "Nixon, I don't ever think I'm going to be okay."

"Did you hurt Bee?"

"The very fact that you have to even ask me that tells me you won't believe me, even when I swear it's the truth."

"Answer the question."

"No," I barked. "I didn't hurt Bee… though I can't promise she won't have a few scrapes from Pike holding a knife too close to her skin."

"Start at the beginning." Nixon sighed. "What did Pike say?"

"Don't you know?" That didn't make sense. Sergio should have told Nixon everything by now.

"No."

"But Sergio…"

It was Nixon's turn to bark out a laugh that sounded more like a hoarse yell than anything. "Sergio's gone."

"What?"

"Gone."

"You killed him?"

"Yes, I killed my cousin." Nixon shook his head. "No, asshole. He's gone, as in, we can't find him. He took off after we left the warehouse."

"But…" It made no sense. Sergio would never bail, not on family, but he was the only one who had the true connection to Pike. And the only reason I knew that was because I knew the family secrets, secrets even Nixon didn't know, secrets Luca swore had to stay within the Nicolasi clan, just in case we needed to use them as leverage back into the States. The folder. Well, shit.

"So… what happened?" Nixon tried again.

"Pike took Bee." I swallowed. "I put a tracking device in her phone and her jacket just in case. I followed the tracking device to the warehouse, and Nick, my right hand man, opened the door, aimed a gun at my temple, and ushered me in. Their plan..." I licked my dry lips. "...their plan is stupid, but it would probably work in the long run."

"Infiltrate?" Nixon nodded.

"Yeah, but in order to do that, they need me shamed in front of the whole Nicolasi family. They were trying to break me, Nixon."

Nixon was quiet for a while then asked the dreaded question. "Did they succeed?"

"No." I choked. "They didn't." But it wasn't for lack of trying. It was because Bee had no common sense whatsoever, and when I'd begged for her to shoot me — she had kissed me instead, sucking away all the pain, the darkness, and for one brief moment, making me feel human.

"Alright then." Nixon stood and walked around the chair to unlock my handcuffs. "I guess we go home."

I rubbed my sore wrists, but, other than that, didn't move, was afraid to even breathe. "What do you mean we go home?"

"Had to make sure you weren't double-crossing us. When Sergio left, well, it's a red flag. I've been watching him a while now... I know he has a shady past, a past that, for one reason or another, has five freaking years where he literally went off our radar. So yeah, I'm suspicious by nature."

"Maybe he just went off grid for a while." It was a lie. The bastard didn't go off grid — not by a long shot.

Nixon snorted. "In the middle of a spat with the feds? Sergio?"

"Shit." I covered my face with my hands. How much did I tell them? Where the hell was Luca when I needed him? "Nixon... Sergio isn't who you think he is."

Nixon stared at me hard before whispering, "I know."

"He's..."

"Not here." Nixon snapped, jerking me up from the

chair. I followed him out the door and into the waiting Range Rover.

Tex, Chase, Frank, and Mil were all waiting inside, their expressions blank. That was, until Tex spoke.

"He tickle you with a feather, asshole?"

"Yeah, and I almost peed my pants," I shot back. "You need new jokes."

"You kissed my sister again."

Mil groaned.

The car pulled out of the parking lot, and with great restraint, I managed not to launch myself into the back seat and give Tex a concussion — returning the favor and all that shit.

"She tastes like vanilla," I said in a taunting voice. "Any more questions?"

"Son of—!" The car freaking moved as Tex jerked off his seatbelt, but someone must have stopped him because nobody touched me.

It was Frank's laughter that broke the ice.

Followed by Chase's.

Then Nixons.

And finally Mil's.

Tex, however, cursed under his breath the entire way home.

CHAPTER THIRTY-FOUR

Sometimes it's easier to focus on the monsters outside than face the scariest one of all—the one in the mirror.

Sergio

I STARED AT THE blinking red letters and swore until my voice went hoarse, and when the pressure in my chest still didn't alleviate, I fell to my knees in outrage.

Activated.

The word blinked up at me over and over again. I still hadn't clicked on the message, because that meant I actually had to admit it existed.

I thought of calling Ax, of telling him everything, explaining the whys, the hows, and then I thought of calling Nixon, but he'd simply shoot me and then feel bad about it later — maybe.

No, this shit was all on me.

All because I had once believed in something.

The difference between right and wrong. But somewhere along the way, I'd gotten in too deep, crossed my wires, and what seemed wrong for so many years suddenly translated into logic, common sense, survival.

The house was dark.

I knew Nixon was searching for me.

He'd called my phone a half-a-dozen times.

It would only be a matter of time before he'd send a crew to check out the house, before he'd turn on my locater.

A teakettle whistled from the kitchen. My heavy footsteps joined the whistling as I slowly made my way into the kitchen.

"So…" He was a huge man, not just muscular but large, commanding, unapologetic about the way his body took up space at our dining room table. He tapped his fingertips against the counter.

I waited for the inevitable.

"…you've been activated." He said in a bored tone. "Yet, you haven't called in yet. Why is that?"

"Oh, you know, I had to pick up my dry cleaning and make sure all my affairs were in order before I walked the plank." I poured myself a hot cup of tea and joined him at the table. "I thought you were above human contact."

"You stopped being human a long time, Sergio. I think we both know that."

I outwardly flinched at the truth of his words. "That may be true, and you only have yourself to thank."

"Oh, I do." He gave a dark chuckle. "Every day, I thank my lucky stars that I have the great Sergio Abandonato in my grasp."

"You'll fail." I sighed. "Phoenix didn't break, the Nicolasis are going to discover Nick's a rat… and Pike? Well, I guarantee if he shows his face again, it won't end well for anyone." Me included, but I didn't say that part out loud. Pike would stop at nothing to bring everyone down with him — the entire operation, even the ones not directly connected to it.

"Are you blind?" He laughed. "Did you really think that was the plan? Allow a punk kid like Pike to lead the entire mission... capture the Cappo's daughter, break a boss who isn't even a threat, who's already broken? Oh, Sergio, if you think this is over, you're so very wrong. We haven't even started."

My stomach clenched. "We?"

"As of today...you're back on payroll."

My teeth clenched together.

"Welcome back to the FBI, Agent Abandonato. We've been simply lost without you."

CHAPTER THIRTY-FIVE

In his arms... where I belong

Bee

I PACED BACK AND forth in my room, irritated that Sergio had bailed, and that I was alone in a dark creepy house.

Tex finally agreed to leave me only after he and Nixon had searched every single hiding spot they could think of for Sergio, and when that hadn't worked, they'd turned on his locator, only to find it had been disabled.

Sergio was gone.

Phoenix was gone.

And I was alone. Again.

Tex promised he'd come back, but it had been over two hours.

As if things couldn't get any worse, it started to thunder outside. I'd always been terrified of thunderstorms — the whole loud noise thing came into full effect again.

The thunder shook the house, making the windows sound like they were going to shatter any minute. I dove under my covers like a total baby and waited for the storm to stop.

It didn't.

I plugged my ears.

Tears streamed down my face.

Alone, I was so alone.

I missed him.

I missed Phoenix.

Heck, I even missed Sergio. At least he carried a gun... then again, what would a gun do? You couldn't shoot thunder and lightning.

Under the blankets with me, my phone lit up. It was Tex, saying he would send someone over to watch me during the night.

Like a little kid.

But I didn't care! At least I would feel safer knowing I wasn't alone in the house... all by myself, just waiting for someone like Pike to come barging in with a knife.

The front door slammed closed.

I held my breath, ready to text 911 to Tex if I needed to. He'd said the entire place was like a compound — no one got in without knowing all the pass codes — but still, fear choked me.

Footsteps sounded on the stairs. I closed my eyes tighter as the door to my room was shoved open and then more footsteps.

"Bee?" Phoenix said in a low whisper. "Are you okay?"

I threw off the blankets and stared. He had his hands in his pockets. Of course, he did. I'd come to learn that about Phoenix; he had to occupy his hands when it came to me. Heaven forbid, he accidentally touched me and liked it.

He bit down on his lip as he took another step forward. "Bee?"

"You aren't bleeding," I pointed out.

He smiled, the lightning flashed, he was so beautiful, a fallen angel, my fallen angel. "Should I be?"

"Well, the guys took you, and you had a concussion, and then they locked me in the house, and Sergio took off, and—"

His fingertips pressed against my lips. "I know."

I nodded, parting my lips against his fingertips.

He let out a curse and jerked his hand back. "I'll be in my room if you get scared."

"Don't go!" I blurted.

His shoulders sagged. "Bee, it's probably not a good idea to be around me right now… after… this afternoon and tonight."

"Please." I scurried off the bed and grabbed his hand, tugging his warm body toward mine. "Please, don't leave me."

He swallowed, his gaze falling to my lips. "I'm going to be completely honest with you right now, possibly in hopes it will scare the shit out of you and make you lock your door, alright?"

He clenched my hand tightly and slowly led me back to the bed, pushing me down onto it and kneeling in front of me. His eyes were dark, his lips full, wet from his tongue reaching out and licking them.

"If I stay, I can't make any promises that I won't touch you. I can't promise you that I won't kiss you. I can't promise that I'll stay in the corner, and because I can't promise that, it also means I can't promise I won't hurt you. I can't promise I won't be the very thing girls should be afraid of, because I've never done it before, Bee. Do you know what I'm saying to you? I've never done tenderness… love. Those words, they don't exist in my world."

"So, don't be tender."

He let out a heavy sigh. "Bee, you're not getting it. I don't know how… to be normal. And right now, I'm not capable of holding onto my self-control, especially when it comes to you." He licked his lips and blew out a curse. "And your damn tank tops and sleep shorts. Good God, woman, we need to get you flannel."

I smiled and toyed with my shorts. "What these old things?"

His eyes hungrily followed the trail my hands made along my thigh. My body trembled. He wasn't trying to hide the way he felt, not anymore, and for some reason, it felt like a huge breakthrough for us.

"Phoenix?"

"Yeah, Bee?" His voice was thick, heavy.

"Kiss me."

"The frog doesn't turn into a prince, and the beast doesn't turn back into a human, Bee." He shook his head. "That's not how life really works."

"I don't mind frogs."

He snorted.

"Beasts are kind of scary... but they can be tamed too."

"Is that your way of saying you can tame me?"

"Aw, do you need a safe word?"

He let out a low chuckle. "Funny."

"It can be bird, you know, because of your name and all."

"How the hell do we go from talking about torture and rape to safe words and birds?" He still hadn't moved from his position, and elation emboldened me. I hadn't scared him off yet. Without a second thought, I gripped his hands in mine and stood.

He hissed out a breath.

"Phoenix..." I moved my hands to cup his face. "...kiss me."

He still didn't move.

"Fine," I whispered. "Typical man, make the girl do all the work." And then my mouth was on his, though I barely remembered moving.

Our lips fused together.

Our bodies touched.

He let out a groan, his lips moving slowly against mine,

carefully, as if he was afraid too much pressure would break me.

I eased back. "You can do better than that," I whispered against his lips, licking the seam, begging entry with my tongue. "Come on, Phoenix... you can do much, much better."

"You're right." His hands tightened on my waist. "I actually can."

I didn't have time to prepare for his kiss.

For what it felt like to actually be truly kissed by Phoenix De Lange, not in anger, not in fear — but absolute desire.

His lips were urgent, his mouth hot as he deepened the kiss, his hands moving down my body, memorizing every square inch, only to move again and again. His tongue dipped in and out.

When he finally broke off the kiss, he pushed me away slightly and cursed. "I need a minute."

I angled my head and raised my eyebrows. "Like a time out?"

His grin was beautiful, free. "Yeah, Bee, I need a time out. Give a guy a break. I'm not exactly... good at this."

"Kissing?"

"For your information, I'm an excellent kisser. I'm just not good at what follows..."

"Ah, your cuddling skills need some work?"

His eyebrows arched. "Right, I'm a shit cuddler. You figured me out."

"Did you ever try practicing with stuffed animals?"

He recoiled in surprise. "Were you dropped as a child?"

I rolled my eyes and crooked my finger. "More kissing."

"Bee..." The tortured look was back. "...I kiss you more, I lose control."

"Wow, you're right, how could I not see it? I mean, you practically tortured that poor lasagna I force-fed you the other night. Dang fork almost didn't make it. The plate... empty." I sighed. "Poor plate."

Phoenix threw his head back and laughed.

It was a beautiful sight.

My breath hitched in my chest.

So, this was the attraction... this man, right here, laughing, smiling, with teasing eyes and that damn dimple.

"We could..." My voice cracked. "...we could always read."

"Read?" he repeated. "First you want to kiss. Now you want to read?"

"Well, I kind of wish you'd show me what all this sex fuss is about, but I'm pretty sure that pushing that particular button will get me stonewalled and tattled on to my brother."

"I would never tattle."

"You told him I broke my toenail."

"You cried."

"I was having a moment," I argued. "Now, what will it be? You aren't leaving me here alone, so either you kiss me, give into all those feelings you know you want to give into.... or you read me *Twilight*."

Phoenix swore.

"Hey, I know which option holds more appeal to me." I held up my hands. "Your choice."

"I've just decided your major."

"Oh yeah?"

"Extortion."

"I am a Campisi."

"Yes, because reminding me that you're Tex's little sister really wins you favor in this argument."

I grinned and took another step toward him. "One more kiss?"

"And then what?" He swallowed, his eyes glazed over. "What then?"

"That's just the thing, Phoenix." I brushed my lips across his. "The world is ours."

"You really believe that." He pulled me closer, his grip

tightening around my hips as his hard body aligned with mine. "That the world is ours?"

"Yeah," I whispered. "I really do."

"Did you mean it?"

"Mean what?"

"What you said at the warehouse." His eyes were uncertain, darting back and forth, unfocused. "Did you mean it?"

"I meant it then."

His grip tightened.

"And I mean it now."

The smile was back.

And so was his mouth.

CHAPTER THIRTY-SIX

Balance is overrated.

Phoenix

I WAS HAVING A really difficult time trying to keep my body under control; it was like every single emotion concerning Bee came surging to the surface, making it physically impossible to pull away.

She really did taste like vanilla.

My new favorite flavor.

The problem with tasting something so sweet was it made you wonder, and I was wondering a lot. What did the rest of her taste like? And if given the chance to taste, should I take it? Or run and hide like a loser?

I was fighting a losing battle.

One I knew I wanted to lose, but at what cost?

Every time I told myself I needed to pull back, she'd make a little noise in the back of her throat, and I'd succumb to the draw she had... one more taste, one more bite. I hadn't kissed a girl, really kissed her...

In years.

I'd stopped kissing them altogether.

Because it had been too personal.

It had been sweet when what I was doing was sinful.

So kissing her?

It was heaven, and I didn't associate it with my past, but I knew, if it went beyond that, I could snap — I felt it in the way my body wanted dominance over her. I wanted to push her onto the bed — with force.

Aggression had always meant I was about to do something I couldn't come back from, so how did I associate it with love?

I couldn't.

I wasn't sure there was even a way.

Bee's hands slowly slid under my shirt. I let out a hoarse groan as she touched my stomach and then lifted my shirt over my head.

Reading. We should be reading.

And then her tank top was gone.

And I was staring at the most perfect breasts I'd ever seen in my entire life, barely restraining themselves behind a black lace bra.

"Shit," I muttered, pulling back and wiping my face, but Bee reached for me again. Our bodies touched, skin to skin. It was searing — painful.

She was soft where I was hard.

Her stomach brushed against mine, her fingers dipped into my jeans. *I should stop her.*

But I didn't want to.

I was being selfish, hoping that it was possible, what she'd said, loving me, being able to experience this moment.

When her fingers tried to unbutton my jeans, I gripped her hands. "No, Bee."

"Don't be bossy," she murmured against my neck.

"It was always..." I pushed her away gently. "They were virgins... like you."

"Okay." She reached again.

"No, Bee, you don't understand. I'm trying to tell you something here. I'm trying to scare you off, and if you keep reaching for my pants, that's it, Bee, they're all that's protecting you from me taking you — all of you — and damning every single consequence or ramification."

She smiled through swollen lips. "I get it. You always had to take control with them. It makes sense... but I'm not them, Phoenix. I'm me."

I exhaled. "I know that."

"Do you?" She reached for my jeans again and pulled me against her.

There was no hiding the evidence of my arousal, not even possible. I was surprised I hadn't already spontaneously combusted and embarrassed myself.

"Because I think if you let someone else have control, you may be surprised."

"Or I could kill you," I said through clenched teeth. It was my last excuse, all I had left.

She let out a low chuckle. "Is that you're way of telling me you don't have the safety on your gun?" Her fingers grazed the front of my pants.

Holy shit.

I stumbled into her, pushing her onto the bed, tangling my hands into her hair as I twisted and pulled, my lips claiming every inch of skin along her neck and then craving more and more.

She pushed me down and straddled me.

It was a position I'd never been in before. Ever.

I didn't like it.

I felt weak.

Powerless.

And then she took off her bra.

And I felt — everything.

The world opening up, my attraction to her, my undying

love for the woman who was willing to risk it all — for me — for someone like me.

She leaned over, her hair falling across her face. "If you're bored, we could always read."

"Screw reading." I gripped her face between my hands and kissed the hell out of her, my hands reaching for her perfect body, forgetting all the horror they'd done, all the things they'd experienced in this same position.

Funny, I thought sex would one day destroy me.

And yet... with Bee...with someone I loved?

I felt anything but destroyed.

Each kiss was like a broken piece getting found and put back together again; each touch was like being reborn.

"Bee..." I breathed against her neck, her skin cooling from my kiss. "...I love you."

"Oh, so now you admit it when you're all hot and bothered."

I burst out laughing and pulled away her shorts. "Oh, I'm hot..." I cupped her ass and jerked her against me. "...but do I feel bothered? Even a little bit?"

"Using the word *little* right now does you a great disservice, Phoenix De Lange."

I groaned when she rubbed against me.

"Now..." She pulled away. "...now will you take off your jeans? I want to see the gun."

"Classy."

"No time for class. Strip."

"Bee—"

"Phoenix, you're lucky I know you love me. Otherwise, I'd be really tired of all this rejection."

"It's not you. It's me," I said lamely, sitting up on my elbows.

With a saucy grin, she undid first the button... and then the zipper, the sound so damn erotic I cursed.

"You're right." She removed my pants. I wasn't wearing

boxers.

Another reason I had fought so damn hard to keep her away.

"It is you…" She licked her lips. "All you."

I gripped her wrist to keep her from touching me. "Bee, think hard about this. Is this what you really want?"

She tilted her head. "I've wanted you ever since I saw you. I wanted you even when I knew it was a bad idea. I wanted you last night when I heard the screams, and I want you now. Any more questions?"

My chest heaved with emotion.

"No words? Not even *bird?* Remember, it's your safe word, Mr. De Lange, in case things get too hard for you."

"Things are beyond hard for me right now," I growled.

"Good." She winked. "You know if my brother finds out, he'll kill you."

I froze. "Did he put cameras in your room?"

"Well, since the door isn't getting broken down, I'm going to say no."

"Thank God."

"Aw, so now you value your life."

I placed her on top of me, exactly where I wanted her.

Bee's eyes rolled to the back of her head.

"I have the sexiest woman alive, on top of me, naked. Of course, I value my life… because with you… it's worth living."

Tears pooled in her eyes. "Never thought I'd see the day you'd stop yelling at me and spout something so romantic."

I gently tucked her hair behind her ear. "It's a day of firsts."

She tensed.

With a smile, I gently pulled her down until I could taste her lips again. Her body shivered against mine. I kicked off what was remaining of my jeans and just focused on our skin, on the fact that I was with the woman I loved, and I was actually able to do the impossible.

Love her.

Dig my fingers into her hair and not see images of hate and brutality.

Kiss her lips, bruise them with pleasure not pain.

I sighed against her mouth, tucking her body into mine, allowing my love for her to take over the past.

"Bee..." I asked one more time. I had to. "...are you sure?"

"Yes." Her voice was quiet but certain. "Yes, Phoenix, with you my answer will always be yes."

I pulled her into my lap and moved into a sitting position so her legs were still wrapped around my waist. My fingers moved to her thighs, cautiously. Not wanting to scare her, I moved them across her smooth skin, the pads of my fingertips enjoying the sensation almost as much as the rest of my body.

"Phoenix..." Bee pulled back. "...stop hesitating."

"Actually..." I choked down a laugh. "...I was lingering, not hesitating. Wanna know the difference?"

She licked her lips.

"Hesitating..." I licked my way from her neck to her mouth. "...means I'm having doubts about what I want to do." My fingers worked their way closer to her core. "Lingering..." I moved further; she tensed. "...means I'm just debating on what to do first."

"I'm confused." She wiggled against my fingers as I moved them against her.

With a jerk, I had her positioned exactly where I needed her to be. "Then allow me to clarify."

"Wha—" Her head fell back as I readied her body. "So good, Phoenix, don't..."

I removed my hand. "Did you need to use my safe word, Bee?"

"Buzz." She winked and reached for me.

"Nope." I lifted her by the hips and slowly dragged her body down, impaling her on me. "You used the wrong word."

I inched into her.

She fought me.

"Bee, I'm trying to go easy on you."

Her eyes blinked open, and then she forced herself the rest of the way with a cry. "You were going too slow."

I kissed her mouth and started to move. "You're extremely demanding, you know that?"

"I'm a girl." She sighed, her forehead touching mine. "You feel so good."

Nobody had ever said that to me before.

I was literally having sex for the first time.

Real sex.

No ulterior motives.

No violence.

I moved her against me, feeling every part of her surround my body. We fit — perfectly.

"Phoenix—" She screamed my name — it was a good scream.

The world around us twisted then faded away, and all I saw were her eyes, her lips. All I felt was her body.

Heaven, after a lifetime of trying to climb out of hell.

"Let go, Bee," I demanded.

"You first," she said through clenched teeth, her mouth finding mine again.

Kissing her while our bodies were joined, there was no greater trust, no better feeling.

The minute her muscles tightened around me, I lost complete control, her fingers dug into my back.

And with a groan... I let go too. Of everything that had been trying to drag me down — and held on to the one thing keeping me afloat.

Bee Campisi.

CHAPTER THIRTY-SEVEN

Buzzkill of the century

Bee

I EXPECTED TO WAKE up in Phoenix's arms; instead, he was pacing the floor, running his hands through his hair, looking about ready to rip it from his scalp.

"Um, good morning?" The sheet fell free from my body.

Phoenix looked up and let out a hoarse groan.

I smiled.

He took a step back and held up his hands. "We messed up. Actually, no, I messed up. Bee, I'm so sorry."

Rejection slammed into me as I tucked the sheet around my body and looked down, willing the tears to stay put. "Um…"

"No, no." Phoenix was at my side in an instant. "Not that, that wasn't a mistake, being with you will never be a mistake, Bee." He cupped my trembling chin. "Damn, you're beautiful." His kiss was tender. "Bee, come on, look at me."

I lifted my head, gazing at him behind my eyelashes, just I case I needed to avert my eyes again and have a good cry.

Phoenix looked rested, so well rested it was almost strange. Gone were the dark circles, his skin had color; everything about him looked alive, better. It was as if his blood had decided to continue pumping through his body, rather than just up and giving in to death.

"I'm not…" He chewed his lower lip and mumbled a curse, his eyes glancing away from me. "I need to test you."

"Test?" I repeated. "For what?"

"Bee…" His eyes filled with compassion, a completely foreign expression on someone so hard. "I think I'm okay. Last I was checked, I was fine, but I just… I lost control last night. We didn't use a condom. I could never forgive myself if anything happened to you because of me. So please… just… don't fight me on this, alright?"

I blinked up at him, still a bit confused.

Until he left and returned with a needle amongst other… things.

"Wait." I wrapped the sheet tighter around me. "What do you think we're going to do? Play doctor?"

Phoenix paused then pulled out a needle. "We're not playing anything. I'm going to draw your blood."

"But—"

"Just sit still and think about…" He lifted his eyes heavenward. "Birds."

"Really? That's what you're going to go with? After last night?"

"Yeah, well…" He fumbled with the needle and pulled a ripped a piece of fabric from his shirt. "…forgive me if I'm not entirely focused this morning."

"Says the guy about to put a needle in my ass!"

"Don't be dramatic, Bee." His smile was blinding. "I'm going to put it in your arm."

"You and that sharp thing get anywhere near me, and I kick you in the balls," I seethed.

He rolled his eyes and sat on the bed. "I need to know

you're okay…"

"Take your own blood!"

"I will," he said in a confident tone, "after I take yours."

"I hate you."

"No, you don't. Give me your arm."

"No." I hid it under the blankets. I'd never actually had any shots since I'd met Phoenix, at least that I could remember, and now I'd had two. I cringed. He knew how I felt about blood — it stayed in the body, not out.

"How about a negotiation?" He put the needle down and grabbed my hands. "Would that work?"

My eyes narrowed. "What type of negotiation?"

"I read to you… and actually let you stay in my room without all the yelling and shit talking… and you let me take your blood."

I chewed my lower lip in thought. "I'm going to raise that to eating a full breakfast this morning, and you have yourself a deal. Just do me a favor and keep the red stuff in."

"Yeah, well, that's the general idea when you're drawing someone's blood, Bee."

"Are you certified to do this?"

"Hell, no." He shrugged. "But I'm good at it, I promise."

With a sigh, I held out my arm. He wrapped the piece of cloth freakishly tight around my bicep and then pulled out the stupid needle again. I closed my eyes.

"Hey," he whispered. "Keep them open. Focus on me, alright, Bee?"

"Right." I said through trembling lips. "Focus on… happy things?"

"Butterflies?" He offered, wiping my arm with something cold. "Turtles crossing the road?"

"Frogs," I blurted.

He chuckled. "Alright, frogs."

"And beasts."

The needled hovered above my arm. "I hope you mean

the good kind, the kind that stay in cages."

"I don't know," I whispered. "I kind of liked letting it out of the cage last night."

"It?"

I grinned. "Yes, it."

"Am I the *it*?" His eyes narrowed.

I let out a laugh just as the needle pierced my skin.

I flinched but managed not to fall into a heap onto the floor while he pulled what looked like my entire blood supply into five separate vials.

"Almost done." He fastened one more on the end. It filled, he pulled it off, and then the needle was gone. Pressure from his hand replaced the sting.

"That hurt." I pouted.

"Don't be a baby."

"Well, don't prick me with things!"

He smirked, his eyes hooded with desire. "Didn't mind it a few hours ago when I—"

"Phoenix De Lange!" I shouted my surprise. "Are you making sex jokes?"

His face went completely blank, and then he laughed. "Yeah, I guess I am."

"I like you this way." I shrugged. "Laughing."

"Me too." The smile fell from his face.

The front door slammed. We shared a brief look before Phoenix tucked the blood he'd collected into a small pouch and then ran out of my room.

Directly into Sergio.

"What the hell are you doing in her room?" he roared.

"Keep talking." Phoenix seethed, his eyes narrowing. "I'm really going to enjoy this." With a roar, he slammed Sergio against the wall and punched him in the face.

Sergio didn't have time to fight back. He slumped to the carpet, holding his cheek. "Damn it! Why did you hit me?"

"You bailed."

"My transmitter broke."

"Bullshit!" Phoenix kicked him in the leg. "You can't lie to me!"

"Yeah, well, believe it. I have proof, and then I was doing recon last night, trying to find your stupid-as-shit right-hand man. I know where he's at, by the way. You can thank me later."

"No ulterior motive? Hmm, Sergio?"

His expression was blank as he glanced up at Phoenix. "Would I betray family?"

The room was thick with tension.

I had no idea what the heck was going on, but I didn't have time to try to psychoanalyze why Phoenix had just lost his mind at seeing Sergio, and why it was such a big deal. My text alert went off.

Big Bro Crappo: *Breakfast in fifteen. Get your asses over here, bring Phoenix, and if the prodigal has returned, make sure he's wearing a bulletproof vest.*

"Aw," I said aloud. "That was a cheerful morning text. Think he'll have fresh orange juice?"

I tossed my phone to Phoenix; he read it with a sneer then shoved it into Sergio's face.

"Judgment day." He tossed the phone back to me. "Apparently, Tex is going to be too focused on killing you to even touch me today."

"You're welcome," Sergio grumbled as he struggled to get to his feet.

"I don't recall saying thank you."

"You will." Sergio's eyes took in my state of undress, and then he glanced back at Phoenix. "Shit yeah..." He groaned. "You really will."

CHAPTER THIRTY-EIGHT

Death by family dinner — of course.

Phoenix

IF BEE KEPT GRAZING my hand with hers, I was going to lose my shit. I'd spent so long not touching her, focusing on anything but the way she made me feel, but now? Now it was absolute torture. Her touch calmed me in a way I'd never before experienced.

It also made me want to lock her back in her bedroom.

Which was such a positive and happy realization that I couldn't help the smile that spread across my face when we reached Tex's house.

"Yeah, I'd stop that shit right now," Sergio muttered under his breath, "before he breaks your hand."

"Stop what?" Bee said innocently, tilting her head to the side, her knee sliding against mine.

Sergio barked out a laugh. "You know exactly what you're doing, Bee. Be careful. Tex doesn't need any more reasons to rearrange Phoenix's face."

She pouted. "But it's such a nice face."

I chuckled while Sergio rolled his eyes and got out of the car.

Bee reached for my hand as we walked toward the doors. I jerked away and glared.

She grinned.

Okay, so maybe breakfast was going to be hell on earth, but how bad could she really make it?

The door opened.

And as expected, Tex came barreling out, and punched Sergio in the face. He fell to the ground for a second time that morning and cursed. Blood poured from his nose.

"Huh." Tex scratched his head. "You already hit him?" He directed the question at me.

I shrugged. "Figured you'd want me to."

"Nice." Tex snickered. "Twice in the same hour." He kicked Sergio in the shin. "Next time, you call. I don't care if you're in deep with Russian drug lords, you call within twenty-four hours, or I order a hit on you. You aren't my family. Hell, you sneeze north when I ask you to cough left, and I'm ending your life. This shit stops now." His eyes found mine. "We gotta get a lockdown on the families before we lose control again, and it's on me, not you guys, if things get screwed up."

I nodded my agreement while Sergio moaned from the ground.

I helped Bee step over his body and walked her into the house where the rest of the guys were already sitting around the table.

My stomach growled at the smells — bacon, eggs, ham — everything smelled too good to be true, like I'd been walking around without any of my senses and now... I just wanted to devour it all.

"Bet you're happy I'm forcing you to eat breakfast, huh, Phoenix?" Bee whispered in my ear.

Nixon watched the entire exchange and bit down on his

lip ring then took a long sip of coffee. Yeah, nothing escaped his notice.

Meaning, we were more than likely going to have a heart-to-heart later that day, during which he would threaten me within an inch of my life if I hurt Bee.

For now though, he was going to act like he didn't notice the way my entire body sang in her presence or the way she huddled next to me like I was the very air she breathed.

"Okay!" Mil clapped her hands. "Time to eat!"

Trace and Mo carried hot plates of food over to the table and set them out in the middle with the orange juice. Steam rolled off each of them.

I closed my eyes and unfortunately let out a little groan.

The table went absolutely still.

Shit.

Trace was the first to talk. "Someone feed him before he starts drooling."

Heat stormed across my face. Holy shit, since when did I blush?

Chase's mouth dropped open, and then his eyes narrowed as he looked between me and Bee.

Nixon elbowed him in the side just as he was about to take a sip of coffee. Steaming, dark liquid sloshed over the side of the cup and cascaded down Chase's hand. He jerked, splashing even more.

"Damn it, Nixon!"

"Slipped." Nixon shrugged, winking in my direction.

"My ass." Chase elbowed him back and reached for the bacon, just as Tex sauntered into the room with Sergio, who looked even worse than when I'd last seen him.

While Sergio slithered into an empty seat, Tex plopped at the head of the table.

"Family breakfast." Tex rubbed his hands together. "Aren't they the best?"

"Sorry I'm late." Frank strolled in seconds later. "Traffic."

"It's okay, Grandpa." Trace rose from her seat and kissed his cheek.

Grandpa seemed way too tame a word to call Frank, assassin extraordinaire. The man had practically invented five new ways to torture people, but sure, now he looked normal.

He was wearing a sweater vest.

A freaking sweater vest.

Talking and laughter erupted around the table. I reached for a piece of bacon just as Bee's hand skimmed my thigh.

I hissed, dropping the bacon onto the plate.

"Hot?" Tex asked, tilting his head.

"Scorching," I said through clenched teeth, praying Bee would remove her hand before I did something we'd both regret.

"Here, let me help ya, big guy." Chase grinned like a fool and tossed some bacon onto my plate, while Nixon chuckled behind his coffee.

I was going to strangle them both.

"So, Bee." Chase leaned forward, his eyes dancing with humor. Shit, this wasn't going to go well. "How'd you sleep last night? Tex said you were pretty freaked, since dipshit didn't come home until this morning."

"Nice," Sergio muttered through a tissue-stuffed nose.

Bee's cheeks pinked as she took a bite of sausage. I refused to focus in on her lips because looking would mean daydreaming, and that would most likely gain me a broken penis, compliments of Tex's hands or possibly his favorite machete.

"Actually..." She sighed. "...I didn't sleep all that great."

"Because of the thunder," Chase prompted.

Mil's eyes narrowed in on her husband then back at me. I stared at my damn plate like it held the secret to world peace.

"No," Bee said cheerfully, "I mean the thunder was bad, and then Phoenix came home and... I was fine."

"Ah, big bad Phoenix, so mean he can scare the storms

away."

"Something like that," I said through clenched teeth.

Thankfully, Nixon started firing questions to Sergio across the table. Where had he been? What had he found out? Why the hell hadn't he called?

I should be paying attention.

As boss, it was my job to pay attention.

But Bee's hand inched up my thigh.

My knees jerked beneath the table, slamming loudly against the underside.

It shook. My orange juice damn near fell over before I rescued it.

"Dude…" Chase's cocky grin was going to end up on a milk carton if he kept it up. "…you okay?"

"Great." I swallowed, forcing another smile. "Just jumpy."

Bee's hand inched closer to where I absolutely did not need it to inch.

Every muscle froze and strained all at once.

Her first touch was tentative.

I let out a hoarse groan and hung my head in my hands. Well, Tex was going to kill me. Absolutely kill me.

"Bee!" Tex barked.

She jerked her hand back. Thank God.

"I'm sorry I left you last night, but I figured you were safe. We have cameras everywhere — hell, they're in every room — so it's not like I didn't know you were fine."

Horrified, I glanced back at Nixon.

He nodded his head once and then elbowed Chase, who winked and then stared into his coffee.

I wasn't sure whether I should be thankful or kill them for seeing her naked; then again, they were both happily married.

And I was screwing the Cappo's sister.

Wow, good one, Phoenix. Apparently, when I go bad, I go

all the way. I don't just play with danger and put it back on the shelf. I keep it all to myself and hope it doesn't explode in my face.

Bee's hand was back.

Speaking of explosions... Son of a bitch, she was trying to kill me! I breathed in and out, focusing on that instead of what her hand was doing to me and what her brother would do to me if he found out.

"This is nice." Mo set down her coffee. "All of us having breakfast. We should do this more often."

Nobody said anything.

"I said—" She glared. "—we should do this more often."

A chorus of *absolutelys* erupted from the table. Mine, however, sounded more like a tortured whimper.

"Are you sweating?" Tex asked from his side of the table.

"Who?" Mo glanced around, her eyes finally finding mine.

"Shithead." He pointed at my face. "You look like you're going to be sick."

"Yeah..." I coughed. "The bacon..."

"He eats green," Sergio mumbled and then ran his tongue over the blood drying against his lips. "The only way he eats real food is if Bee tricks him."

"Is that so?" Tex chuckled. "Bested by my little sister?"

Her fingers dipped into the waistband of my jeans.

I stilled. "Yeah, she's... talented."

Her fingers went lower.

"I bet." Sergio's eyes narrowed.

"I didn't say you could talk." Tex spat at Sergio and sent a loving glance toward Bee. "I'm glad you're okay, sis. Promise you slept alright? No bad dreams?"

"Birds," she said in such a sweet voice I nearly choked. "I dreamt of birds... lots and lots of—"

"Birds." I interrupted. "We get it."

"Good to know he's still being an ass to you." Tex

chuckled into his coffee.

"Phoenix is always hard on me." Bee's fingers tickled my sensitive skin. "Demanding." More tickling, deeper. "Forceful..." Her palm pressed against my hip. "And hard to please."

Slowly, I turned to Nixon, shooting him a look of pure helplessness.

He smirked then stood. "So, we should probably get down to business. Ladies, if you'll excuse us."

"Hey!" Mil shouted. "I'm a lady."

"With balls," Chase clarified. "Therefore, you stay."

"Why does Chase get to stay?" She glared at him and stuck out her tongue.

"Love you too, sweetheart," he sang, leaning back in his seat.

"Bee..." Nixon's eyes fell to her. "...why don't you help Trace and Mo with the dishes? It will keep you out of trouble." His eyebrow arched.

Smiling, she removed her hand and stood, as if she hadn't just been trying to kill me. "If you say so." She grabbed a few plates then bounced out of the room.

With a sigh, I leaned back and mouthed *"Thank you"* to Nixon.

Chase caught them and about fell out of his chair, laughing.

"What?" Tex coughed from his end of the table. "What's so funny?"

"Life." Chase answered. "Gets me every time."

I flipped him off behind Frank's chair.

CHAPTER THIRTY-NINE

Lying about my feelings... bad sign?

Bee

"SO..." TRACE HANDED ME a clean plate. I dried it and tried not to think about Phoenix — about his hands, his mouth, any part of his body that I wanted to touch. "Even after everything... you still aren't afraid of him?"

"Who?" I put the plate down. "Tex?"

Mo let out a snort. "Please, he's as tame as a housecat."

In the living room, Tex's voice rose another octave, this time in Italian. Pretty sure Sergio's name was on the other end of an insane amount of expletives.

She winced.

"Yeah, I bet he coughs up hairballs on a daily basis." My eyebrows arched as I reached for another plate.

"Phoenix."

The plate almost fell out of my hands.

Trace's eyes narrowed. She put her hands on her hips. "What's going on between you two?"

"Um..." I swallowed and continued drying the plate.

"…nothing."

"You sure?"

I worked the towel harder against the ceramic. "Yup."

"Careful, liar pants," Mo whispered, taking the plate from my hands. "You're going to rub a hole through the already dry plate."

Trace leaned back against the counter. "He's fragile, Bee. You know that, right?"

I fought the urge to roll my eyes. "Trust me, I practically live with him. I know all about how you guys feel."

"It's not just us," Mo defended. "It's everyone. Yes, he's fine… for now, but what happens when something sets him off? What happens when he gets pissed? He's a time bomb, Bee. It's good for you to remember that."

Angry, I threw the towel against the counter. "Why don't you guys just lay off him already! He can't be better when everyone who supposedly cares for him keeps making him feel like crap all the time!"

Mo's eyes almost bugged out of her head while Trace grinned at me like I'd just proclaimed undying love.

"So…" Trace smiled wider. "…you like him."

"No…" I crossed my arms defiantly. "…I love him."

Trace stopped smiling, and Mo took a step back from me like I was diseased.

"You love who?" Tex asked from the doorway behind me.

My heart stopped. I gave a pleading look to Mo, who immediately flashed Tex a smile and said, "You. She loves you… though it still escapes me why."

He rolled his eyes then crooked his finger. "Come here, baby."

"No."

"Now, damn it."

"Campisis…" She flounced across the room. "…so demanding."

He pulled her into his arms and kissed her hard on the mouth.

Trace put her hand on my shoulder and whispered, "I'm happy for him… for you both. I really am."

Guilt slammed into me. "But he… I know what he did." I hung my head.

"Did," Trace repeated. "Past tense. If I can get beyond it, then so should Tex. Just… give him time before you start making it known and popping out kids."

I laughed with her.

And then choked on that same laugh.

Kids.

That morning.

Phoenix had said we hadn't used protection. He'd been worried about STDs… but he'd never said anything about pregnancy.

I briefly touched my flat stomach.

Once. Once wouldn't be enough, would it? The last thing I needed to do was freak him out by bringing it to his attention. We were probably fine, but Trace was right; Tex would freak.

We needed more time together before we announced it to everyone. And a part of me felt like Phoenix and I deserved a bit of normal before my brother went and ruined everything again by being himself.

"Bee," Tex said, releasing Mo and sauntering over to me, "Phoenix has strict instructions. You'll go back to school, but he doesn't leave your side. You have to go pee, you raise your hand, he freaking follows you to the stall and sings to you if you get stage fright. He's also going to sleep on your floor…" The last part made his jaw clench. "…not that I'm happy about it, but it's better than you being by yourself, and I don't want to take any chances. We're going on total lockdown until I have both Pike's and Nick's heads. Alright?"

"Alright." I agreed and wrapped my arms around his

neck. "Thank you… for protecting me."

Tex sighed and lifted me against him, returning my hug with a fierceness I'd never experienced from him before. "Bee, next to Mo, you're my life. I'd do anything to keep you safe."

"I know." That was what I was afraid of.

Because, according to Tex, Phoenix was anything but safe. He was fire itself. And I was playing with it, hoping to end up unscathed.

"Bee." Phoenix came into the kitchen. "You ready to go?"

"Yeah." I nodded. "I have an afternoon class, after all."

"And your professor's an ass who gives out tardy slips just because he can," Sergio sang from the door. "Get a move on. I have to fix my face before my next session."

"Can't fix ugly." Tex whistled under his breath.

"One day…" Sergio swore. "…I'm going to grab your balls and twist."

"Just try not to enjoy it too much, Serg." Tex winked.

Sergio lunged, but Phoenix held him back. "Alright, family breakfast is over."

CHAPTER FORTY

I'd waited for death my whole life. Now that it was here?
Kind of anticlimactic.

Sergio

MY LIFE WAS OVER.

I was finally forced to face my own impending demise, and it wasn't pretty. There would be no come-to-Jesus moment, no light, nothing. Just blackness and a sickening feeling that I was leaving a horrible legacy behind.

They'd remember me for my betrayal.

And they'd be right to.

I hung my head in my hands as students started shuffling into the classroom. My heart wasn't in it, not that I'd been enthusiastic about teaching US History, but at least it gave me a purpose outside of the family, outside of my job with the FBI.

Shit.

Nixon was going to shoot me in the head. Execution style.

I couldn't fix it.

And the worst part was Phoenix knew who I used to work for; he knew all the dirty secrets because, once upon a time, I was the man who needed saving, not Phoenix.

Once upon a time.

Luca had saved me too.

"You have two choices, son." Luca held the gun to my temple; *his finger squeezed the trigger. "Shall I lay them out for you?"*

I said nothing.

"I pay some people off... but I own you. I own your very soul. Not the Abandonatos, not the Alferos, but me. I'm your boss, Sergio. My family is your family. I get you out of this... predicament, clean up the mess you handled so horribly." He sighed, pulling the gun away. *"Do we have a deal?"*

"You can't." I shook my head and looked around at the dead bodies scattered at our feet. *"You can't just walk into the FBI and say I screwed up."*

"Whoever said you screwed up?" He balked then pointed his gun at the dead bodies. Over and over again, he fired until no shots were left. *"Looks like the Nicolasi boss was at it again... I'm ever so... trigger happy."* His grin was ruthless. *"Now, run back to your shiny little office and tell them you want to be activated... tell them your family trusts you again. They want you in. You are a ghost no longer, Sergio. From here on out, you're a double agent."*

"But Nixon—"

"Will be fine."

I had no choice. Either take the fall for all the dead federal agents around me, or go back, blame it on the Nicolasi family and solidify myself as a trustworthy federal agent, and go deep under cover within the family."

Either way, I was a dead man.

"Fine," I snapped. *"I'll do it."*

"Of course, you will..." Luca grinned menacingly. *"Because blood always wins, doesn't it?"*

"Wow, you're either really deep in thought or your dog

died this morning." Andi knocked on my desk with her fingers and grinned.

"I don't like pets."

"Shocker." She winked. "Though it would probably be good for you to hug something other than your own pillow at night."

"Keep going. You're just begging me to kick you out of class, Andi." I was pissed, pissed that I was dying and so was she; yet a smile — a freaking smile — and jokes? Unbelievable.

She leaned in, her eyelashes fanning across her face. "One day... you'll regret pushing me away. One day, very soon, you'll be eating your words."

My head snapped up. Was a student actually threatening me? My eyes narrowed as she crossed her arms.

"Find your seat, Miss Smith."

She shrugged and walked off.

Leaving me even more irritated than before. Class went by in a blur. I said all the right things, assigned homework, then locked the door when my phone rang.

"Next week," the voice said. "...make sure he's present. We'll do the rest."

"And if I can't get him there?" I asked.

"You can... unless you're in too deep. Are you?"

"No," I barked. "I can do it."

"Great, we'll hand him exactly what he wants in return for something we want. No lives need to be lost."

"No. But they will be lost, won't they?"

"What's one person in the grand scheme of things?"

"Right." I hung up my phone and stared at the door. I was going to lead my friends, my family, into a trap.

And now that Phoenix had finally found life...

I was going to deal him his death.

How was that for irony?

CHAPTER FORTY-ONE

I want him — badly. Every second. Of every day. My world is Phoenix.

Bee

CLASS HAD BEEN ABSOLUTE torture. I didn't realize that one experience with Phoenix would make it so the whole world could crumble around me, and I'd still only be focused on his lips, his rough hands.

By the time we made it to the car, I was so elated I could have skipped.

I think Phoenix was trying to play it off like being around me wasn't a big deal. At least, I hoped that's what he was doing. I couldn't really tell since his face had remained expressionless all through class.

He opened my door for me and ushered me in.

When the car started, I sighed and leaned back against the smooth leather. "So, what's the plan?"

"The plan?" he repeated, his eyebrows arching. "We drive home, you do your homework, and, if you're really good, I let you have ice cream with dinner."

I rolled my eyes. "Same old Grandpa Phoenix."

"Grandpa?" His voice rose. "Did you just call me a grandpa?"

"Quick! Turn on Mozart before I start rapping!" I fumbled with the controls and turned on the classical music. "Ah, isn't that better?"

He opened his mouth, but I interrupted him.

"But wait... maybe my shirt's too open again. I know how you feel about buttons." I undid the first two then the third. "Whoops, going the wrong way."

The car swerved. "Could you not?"

"What? Trouble concentrating, Grandpa?"

"Holy shit, stop taunting me! So what if I like classical music."

"Liar... you hate it."

"It's..." He coughed. "...educational."

"Favorite composer—"

"Mo—"

"Other than Mozart."

"Uh..." He blinked. "...you're just putting too much pressure on me."

"Alzheimer's already getting to you?"

"For the love of God, stop saying I'm old!"

"I almost bought you a cane then realized you'd actually use it... not spank me with it so..."

The car swerved again, and then we were in an abandoned field, still three miles from home.

I didn't have time to yell at him for nearly killing us — or the corn.

Because within seconds, his mouth was on mine, and he was undoing my seatbelt. "Damn, you drive me crazy."

"A good crazy.

He grunted against my neck. "I'm still deciding."

"Can we make all big decisions this way?" I wasn't against begging, especially when his hands found my breasts and started massaging.

"Whatever you want, it's yours." His hungry gaze met mine briefly before he kissed me again, his tongue tangling against mine, his body not nearly close enough.

I tugged him harder against me. The console kept getting in the way.

I growled.

He laughed at me.

I bit his lower lip.

And all laughing stopped as his hands dove into my hair.

I tried to move so I could straddle him, but it was like the car was working against us.

"Home," he said against my lips. "Wait until we get home."

"No." I tugged his shirt, nearly ripping it form his body. "Now."

"Bee…" His voice had a warning edge to it. "…pretty sure your brother's already going to put a shotgun-sized hole in my chest. Don't make him run me over with a car for good measure because I felt the need to pull you into the back seat."

"Ooo, back seat! Good idea." I started to move.

Phoenix groaned and buckled my seatbelt back up. "Stay."

"Boo. You're no fun."

"Oh, I'm loads of fun — when I'm living. And I won't be living if your brother happens to drive by."

"You could always run through the corn."

"Not how I envisioned telling him, Bee."

"Wait, what?" He pulled the car out of the field and started driving back toward the house. "You're going to tell him? About us?"

Phoenix sighed, tapping his fingers against the steering wheel. "Bee, I can't be that guy… I'm not that guy. I refuse to go behind his back just because I'm afraid of him spilling my blood."

"But—" Panicked, I reached for his hand. "—Phoenix… he'll kill you."

"You're worth that risk, Bee."

Suddenly embarrassed, I shuddered, despite the warmth invading my face. "Are you going to tell him about last night?"

"Hell, no." Phoenix swore. "Last night was about you and me, Bee — not your brother, the mafia, or anyone else in this godforsaken world. Just you and me…"

"And birds." I laughed.

He groaned. "The word *bird* should never give a man an erection, Bee. Ever."

"Aww… having a rough time when they chirp by your window?"

He shook his head. "Yeah, something like that."

When he put the car in park, I leaned over and kissed him on the cheek. "My room… five minutes."

"Bee—" Phoenix gripped my arm. "—we have to be careful. Sergio…"

"Isn't even here." I pointed to the empty parking spot. "He drives his Lexus to school, and it's still not here. Therefore, we're alone, though you should probably make sure those cameras aren't on in my room."

He let out a heavy sigh. "They're going to put on my tombstone… *And he loved her so much he never said no.*"

"Good." I grinned like a happy fool and marched off to my room, getting rid of my school clothes and getting ready for more bouts with Phoenix, my best friend turned…

Everything.

CHAPTER FORTY-TWO

Big Bird. Funny, I never thought yellow would cause me to lose my mind.

Phoenix

I WAS ABOUT TO knock on her door like an idiot, when it swung open. Bee was on the other side in shorts that had Big Bird on them and a white tank top.

"Ah, so now it's going to be *Sesame Street* that does it," I muttered, running my hands through my hair. It was all so new to me. Having a girl I loved, spending time with her, not puking after sex.

I'd never spent the night in another woman's arms.

Until Bee.

She tilted her head, her pouty lips taunting me by merely existing.

I slammed the door behind me and picked her up into my arms, my mouth finding hers in seconds.

"I love you..." The words rumbled from my chest. "...more than anything."

"I love you too." She hooked her feet around my waist.

"Now kiss me, Phoenix."

"I am."

She ground her body against mine. "Harder."

"Damn, you're not easy to please," I grumbled, kissing her so hard my lips were going to be bruised in the morning. I'd forgotten to shave, so I knew she was going to be tender around her mouth from the force of my kiss, but I couldn't stop, didn't want to.

When I tossed her onto the bed, everything was fine.

And then...

All hell broke loose as an image of another girl flashed through my brain. Horrified, I backed away from Bee.

The girl had worn a white tank top just like Bee's.

I shook my head, bile rising in my throat.

"Nope." Bee clung to me and brought my face down to hers. "Stay here... with me. It's just me, Phoenix."

"But—"

"Let it go." She sighed, running her hands through my hair. "It's us, only us. Make love to me."

I sighed as the heaviness started to peel away from my body. She was right. Her, I could focus on her — on pleasing her, on her pleasure, on her body.

"A man could die worshipping your body, Bee."

"Are we back to the grandpa theory again?" she teased, tugging my bottom lip with her teeth. "Don't go having heart failure."

"At least I know I have a heart now," I confessed.

"Of course you do." She gripped my face with her hands. "But I've always known that."

"Even before I did," I whispered hoarsely.

"I'm the smart Campisi." She winked and then glanced around the room. "Tell me you took care of the cameras."

I rolled my eyes. "The very second we got back to the house. Nixon already destroyed the others. Thank God."

"Nixon knows?"

"Yeah…" I cringed. "…so does Chase."

"What the heck, Phoenix!" She smacked me in the chest. "When were you planning on telling me?"

"That would be never." I hovered over her and kissed her neck. "They won't say a word, at least not yet, and maybe, possibly, when Tex aims his gun for my head, they'll defend me."

"Mmm…" Her body arched off the bed as I tugged her tank top away and stared greedily at her naked body. "…it feels good when you look at me like that."

"I'll make you feel better than good," I vowed, kissing her again, removing every article of clothing and showing her over and over again that I wasn't who I used to be. I'd been reborn.

I was hers.

Owned completely by Bee Campisi.

CHAPTER FORTY-THREE
Coming clean

Bee

"DO YOU STILL HAVE nightmares?" I whispered, tucking my head into Phoenix's shoulder, my fingers splayed across his naked chest. We'd spent every waking moment together since the family breakfast. When we weren't at school, we were at home. Each moment was precious because I knew it was only a matter of time before he really did talk to my brother.

And though things were... better with the rest of the guys, I was still afraid they would take him from me, my only friend, the man I loved.

Sergio had said he knew the location of both Nick and Pike, but he was waiting on more intel to come in, whatever that meant. And because Phoenix was chomping at the bit to end their lives for putting mine in danger and trying to double-cross him, I had to distract him — in the best way possible. He'd complained of dehydration and sore muscles, and I'd called him Grandpa, at least out of bed. In bed, he'd said that was the fastest way for him to lose concentration.

"Yeah." He pressed his lips against my temple as he finally answered my question after a long hesitation. "But they aren't as bad when you're here."

I swallowed, the rattle of rain hitting the house was the only sound making it into the dark room. "Can I ask you something? And promise not to yell?"

"Bee, when was the last time I yelled at you?"

"This morning."

His warm chuckle did amazing things to my body, making me smile against his skin. "You weren't wearing enough clothes and purposefully dropped your granola bar onto the ground three times."

"I'm clumsy."

"You were also wearing underwear that said *bad ass* on the actual ass and flashed me each time. But sure, it's because you're clumsy."

"I have a fondness for that pair of underwear."

"Funny, me too."

"So…" I chewed my lower lip. "…my question."

"No yelling. Promise." He kissed my head again. "Though if you asked it sometime this year before I really do turn into a grandpa, that'd be great."

"Ass."

"I never claimed to be anything but." He laughed softly.

"It's about your past."

His arm tightened around me. "Okay."

"And what you… did."

I could feel his heart start to hammer against my ear as his entire body went tight with tension. "Damn it, Bee, just ask before I lose my mind."

"I know you feel bad now. I know you hate yourself still, but in the moment… back then, did you feel guilty? Or was it just a job?"

With a shudder, Phoenix released me and pushed up from the bed, resting his elbows on his knees. The sheet fell away from his muscular body as he exhaled deeply, pressing his hands against his face.

"I'm sorry," I said quickly. "I shouldn't ask things like that I just—"

"Bee," he said in a low tortured voice. "Don't ever apologize. You have every damn right to ask questions like that."

"But I shouldn't"

"Don't." He removed his hands and leaned his chin on his knees. "Don't apologize for wanting to know. It's hard, though, letting you see the worst parts of me, having to actually admit those things happened, that I was the one that did them."

I touched his arm.

He didn't flinch, but he didn't reach for me either.

"In the moment..." He sighed. "I felt so much fear, at least at first, and then anger at myself, my father, at the situation, and it was only too easy to transfer it into what I was doing. It's easier to blame the victim for your own shortcomings than to admit to yourself that you're the monster, you're the evil. People can justify anything, and in the beginning, I justified that it was my job. The mafia's dark, you know?" He licked his lips and shook his head. "So I told myself I needed to man up, do the job, and then I convinced myself it was better *I* did it than my father. After a while, I became so numb to everything that I snapped. And then... when I tried to have a real experience with a girl, my freshman year of college... I couldn't even—" He swore. "Do you really want to hear this?"

I nodded, afraid to speak.

With a deflated sigh, he kept talking. "I couldn't perform... in any capacity. I refused to kiss her, just wanted to use her for sex, prove to myself that I could have sex outside of what my father had me do. And I couldn't do it. I think that's part of the reason I snapped, or maybe it was the beginning of the end. There's nothing more terrifying than when you can only associate violence with something that should be beautiful. When you mar a thing of beauty and know that you'll never be like everyone else, it's heartbreaking. Huh..." He snorted. "...and maybe that's it. In breaking those girls, I broke my own heart. It didn't work anymore."

"You work now," I choked out, my voice heavy with unshed tears.

"Yeah, well..." He reached for my face and tilted it toward him until his lips were inches from mine. "...someone offered to fix it."

"Is that your way of saying you'll keep eating the lasagna I toss in your face?"

A toothy grin flashed across his face; the dimple I was obsessed with dug into his cheek, making him look so much younger than I'd ever seen him. "Yeah, Bee, but let's try a different food."

"Bite your tongue!" I jerked away from him. "We're Sicilian. We eat pasta, pasta, wine, and more pasta."

"Don't tell anyone," Phoenix said, tugging my body closer to his. "But pasta's my least favorite food."

My mouth dropped open in shock.

He closed it with his thumb and pressed a kiss to the corner of my mouth. "But I would love if you could make a hamburger."

"Or we could just go to a drive-through?"

"We could do that too."

An abrupt knock sounded at the door. Phoenix froze. We'd been careful, more than careful. Sergio's schedule was so predictable that it was almost easy to fly under the radar, but he wasn't supposed to be home yet. It was only ten on a Saturday night, and that was usually when he met with Nixon.

"Shit." Phoenix glanced from me to the door then slowly got out of bed, threw on a pair of jeans, and faced the music. When he opened the door, it wasn't Sergio on the other side, but Nixon.

I wasn't sure if we were supposed to be relieved or terrified that he hadn't brought my brother with him.

"Hey," Nixon croaked, then looked over Phoenix's shoulder and gave me a knowing grin, "sorry to interrupt, but neither of you were answering your phones and yeah… I needed to talk to you about something… important."

"Yeah…" Phoenix coughed. "…sure, just let me grab a shirt."

He walked back toward me, threw on a shirt, kissed me on the head, and left.

My body shivered at his absence. I reached for my phone and saw two missed calls from Nixon and at least ten unchecked texts from my brother. Yeah, he couldn't be pleased about that.

It was hard lying to him. He was the only family I had left, and even though I loved Phoenix, I still felt like I was doing something wrong. I clicked through my texts and sent him one that basically said I was fine and to keep his pants on. With a yawn, I clicked on my calendar notifications and froze.

A little red dot and a sad face were bouncing up and down on my notifications, showing me the date of my supposed time of the month.

Three days ago.

Don't panic. I squeezed my eyes shut then opened them again, praying I would be on the wrong month or date.

Nope. It still said three days ago.

Three days late.

Which could mean anything. I'd been captured and nearly killed, for crying out loud! My body had been under a lot of trauma…

That was it! I was traumatized.

Yet, all the warnings the girls had given me surged to the forefront of my mind.

"It's only a matter of time before he snaps."

What if I caused that? What if… if I was the reason he finally went off the deep end. What if I had no one to blame but myself and my love for the beast?

CHAPTER FORTY-FOUR

I'd die to protect her — even if it meant I didn't actually deserve it this time.

Phoenix

"YOU'RE LUCKY AS SHIT that I'm the one knocking on her bedroom door and not Tex." Nixon slammed the door to my room closed and started pacing back and forth, running his hands through his hair like he was contemplating pulling out every last strand.

"Yeah, well..." I choked back a smart ass retort because really, what leg did I have to stand on? I was going behind Tex's back; he entrusted his sister's safety to me, and there I was, every night, putting her in jeopardy, just because I couldn't stay away. No, it was more than that — because I loved her, because I craved her, because she was my reason for breathing after spending a lifetime suffocating. "...I'll tell him. Just give me time."

Nixon snorted and shoved his hands into his pockets. "Make sure I'm there so he doesn't actually kill you. Tex doesn't really think before pulling the trigger anymore. He'd rather apologize after shooting you than not shoot you at all."

"Good pep talk," I grumbled.

Nixon licked his lips then finally met my gaze. "She's safe... right?"

I knew what he was asking. Shame, the same shame I'd been trying to ignore for the past five days charged to the surface, making me wince with the darkness it put on my soul, making me want to scream. "She's safe," I finally snapped out, my voice hoarse, "from me, since that's what you're really asking."

"One of us has to, Phoenix."

"Ah, so you pulled the short straw." I popped my knuckles. "I wouldn't lay a hand on her... ever. I thought at first..." I clicked my tongue. "But, it would be like killing a part of myself. She's in me, man. I could no more harm her than I could take a knife to my own heart."

Nixon was quiet, staring at me for a few minutes, then he took a seat across from me. "Moving on to question number two."

I leaned back, waiting for the next chip to fall.

"Sergio..." He sighed. "...can we trust him?"

"What is trust... really?" I drummed my fingers against my thigh. "Especially in our line of business. I trust you today, don't screw me tomorrow?" I bit back a laugh. "It's a fantasy, trust."

"It doesn't have to be."

"With some people—" I gave him a deadpan expression. "—it is."

"Some people being Sergio?"

"Sometimes..." I cracked my knuckles. "...we see only what we want to see, Nixon."

"Shit." He rubbed his hands across his face. "It feels like something bad's going to happen. I hate that feeling, and I can't stop it. Whatever storm I thought was over, it feels like someone just threw C4 back into the clouds and lit a match."

"I'll do it."

"Do what?" Nixon's eyes narrowed. "I didn't say anything."

"I'll tail him." I exhaled. "It's the least I can do after… everything. After all, he claims to know where Nick and Pike are located. Maybe I'll discover three birds with one stone."

"You mean bullet."

"Yeah, but stone sounded better."

Nixon snorted a laugh and rose from his seat. "So you discover something bad, what happens?"

I swallowed the bile in my throat at hurting family; I didn't hurt family, not anymore, but I might have to.

"Phoenix," Nixon said, putting his hand on my shoulder. "I can't ask you to do this if you aren't ready."

"I offered…" I pushed his hand away. "…and I'm ready." I swallowed the emotion tightening my throat. "A long time ago you didn't let me prove myself. Let me do it now."

"I think you've gone and proved yourself over and over again, Phoenix. When will it stop?"

"When the guilt stops," I said honestly, blowing out air through my lips. "When I stop seeing their faces… when I stop hating myself… when I finally have peace. That's when it stops."

"Never." Nixon cursed under his breath. "We aren't gifted with peace."

"Which is why we need to be comfortable with war." I put my hand on his shoulder then pulled him in for a hug. I kissed each cheek the way a boss would with another boss — out of total respect. "Which is why you're going to stay back this time and let me do my job, Nixon. If it ends badly, it will be on my head. The families will be much more forgiving of me eliminating three individuals. You? Not so much. There's been too much heat on the Abandonatos. The last thing you need is to draw more attention."

Nixon nodded, his jaw clenched. "Thanks."

"You don't ever have to thank me for doing the right thing."

"Yeah, but I will. Every time," Nixon whispered and walked out of the room, only pausing at the door to say, "Oh, and... tell Tex next week. Wait until this mess is fixed before you heap more gunshot wounds onto yourself."

My face cracked into a smile. "I'll think about it."

"Your funeral.

"Probably."

Nixon smirked. "Worth it?"

"Hell, yeah."

"That's what I thought." He chuckled and closed the door behind him, leaving me alone in the silence.

I was going to sniff out a rat. I was almost one-hundred-percent sure I knew what was going on with Sergio, but I had no proof, which meant I first needed proof, then needed to silence him without bringing the FBI down on our families.

A long time ago, it had been my job to do the ugly.

A long time ago I'd hated myself for being so damn good at it.

But now? With Bee sleeping in her room, a smile on her lips, her naked body just waiting for me? Yeah, I was more than grateful, because Nixon was right, I would do anything for family.

Anything.

And I was about to do the unthinkable for her.

I was going to kill Sergio.

CHAPTER FORTY-FIVE

Trust and love two things he did well.

Bee

BY THE TIME MONDAY of the following week rolled around, I was officially freaking out. Still no period. And I still hadn't said a word to Phoenix. I trusted him, I loved him, but the girls' warnings were like little bombs going off in my head, and I couldn't help but worry that this one thing would cause him to fly off the handle.

My last class was canceled, giving me adequate time to sneak out of Elite and run down the street to the drugstore. It was only a matter of time before I was supposed to meet Phoenix, and I knew he would flip his lid if I was late — again. As it was, he monitored the little dot on his phone like crazy — swear, if I was in the wrong spot, he knew it within fifteen minutes — thus my reason for sprinting.

We'd been doing the whole *I'm your security guard you may not pee unless I say it's time* thing for the past week and I was getting sick of it. He was polite, yet distant at school and then a totally different person at home.

It helped that Sergio was rarely even there anymore.

When he did manage to crawl back into the house, he never wanted to hang out. Not that we had been all buddy-buddy before, but at least now Phoenix wanted to enjoy life.

Case in point: the man ate popcorn.

It was a miracle; I believe I even said something like "There is a God."

When he took more than one bite, I pretended to swoon.

And when he added chocolate chips to the next batch, a tear all but trickled down my cheek. He rolled his eyes, caught the tear with his thumb, and kissed me.

His taste mixed with chocolate was my new favorite obsession. I even offered to bathe him in it. He declined, saying he didn't like messes.

I told him I'd drug him then toss him in the bathtub.

He said he'd like to see me try.

Ha, he really shouldn't have doubted me at that point. I smiled at the memory, my hand resting on the pregnancy test. It was just a test, a silly little box. It held no power over me. So why was I hyperventilating?

With a curse I grabbed it, hurried over to the cash register, and pulled out my shiny card — the one big brother had given me.

It was titanium.

And looked bad ass.

And I hadn't even had a chance to use it yet. Funny, my first time just happened to be at a drugstore because I'd slept with the enemy.

Good one, Bee.

I slid the card through the slot. It immediately asked for my PIN. Crap. I had no idea what my pin was! I hit credit and prayed it would go through.

It did.

Note to self: find out PIN from brother or Phoenix.

I guess either one of them could help me figure it out, but

I hated feeling stupid and helpless when it came to things someone my age should typically know, like my own personal identification number.

The minute the clerk handed me my receipt, my phone went off, with Phoenix's ringtone, which just so happened to be a chirping bird.

He said it wasn't funny.

I, however, found it hilarious. Every time.

"Hey!" I croaked, all too aware of the guilt in my voice. "What's up?"

"Where the hell are you?" He barked loud enough for me to have to physically pull the phone from my head lest he shattered an eardrum.

"I'll be there in ten minutes. Geez, I'm not even late yet!"

"Your class was canceled, Bee."

"Aw, you stalking me now?"

"Bee," he growled. "If you aren't here in five seconds I'm going to—"

"Spank me?" I offered. "Mud wrestle until I say uncle?"

The clerk's eyebrows shot up into his hairline.

My cheeks heated as I waved and bolted out the door in a full-out run.

"Why are you panting?" Phoenix asked in an annoyed tone.

"I… er, was thinking about you in the mud. Naked."

He cursed. "Bee, please… I need to know you're safe. I don't do this to irritate you. I need to keep you safe — alright? Don't take off without asking permission first."

"You're lucky…" I heaved as the university came into view. "…that I like bossy bastards."

His warm chuckle had me grinning like a fool as I made it back onto campus in one piece.

"Hmm, have I told you how hot you look today?" I whispered into the phone, my eyes drinking him in. He was waiting by the student center, hands on hips, sweater off, white T-shirt wrapped tightly around his body. Damn, the man was delicious to stare at. And I wasn't the only one who thought so; I'd almost gotten into a fight the day before when a girl tried hitting on him.

He couldn't be less interested, but still, it was the principle.

Girls openly stared.

"Playing games, Bee?" Phoenix asked in a teasing voice and then disappeared from sight.

He ducked behind the student center. Where was he going? I quickened my pace and then started to jog around the building when warm arms wrapped around me, pulling me into a familiar chest.

His voice rumbled against my neck. "If I look hot today, then you look sexy, Bee... so sexy." His lips nibbled my ear.

With a shiver, I dropped everything in my hands and wrapped my arms around his neck.

"I love your mouth." I captured his lower lip between my teeth and bit down.

With a groan, he pushed me against the brick wall and slid his hands up my sweater. "Damn, I love..." He cursed again. "...you." His tongue slid into my mouth then pulled back. "Everything about you."

"Oh good..." I pushed at his chest. "Because I was getting worried."

He rolled his eyes and looked down.

And paled.

Crap! I tried to wrap my arms around his neck again, but he gently pushed me back, his eyes still trained on the ground, and I knew it wasn't my shoes he was staring at.

Twisting my hands together, I waited for him to yell.

Instead, he leaned down, and picked up the box that had fallen out of the paper sack. "Bee..." His voice was so quiet I almost didn't hear it. I think I would have preferred that he'd yelled. "...what's this?"

"A new pen?" I joked, trying to swipe it from his hands.

He pulled away from my body, taking the box with him. He swallowed slowly, his eyes still staring at the little box, probably the same way I'd been staring at it earlier in the drugstore. "How late are you?"

"A few days." I forced the words from my mouth; they tasted wrong, like I was in trouble for something, like I should feel shame for being in that situation. "But I've never been super regular, you know how it was with my dad... weird eating schedule, hearing people get murdered, then getting captured here. It's not like my body is calm and able to produce hormones in a totally carefree way."

"Let's go." He grabbed my backpack and started walking.

I had to run to keep up with him. "Phoenix, wait..." I put my hand on his shoulder, but he jerked away. "I'm sorry—"

"I don't want to talk right now, Bee."

"But—"

"Get in the damn car." He nearly took the door off the hinges as he held it open.

Trembling, I got in and buckled my seatbelt.

When he got in the car, he slammed his hand onto the steering wheel and started mumbling in Sicilian. I didn't even try to decipher what he was saying. By his tone, I knew it was bad.

And it felt like it was my fault.

He was pulling away.

He was angry.

And I was terrified that what the girls had predicated to be true was about to happen. Because the Phoenix I'd grown to love wasn't present on the way home.

The haunted look was back.

And I could no sooner stop it than I could stop breathing.

When we pulled up to the house, he didn't say anything, simply opened my door, led me through the kitchen and up the stairs, then handed me the test.

"Do you need water?"

"What?" I shook my head. "What for?"

He braced his body against the bathroom door. "Can. You. Go. To. The. Bathroom."

"Y-yes." I mumbled, choking down tears. "I mean, I can manage. I don't need water."

"Good." He shut the door in my face, leaving me alone to face the music.

I was a planner; that was how I was put together. I'd constantly made just-in-case plans because I'd never known when my dad was going to snap. I'd never known if it was the last day I would see sunlight or if he would throw me at one of his men.

So I'd planned.

I'd had escape routes.

I'd had detailed versions of what could happen to me and choices to make if they did.

But in this situation? I had no plan. Because I'd never noticed the danger. I didn't think. And that was the problem.

My heart was invested.

So my head had taken a siesta.

I braced my hands against the sink.

If I was pregnant, what would happen?

If I wasn't? Would it ever be the same as before?

Shaking, I quickly pulled the test from the box and peed as fast as humanly possible then sat it on the table and waited.

Two minutes was a long time.

It sounded short. Most TV commercials were under two minutes; I mean, it took longer to walk from my room to the kitchen.

But those two minutes were absolute hell. I kept checking my watch.

When the two minutes were finally up, I couldn't look.

I simply picked up the test and opened the bathroom

door.

Phoenix was slumped against the wall, bracing his head in his hands like it would fall off if he didn't have the extra support.

When the door shut behind me, his head jerked back. "What's it say?"

"I didn't look." I handed him the test with shaking hands.

He stared at the test, his lips trembling, then very slowly pulled it from my grasp and looked for both of us.

When a smile replaced his frown, I wanted to beat him with my fists. So what? I wasn't pregnant and now everything was right in the world? I was about to yell at him when he said in such a low voice I had to strain to hear.

"Redemption."

CHAPTER FORTY-SIX

The moment everything in my world — clicked.

Phoenix

IN THE SPAN OF a half-hour, I'd gone from complete shock to rage, back to shock, then something had twisted in my chest, like a part of it had broken off and floated away.

Because the rage had been replaced with hope.

The shock with elation.

And the anger… with complete terror.

It was my fault she was in that position. The hate that I felt for myself was suffocating, and then to see her face… I knew she thought I was mad at her, like it was her fault. But I didn't trust myself to speak. I couldn't. I was afraid I'd scare the shit out of her. As it was, I was scaring myself.

STDs had crossed my mind because of the women I'd dealt with in the past, but pregnancy? Yeah, long ago I'd given up on that particular worry because none of the girls had ever gotten pregnant.

And I knew that for a fact.

That had to mean that God had been punishing me

physically, or maybe at the time just giving me a blessing. When I'd talked to my father about it, he'd laughed and said that when I'd been out for my sixteenth birthday — after a failed overdose on my meds — he'd asked the doctors to sterilize me.

He'd said one son was enough. For *me* to carry on the seed of our family would only disappoint him.

I'd never felt so angry in my life, wanted to murder him so badly. Because he'd taken that choice away from me. Made it so that I was ashamed of my own bloodline. Not only had I been ashamed of what I was doing for him, but it appeared as if he'd been protecting the women we'd used — from me.

As if I had been the real monster.

Not him.

I'd never told a soul what my dad had done to me. Somehow, it felt like saying it out loud only solidified the truth, and the more I'd thought about it, the more I'd wanted to scream in outrage.

Because I would have loved a second chance.

And to me, life? Giving life to someone? That was a second chance. And he'd taken it from me — purposefully.

I'd slumped to the hardwood after Bee had gone into the bathroom. I hadn't trusted myself not to burst into tears.

I hadn't trusted myself not to yell then crumpled to the floor and pounded my fists until they bled.

With trembling fingers, I'd gripped the test in my hand and read the result. A smile had erupted across my face before I could stop it.

Bee had clenched her fists.

"Redemption," I'd whispered…

"What?" she choked. "What are you talking about?"

I licked my lips and met her gaze. "You're pregnant, Bee. We're… pregnant."

She nodded her head, once, twice, then burst into tears.

"Shit." I shoved to my feet and pulled her into my arms,

taking her and the test with me into my bedroom. The door slammed behind us. I kissed her cheeks, the salty taste of her tears making me feel like more of an ass because she was so upset. "It will be fine, baby. Just take deep breaths."

Bee's eyes were wild as she tried to inhale, only to start coughing against my chest.

"I love you…" I choked. "I was scared… I love you though, Bee. You need to know something." I pulled back and gripped her face tightly in my hands. "You are never alone. Do you understand?"

More tears streamed down her face, colliding with my fingers.

"Bee, look at me."

"I… am," she whimpered.

"I'm never leaving you," I vowed. "Ever. Pregnant or not pregnant, nothing will ever change the way I feel about you." I kissed her mouth. "You own me, Bee Campisi, and I wouldn't have it any other way."

"Y-you scared me so bad." She huffed, her tears melting into her pouty lips. "I thought you were going to hate me, and I'm so sorry. I just—"

I kissed her. Hard.

Molded my mouth against hers, pressed my body so tightly against her that there was no clear indicator where she ended, where I began.

Her lips were soft against mine.

My hands tangled in her hair as I deepened the kiss, sucking on her tongue, drawing her sadness out, praying I could take away every inch of pain she was experiencing, hating myself because I knew the only reason it was there was because I'd panicked when she'd needed me to be at my best.

"I…" A kiss across her lips. "…love…." Both cheeks. "…you." Her forehead. "I may not react perfectly in every moment. Hell, I may look terrified, angry, frustrated, but Bee, I would never walk away from you. Ever. I don't have it in me.

Don't mistake my silence or anger for a lack of love — most of the time it's because I love you so much that I react. I know that's no excuse, but you're the most precious thing in my world." My throat caught. "Both of you." I placed my hand against her flat stomach. "God…" The words caught in my throat.

"Why?" she whispered in a cracked voice. "Why were you so upset?"

"Because…" I kept my hand where it was, afraid that if I took it away, it would all be a dream. "…my father said I wasn't able to have children. I was operated on after being in the hospital. He wanted the bad seed, the curse, as he'd called it, to end with me."

Bee covered her mouth with her hands. "I'm so sorry!"

"So…" I went down on my knees and pressed my head against her stomach. "…right now… I'm pretty sure I'm witnessing a miracle."

She tangled her hands in my hair; now that it was longer, it was possible for her to grab it. "Yeah." Adoration shone in her eyes. "I think I am too."

CHAPTER FORTY-SEVEN

Killing friends, never part of the plan.

Sergio

I WAS GOING TO have to kill Phoenix.

No matter how I looked at it, the scenario was the same. The feds wanted in, and the only in they could get would be me.

I'd have to set him up. Make it look like he trusted me enough to take over the Nicolasi family. I'd have to lie, cheat, steal, murder. All because it was my life on the line.

When did I turn so selfish? Did I suddenly wake up one day and decide that I would live life for myself and only myself?

I clenched the glass of whiskey in my hands.

The problem was it would be too easy, a few alterations to the contracts Phoenix already had drawn up — that every boss had drawn up just in case he was killed, so the family wasn't left in chaos.

My name replaced with Nick's.

After all, he was old news, and I'd be the one to bring his

treachery to the family, only I'd make it look like he was selling secrets to the feds right along with Phoenix and Pike.

Well, Pike was just an unfortunate loose end. He made it easy for the feds to kill him without making it look like it was on purpose.

He'd cut a deal, given them all the intel they'd needed, and now they were finished with him.

And I was going to be the one to end him.

No loose ends.

See, the thing about the mafia? People always judged us; they said we're the evil in the world; we're heartless.

Bullshit.

The mafia was a freaking parade compared to what I was dealing with. The feds? All they wanted was power and more power, and they didn't care who they killed in order to gain it.

My fingers went numb from the ice in the glass as I continued to stare at the clock in the kitchen.

Bee was going to be devastated.

Nixon was going to suspect, but he'd always suspected, never truly knew why I'd kept things so hidden so close to myself.

I took another sip of whiskey, letting the burn trail all the way down into my stomach.

I'd stopped living for my family.

And had started working for the devil.

And I hoped one day someone would kill me for it — the way I wanted to kill me.

But it was either Phoenix, or it would be me.

And apparently, I valued my life more than his — or maybe it was just the fact that I knew he wanted to be put out of his misery.

I hadn't seen him in two weeks. I'd stayed away on purpose; it had made the job harder.

Laughter erupted from the upstairs and floated down.

It got closer.

Until both Phoenix and Bee were in the kitchen.

She jumped into his arms, wrapping her legs around him, and kissed him. I expected Phoenix to freak; he hated being touched, and I'd assumed their fling was long over.

Instead, it looked hotter than ever.

He groaned and then laughed against her mouth.

I cleared my throat. Slowly, Phoenix inched her down his body and glared at in my direction. "Catcha cold, Serg?"

"Cute." I lifted my glass toward him. "Playing with the Cappo's sister, Phoenix?"

"Playing would mean I was about to stop... or somehow get bored." He tilted his head, his eyes murderous. "And considering she just agreed to marry me, I'd say that's not going to happen."

I spat out the contents of my drink and slammed the glass onto the table. "What?"

"Married." Phoenix grinned. "The normal reaction is a toast, but choking is fine too... I guess."

"Married," I repeated. "To Bee?"

Bee burst out laughing. "Um, do you see him kissing anyone else?"

No. Then again, Phoenix avoided women like the plague. I'd started to actually put stock into the idea that he swung the other way.

"Does Tex know?" I cleared my throat and put the ice that had spilled out of my drink into my hand.

"Not yet." Phoenix flinched. "I'm meeting with him later this week."

No. He wasn't.

He wouldn't get the chance.

Because he would be dead.

By my hand.

"Well..." Words felt funny crossing my lips. I tasted blood, must have bitten my tongue. "I hope all goes well."

"It will." Phoenix leveled me with a glare. "Why

wouldn't it?"

Because... friend. I'm going to end you and quite possibly take away Bee's only reason for living.

"It will," I lied. "I have to go out. I'll see you guys... later."

I brushed past them and jogged out to my car. I was surprised that it only took ten seconds before I pulled off the side of the road and puked onto the gravel.

As if sensing my hesitation, my phone went off.

Agency: *Tomorrow night. Eight. Don't be late, and bring a friend.*

It looked like a friendly text.
It was an invitation to certain death.

Me: *Can't wait.*

I texted back and puked again. My hand hovered over my contacts list, but that was the thing... I had my brother, but he had Amy... I had Nixon, but he had Trace.

No friends.
No close family.
No one.
I had no one.
And now Phoenix did.
So why... why was *my* life more precious than his?

CHAPTER FORTY-EIGHT

Just when everything starts to look good…

Phoenix

I STARED UP AT the ceiling and planned, plotted was more like it. I knew that look on Sergio's face.

It was only a matter of time.

I'd planned on tailing him all day and hadn't told Bee that I wouldn't be going with her to school. Chase said he'd cover for me.

Funny, because I'd wanted Nixon and had gotten Chase instead, and he'd said I was lucky he was doing me a favor and not telling Tex.

I trusted Chase.

I just knew he hated me.

Nixon, somehow, was able to push past things; Chase had the tendency to chew on them a while, pretend to swallow, then cough them back up and go to town again.

"Phoenix," Bee whispered against my chest. "What time is it?"

"Morning." I turned and looked at her. Dark hair fell

across her high cheeks. My breath hitched. I'd do anything to keep her safe.

Chest clenched, I reached for her and took possession of her mouth.

"Hmm." She pulled back. "A very good morning."

"The best." I chuckled against her lips. "I think I know a way to make it better, too."

"Oh?" She crawled over until she was straddling me. "And what's that?"

"Mind reader," I growled, gripping her hips with both of my hands.

She threw her head back and sighed. "Yes, well, that's not my only talent."

"Believe me," I growled, "I'm well aware."

Last night had been an absolute dream — or nightmare, depending on how you looked at it. It had been years since I'd let a girl touch me.

Even knowing that, Bee hadn't just touched me; she'd stroked, played, and, when that hadn't satisfied her curiosity, she'd tasted.

I died a thousand deaths.

And lasted all but five seconds with her mouth on me before I'd had to be inside her.

We hadn't gotten much sleep — and part of the reason had felt desperate, like if we'd spent any of those moments we had together doing anything but kissing, making love, then we were being wasteful. Maybe that was because I'd felt like I'd wasted so much of my life so far.

"Phoenix!" Bee clapped her hands in front of my face then rocked her hips into me. "Focus, man. We've only got ten minutes."

"Bossy." I reached for her but was slapped away.

"Get your head in the game, son." She winked. "We have ten minutes before I have to get ready." She slid her body against mine.

I moaned. "Got it. Ten minutes."

"Maybe nine now." She giggled then slid against me again. Bee rubbing her naked body against mine was so damn erotic, I just wanted to sit back and watch, and then she slapped me against the chest, killing the moment. "Dude, we're running out of time!"

"Did you just call me dude?"

"Yeah, like we're on a farm, a dude ranch!" She clapped. "Get it? Because I'm on top of you and—"

"Bee..." With a tug and a bit of shifting, I had her flat on her back. "...shut up."

"But—"

My tongue plunged inside her mouth as I covered her body with mine; our hands gripped each other tightly as I made love to every inch of her, paying special attention to every place, worried I'd missed a spot of skin that hadn't yet had my lips.

"I like it when you make me shut up." She tugged me by the hair and damn near drew blood with her teeth when she kissed me. "More."

"I'll always give you more." I rocked into her. "Always."

"Good." Her head fell back against the pillows as my movements went from slow and fluid to frenzied. "That's so good."

When she hooked her ankles behind me, I lost complete control, forgetting about her pleasure or anything else. I let her grip carry me off the ledge.

"Selfish bastard," she hissed.

"What?" Horrified I glanced up at her. "Bee, I'm so sorry I—"

"Kidding." She held up her hands. "But it was worth it to see that look on your face."

With a growl, I spanked her. Hard. And tilted my head. "We still have five minutes, Bee..."

"So use them." She wiggled against me. "And make 'em

good, Phoenix."

"I don't know how to do bad."

"I know." She laughed. "Oh, and I love you, just in case you were curious."

"Good, because when you screamed my name just now, I was afraid your heart wasn't really in it."

"Yeah, well, not all screams are created equal."

I laughed against her neck. "Probably two minutes... shower or make out?"

"Silly boy with his funny options." She slammed her mouth against mine.

And I spent the next two minutes making both of us forget everything but us... together.

CHAPTER FORTY-NINE
Heart. Broken.

Bee

"SO…" I GOT OUT of the car and checked my cell. Surprisingly no freak-out texts from the brother. Things were looking up! You know, until I told him that my security guard, family enemy, and his least favorite person was going to be a dad.

Yeah, maybe I should tell Mo first so she could pave the way with lots and lots of sex. Ew. He was my brother, but I was desperate that he be as calm as possible when Phoenix and I sat down with him and gave him the news. I even thought about bringing in a puppy.

Because puppies screamed innocence, and really, who could shoot someone in front of a puppy? A heartless bastard, that's who.

Oh look! Tex's name next to that definition in *Webster's*. Oh well, I tried.

"So, what?" Phoenix checked his phone and didn't take off his sunglasses or his jacket.

"Er, we going to class first, or do I get the coffee promised to me beforehand?"

"Coffee." A voice chirped. "Ah, I forgot how much fun it was to be a little errand boy. Chase, get me coffee. Chase, grab my books."

Phoenix smirked. "Trace never ordered you around like that."

"True." Chase sighed. "I think I may have made that up in my head to make myself feel better about being her security guard. You know, since my balls all but disappeared during that sad, sad time."

"Chase?" I crossed my arms. "Why are you here?"

"You're smaller than I remember?" He glanced at Phoenix. "Does she look smaller?"

"Right here," I sang out, raising my hands.

"No." Phoenix tapped his chin. "Prettier though. Definitely prettier."

"Tsk, tsk, don't let the Cappo hear you say that lest he castrate your parts and feed them to the birds."

"Bird." I laughed.

Phoenix glared.

"He loves that word." Winking, I uncrossed my arms. "No, but seriously, why are you here, Chase?"

"It's the job, little one."

"Little one?" I repeated.

"Seriously though, I thought you were tall." Chase shook his head. "Alright, let's go coffee you, since clearly your growth is already shot to shit, and then we'll go to class. I can't wait to pick on your least favorite students. Don't tell me who they are; I'll figure it out then make a cutting motion with my finger and see if they piss themselves."

Phoenix rolled his eyes. "Sorry, Bee. I have some things I need to do today, so Chase is going to make sure you get to every class on time."

"And pee during the allotted breaks," Chase piped up. "But it's weird that Phoenix actually wrote that down."

Panicked, I was about to freak out, or say something like, *"Don't leave me!"* when Phoenix pulled me into his arms and kissed me, silencing all the worries before I could even voice them.

"Baby—" He kissed me harder. "—you're safe. Just trust me on this, okay?"

"And..." I had trouble finding my voice. "...you'll be right back? Tonight? As promised?"

"Yes, yes, and yes." He kissed my nose. "I love you."

My eyes watered with tears. Stupid hormones! "Love you too."

When he released me and stepped back, I expected Chase to charge him or say something smart. Instead his mouth was ajar, and he was looking between us as if we'd just told him we were from Mars and taking him back to our leader.

"Dude..." Chase scratched his head. "...Tex is going to flip his shit... but... I'm happy for you." He licked his lips and looked down. "I didn't think... it was... like this."

"Like what?" Phoenix gripped my hand and kissed each finger.

"Real." Chase snorted, finally looking up. "I didn't think it was real."

"And now?" Phoenix asked, releasing my hand and pulling out his keys. "Now what do you think?"

"I think you better stop looking at her that way before she ends up pregnant." Chase chuckled. "That's what I think."

I fought to keep my laugh in while Phoenix chuckled under his breath. "Alright then... you guys have fun."

"Please." Chase waved him off. "I'm the best bodyguard around."

"You got shot last time." Phoenix rolled his eyes. "Just sayin'."

"Flesh wound, bitch." Chase gave him the finger. "Just sayin'."

"Alright, girls." I clapped my hands. "Can we go now?

Before one of you ends up comparing gun sizes?"

"Like it's a contest," Chase grumbled.

"Bite me!" Phoenix charged toward him.

Laughing, I pushed at Phoenix's chest and shoved him toward the car. "Get in, big boy. Apparently, you've got work to do."

"You let her anywhere near your gun, and I end you," Phoenix called over my shoulder then kissed me possessively.

"You do realize he's happily married?" I pointed out when he drew back.

"Don't care." Phoenix kissed me again, this time harsher. "The man could charm anything with a pulse."

"Thanks!" Chase called over. "I'll let my wife know you appreciate my skill."

"Weirdest conversation ever," I mumbled. "Go, Phoenix, we'll be fine, all three of us."

His face softened. "I'll miss you both."

"Go already."

He kissed me again then shut the door to his car and drove off.

It was hard not to feel his loss like a physical blow to my body. I'd become so used to having him around that his absence next to me felt strange; even when he'd been annoying and cruel to me, he'd still been there.

"Chin up, buttercup." Chase threw on a pair of sunglasses and popped his knuckles. "You're with Uncle Chase now."

"Ew!" I held up my hands. "I'm sure you meant that as a weird sort of familial gesture, but all I felt was the intense need to punch you in the face."

"Aw, you really are Tex's sister. I'm so proud. But don't punch the face. Mil will get pissed. Apparently, only she's allowed to bruise me."

"Happen often?"

"More than I'd care to admit." He laughed.

I'd always liked Chase's laugh; it was easy, fun, comfortable. It was almost comfortable enough to forget that he was a trained killer, who was also skilled in the art of torture and enjoyed shooting things.

Add that in with his crazy good looks, and a girl felt anything but comfortable around the guy. More like petrified and oddly curious as to how he kept his hair styled so perfect all the time.

"Do you wax?" I asked, once we reached the campus coffee shop.

Chase smirked. "Do I wax? Where did that come from?"

"Up here." I tapped my head. "Now buy me a coffee and answer the question."

"Are we talking wax my eyebrows or my…" He grunted. "…ass."

"You have a hairy ass?"

"Wouldn't you like to know?"

"No, I really wouldn't. Just curious how you keep…" I pointed at his face. "…all this so perfectly groomed."

"Aw, shucks, she called me perfect." He winked at the barista who, in turn, looked ready to choke on her tongue and pass out head first into the milk wand. "Keep the change," he whispered.

He'd given her a twenty.

"Shameless little whore," I said under my breath. "Flirting with the coffee lady."

"She's fifty." Chase rolled his eyes. "And has worked at Elite for the past four years, has three grandchildren, can't afford health insurance — or couldn't until we hired her — and her social security number is—"

I plugged my ears and winked. "You made your point. You know everything about everyone."

"Care to play a game?" He gave me his coffee and held out his arm.

I took it and narrowed my eyes. "Ah, doubtful of my

skill?"

"Maybe."

"Name a teacher."

"Mr. Hibland."

"Horrible man." Chase shuddered. "Actually tried to kill his own wife in order to get life insurance. When it was discovered by the university that he tried to spook her horse, we spooked him, cut out his tongue, offered him a lovely salary to teach sign language so we could keep him under our thumb if we need quick cleanup on campus. His social security number changed — after all his wife thinks he's dead. Oh, and we gave her the life insurance money. Last I heard, she was on her second honeymoon in France."

My mouth dropped open.

"What?" He shrugged. "Just because they're teachers here doesn't mean they're clean. In fact, we have more dirty teachers than clean ones at Elite, but we like it that way. basically means we can burn down the entire school and they'll simply nod their heads and ask if we want to burn them as well."

"Scary."

Chase took a sip of his coffee. "Not really, but it is necessary."

"To control everyone and everything?"

"If we don't..." He stopped walking. "...people get hurt. Therefore, we control, we play puppetmaster, and hopefully, when things go to hell, we're able to fix them."

"Huh." The coffee was warm against my lips as we walked in comfortable silence all the way to my first class. "Do you know what Phoenix is up to?"

He snorted. "Phoenix is all kinds of scary. I'd no sooner ask him than tell Nixon I want a swift kick to the balls. Nixon knows, and that's enough. Though, if I were a betting man, I'd say it has to do with Sergio."

I paused. "Why Sergio?"

"Keep your friends close… and your enemies closer." He flicked my chin with his fingers and led me into the building.

"And you guys think Sergio is our enemy?"

"Think, suspect, ponder…" Chase shrugged. "…regardless, Phoenix is the one that has to figure it out, not us. After all, he's the only one who truly knows anything about Sergio. The rest of us were left in the dark, thank God."

"Wait, I don't understand."

Chase sighed and rubbed his face with his free hand. "Think of it this way… our family has secrets, lots and lots of secrets. Secrets are like currency in our way of life. But the gatekeeper? That was always Luca. That was why people were so terrified of him. He knew everything. Hell, I still don't know how the man slept at night. But he made it his life goal to have something on every family, on every individual. The day he died, those secrets made a little transfer — directly into Phoenix's hands."

"Doesn't that put him in danger?" I swallowed the fear that was slowly rising in my throat.

"No, sweetheart." Chase chuckled. "That makes him a powerful son of a bitch. And the last thing you want to do is piss off a man who finally has something to live for."

"Huh?"

"You," Chase whispered. "I'm talking about you."

CHAPTER FIFTY

Secrets kill.

Phoenix

I DROVE IN TENSE silence, following my GPS until it finally stopped moving. I parked my car across the street and glanced up at the building. Well, shit.

The Federal Building.

A part of me knew.

And that part was wishing like hell I was wrong.

With a loud sigh, I made sure I put both of my guns in the glove box and tossed my sunglasses onto the dash.

The folder sat on the leather seat next to me, mocking me, staring at me. Luca's handwriting was scrawled across it.

I pulled the note from the top of the pile and read it over again.

Open and proceed only if he's reactivated. It's the only way. Be smart. Be safe. You're a Nicolasi now. Do what needs to be done. Think about it later.

"Ha, easy for you to say, you crazy bastard." I wiped my face with my hands and slowly got out of the car, locking the door behind me. I glanced up at the building and made my way across the street.

By the time I made it into the building and through the metal detectors, I was sweating.

A De Lange — the boss of the Nicolasi family — was officially walking into enemy territory.

Had someone told me I'd be walking into the FBI building a year ago, I would have thought they'd meant in cuffs.

Not as a free man.

I took the elevator to the fourth floor.

The doors to the elevator opened. I looked up. Activity blurred around the office — papers flew, phones rang.

But the minute I stepped off the elevator, all activity… simply… stopped.

That was the problem with the government; they took such crap pictures of people that when the feds actually saw me in person, they had to stare a good five seconds before they realized who the hell I was.

Nobody moved a muscle.

I smirked and made my way toward the back office.

Whispering commenced. I had the sudden urge to turn around and say something like *"Boo!"* But they'd probably mistake it for bomb and use that as a reason to arrest me.

As it was…

I was clean.

As a freaking whistle.

I knew it. They knew it.

I could strip naked and do a little dance, and they'd still have to let me go on grounds that I knew too much.

To the feds, I was too dangerous.

Because what Luca had known — I now knew.

And it could get them shut down.

By the time I made it to Director Smith's office, the rest of the room started talking again, though it was hushed as if they were afraid to speak too loudly.

I knocked twice.

He looked up.

And paled.

I angled my head. "Care if I come in?"

He opened his mouth, but all that came out was a croak.

"What? No, it's nice to see you." He swallowed and moved to stand.

"I'd rather you sit." I held out my hand. "Don't give me a reason to shoot your head off and mess up that lovely picture of..." I peered around him. "...Andi, isn't it? The adopted daughter you planted in Elite? Blond hair... really pretty brown eyes..." I chuckled. "And dying — am I right? From... what is it?" I snapped my fingers. "Leukemia, that's it."

His face turned bright red. "You know nothing!"

"Oh..." I took a seat and put my feet up on his desk. "I know a little bit of everything, so let's not play that game. I'm already bored." I yawned. "Government jobs pay like shit, don't they?"

He looked down.

"But me..." I chuckled. "...I'm loaded. But wait—" I pointed at him and gave my finger a little shake. "—you probably already knew that, right?"

More silence.

"So..." I nodded. "...I kept thinking, what could possibly cause Sergio to freak out, to just up and leave for days and then suddenly say he knew where to find Nick and Pike?"

"Phoenix, I—"

"Shut up." I snapped. "I'm talking."

His nostrils flared.

"How much?" I asked.

"How much?"

"Play dumb one more time, and I'm going to cut off your

thumb." I reached for a letter opener on his table. "Kinda dull, but it may just do the trick."

"One million," he said so softly I almost didn't catch the words. "The Russians were going to pay one million. All I needed to do was set up Pike, make it look like an accident, then infiltrate the family."

"My family."

"The Nicolasi family."

"With?"

"They're bleeding money. They need a new trade route… thought the best way to ship drugs in and out was with the Nicolasi brand. You own seven harbors in the US."

"I do."

"And…" He pulled at the neck of his shirt. "…Sergio would naturally take over operations for me, stepping in as the next boss."

"One you controlled."

He licked his lips and glanced out the window. "I would do anything to save her."

"Anything?" I tilted my head. "Do you truly mean that?"

Smith paused. "What are you getting at, Phoenix?"

"I'll deal with your problem. Eliminate the players, take out the ones that need taking out… and I'll protect you from Petrov." I captured his eyes with a pointed stare. "But it will cost you. After all, you nearly destroyed my life, so it's only fair if you make me bleed… I make you bleed."

"What about Sergio?"

"You let me deal with Sergio."

"You'll kill him."

"Your time's up." I stood. "I'll call you later today to ask for your answer. Just know this isn't a war you'll win. You end up dead trying, and your daughter dies… or I save your pathetic ass, and your daughter lives."

"Will I ever see her again?" He didn't meet my eyes.

"Don't you think it's a little late to start acting the part of worried father? Granted, a million dollars would go a long way for her treatments, but you probably should have thought of that before you started embezzling money and dabbling at the Russian's casinos, am I right?"

"I never meant—" His body shook. "—I never meant for it to get this far. My job, my career, my little girl—"

"All your choice." I nodded. "I'll be in touch, and don't try fleeing the country or calling your superiors, or I'll have a gun trained on that clammy forehead before you even finish the damn call."

I slammed the door behind me and whistled while I walked all the way back to the elevators. The little dot on my phone paused again. Sergio's office was one floor down.

Deciding against the elevators, I took the stairs and made my way into the maze of cubicles.

When I found his…

I sighed.

He froze, not turning around. "Just do it already."

"Do what?" I asked, calm, though I felt like ripping his freaking head off.

"If you don't kill me, Nixon will. I had no choice."

"Don't," I spat. "Don't you dare say you didn't have a choice, not to me of all people. Not to me, Sergio." I pulled his chair around, and gripped his chin with my hands.

People around us gasped.

"Do it." His nostrils flared. "I was activated. That was the deal with Luca. I get activated. He comes for me. It was only a matter of time."

"Were you going to kill me? Would you have followed through with the plan?"

He didn't hesitate, simply said, "Yes."

"Why?"

"Because I wanted to live."

"And I don't deserve to?"

"You're Phoenix De Lange. When did you ever deserve

life?"

I punched him across the face then pulled him to his feet. "I think I'm going to enjoy this."

"What?" Blood sputtered out of his mouth. "Enjoy what?"

Grinning, I half dragged him to the elevator and pressed the lobby button. When the elevator doors opened, I pushed him in then punched him again. He was letting me hit him, and in that moment I didn't care.

He slumped to the floor.

I ignored the blood and dialed Nixon.

"Problem?" he asked.

"Meeting. The Space. Bring company."

When I hung up, I tossed the phone at Sergio. "Call Nick and Pike. We do this now."

"So what? You kill all of us, and then what? Petrov still wants in the Nicolasi family."

"Who said I wasn't letting him in?" I snapped.

"But—" Sergio's eyes widened. "—he's Russian trash!"

"Money... always speaks. I give him what he wants. He leaves us alone. Come on, Sergio, you let your own fear get in the way. He wants a shipping company. I give it to him for a price. Heads don't have to roll, not unless I say they roll."

"But—" Blood trickled from his lips. "—are you saying if I had told you from the beginning what was going on...?"

"Maybe then..." I sighed. "...you would have been spared."

"And now?" he choked.

"Now," I said with a nod, "I'm handing you over to the executioner."

CHAPTER FIFTY-ONE
Out of the bag

Bee

"IF YOU DON'T EAT, Phoenix is going to get pissed." Chase sang, dangling a Cheetos in front of my face. "Seriously though, eat some food."

"I, um…" Rubbing my stomach I tried to smile. "…I'm just not super hungry."

"One chip." He handed it over to me. "And drink some water. Damn, you look pale. You can't drop dead on my watch. Seriously, I have a reputation to uphold."

With a tense smile, I grabbed the chip, choked it down, and followed it with water.

And ten seconds later, I puked it onto the ground behind the tree.

Chase was there in seconds, rubbing my back. "Whoa there, little one, you can't even stomach one chip?" He laughed. "Geez, it's like your preg—"

He didn't finish the sentence.

He stopped rubbing my back.

"Bee…" His voice turned serious. "…tell me you have the flu."

"I have the flu." I rolled my eyes and wiped my mouth.

Chase narrowed his eyes. "Great, now stop looking so guilty and say it to my face."

For some reason — maybe it was the concern in his voice and the pitiful look he was giving me or maybe it was just the stress of having Phoenix gone — I burst into tears. I mean, completely lost it and sobbed against his chest.

"I'm going to kill him!" Chase raged, patting my back a little too hard. "Tell me where to shoot him. Scratch that, I'm taking off the man's penis. Son of a bitch, he's a dead man!"

"He knows…" I sobbed. "I'm happy."

"If he hurt—" Chased pulled me away. "What did you say?"

"Happy. I'm happy." I snorted. "I just miss him."

"I'm sorry. Did you just say you were happy… with Phoenix? And you're having his love child?"

I nodded, wiping at my cheeks.

"And he took this news… how exactly? Shot a squirrel? Punched a wall? Kicked a puppy?"

"He smiled." I shrugged.

"You've got to be shitting me."

"No." I furrowed my eyebrows together. "It's a long story but… he asked me to marry him."

Chase held up his hand. "I need a minute to digest this." He placed his hands on his knees and took a few deep breaths. The man looked like he was ready to be ill right next to where I'd just thrown up.

"Do you, uh, need to sit down?"

"No," he said in a strangled voice. "I'm good. Just swallowed a bug."

"Or a bird." I rolled my eyes. "Seriously, Chase, you look pale."

"Phoenix?" He shook his head. "The same Phoenix who

just left you to go play doctor and rearrange people's organs? That Phoenix?"

"Yeah." I cringed at the mental picture.

"Well, shit me sideways," Chase muttered then finally stood. "Clearly your brother has no idea."

"I'm thinking I'll tell Mo first."

"Won't save his life." Chase shook his head. "Your best bet is to go to Vegas and back, ask for forgiveness later, and tell Mo to lace his whiskey with X."

"What would that do?"

"Probably nothing, but it's worth a shot." Chase flashed me a devastating smile. "You're really okay?"

I nodded. "I'm happy."

"Then I'm happy for you." He pulled me in for a hug. "Holy shit! I'm going to be an uncle!"

"But you guys aren't all really related—"

"Uncle Chase! Damn, I hope it's a boy. That would seriously piss Tex off, for Phoenix to have a boy before him. I'll pray for it tonight."

"Surprised God still hears you."

"Yeah, well, fingers crossed." He winked then reached for his cell phone. The smile immediately fell from his face. "We gotta go."

We climbed into Chase's SUV but didn't make it far. He pulled up to a spot on the far edge of campus that looked semi-deserted.

"Stay." He placed his hand on my knee. "You'll be safe out here, safer than if you were in there. I just... you need to stay, lock the doors, take a nap — whatever. I don't have time to take you back to the house to grab one of the men, and I don't want you to see—"

"See what?" My heart dropped to my knees. "Is it Phoenix? Is he okay?" Panic welled in my chest. "Chase, what aren't you telling me?"

"He's fine." Chase sighed. "Phoenix is okay. He's

probably inside already, just… stay here until we can figure some stuff out, alright?"

"Okay." I still felt panicked but did what Chase asked, because really, I didn't have any other choice in the matter.

I locked the doors and crossed my arms as I watched him walk up to a small building, knock twice, and then walk in and slam the door behind him.

Students were still milling around, but they gave what looked like an abandoned building a wide berth. I could only guess what went on inside; I almost didn't want to.

I'd ask Phoenix later.

Once he was okay.

Once he was in my arms.

CHAPTER FIFTY-TWO
Web of lies

Sergio

SOMEHOW, I'D BLACKED OUT between my transfer from downtown to where I was currently tied to a chair. My head was heavy, my mouth full of blood. I tried to spit it out, but I was so dehydrated it was like spitting sand.

"Ah, you're awake." Phoenix said in a taunting voice.

I rolled my eyes. I could really go without the dramatics. Besides, I didn't need to be toyed with. It would be impossible for me not to know what was happening next. The guys would question me, torture me, then kill me.

All because, a long time ago, I took a deal with the feds. Not that I knew at the time what I was protecting, who I was protecting, or how it would come back to bite me in the ass.

I blinked as a light turned on over my head.

"Nixon?" I coughed as he stepped into the light along with Chase, Tex, Frank, and Mil. Great. All five bosses, and it sure as hell wasn't a potluck.

Phoenix stood in front of me and slowly pulled out a

knife. Shit. I tried not to look afraid but no man — I don't care how badass he was — stares death in the face and actually laughs James-Bond-style. Pain is still pain.

The knife was cold against my lips as Phoenix slid it across my jaw and then with a jerk made a vertical cut down the side, crossing both my upper and bottom lip. A sharp pain, like a horrible paper cut started radiating from my skin as fresh blood poured down my face.

"When rats talk," Phoenix said in a low voice, "they get punished."

"You would know," I spat.

His fist flew so hard against my temple I almost fell out of my chair. Blood roared in my ears as the pounding in my head continued.

"So..." Nixon stepped forward, pulling a cigar cutter from his pocket. "...I'm not even going to ask if you want to do this the easy way or the hard way, Sergio. I'm just going to ask point blank — what the hell were you thinking?"

Tex snorted. "Or were you thinking at all?"

Frank held up his hand, pressing it against Tex's chest. "Let him speak."

Surprisingly enough, Tex backed off and crossed his arms while Frank approached, pacing in front of me.

I'd never liked Frank.

Frank or Luca.

They knew too much.

Swear, their wrinkles were full of secrets, and it pissed me off that they knew the real reason why I'd done what I had, yet never seemed to care that, in the end, I'd been the one who'd saved their asses.

"You know why," I said in a detached voice. "I made a deal with the feds... I told them I'd feed them valuable information."

"In exchange for what?" Frank's eyes narrowed.

"Ask Phoenix."

Phoenix smirked. "I think it's best you tell them, sunshine."

"Blood always wins." My voice was hollow, my chest tight. "Isn't that our motto?"

Nobody said anything, so I kept talking.

"The feds knew you went into hiding, Frank. When I was old enough to start working for the family, I started hacking. Small stuff here and there, but I finally got smart enough to hack their system. I pulled every damn thing they had on us."

Phoenix kicked my chair. "Keep talking."

"It was too late," I whispered. "They knew where the Alfero boss was hiding out, and it was only a matter of time before they eliminated him."

"When was this?" Nixon asked.

"Five years go." I shook my head as more blood filled my mouth. "So I offered them something they couldn't refuse."

"You." Tex finished for me.

With a nod, I slumped forward, my head hurting too much to hold it up anymore. "But making deals with the devil — that never really works out the way you hope. I pretended to be a double agent, worked for the family and the feds, kept us clean, kept them happy by feeding them information that would satisfy them enough not to make any movements."

"What went wrong?" Frank asked. "Because something had to have gone wrong."

"They wanted to infiltrate, put some of their own men in the family. I said it was impossible. You can't simply will yourself into a blood-owned family. They threatened retribution and then went after me... my own guys. The ones I'd worked side-by-side with for years went after me."

"And you killed them all?"

I bit my lip, tasting blood. "I killed them, but Luca... he took the fall, told me to go back and say I was out, that I was a *cafone*... making it so I was no longer useful to the mafia. I told the feds that the family was forcing me into hiding."

"And yet you came out." Frank sighed heavily.

"You needed me." I felt my emotions crack in that moment. "The family needed me, and you don't turn your back on family." I sniffed. "The feds reactivated me once they saw I was no longer a ghost, once I was valuable again, just like I knew they would."

"Why take the chance?" Nixon asked. "It makes no sense, why take the chance that they'll reactivate you? Hell, why not come to us?"

Shrugging, I swallowed and looked away. "I got myself into this mess. I was going to get myself out of it."

"Oh, good to know you had a plan." Tex rolled his eyes.

Phoenix slapped me on the back. "I knew you could come clean, now I won't have to slit your throat."

All eyes fell to him while I blinked in confusion. "What?"

"I took care of it." Phoenix was way too calm.

"What the hell do you mean you took care of it?" I roared.

"Director Smith..." Phoenix said, shrugging, "...has a little gambling problem... in deep with the Petrovs. They offered him one mil to infiltrate the Nicolasi family, which Sergio was going to help them with. Thanks, by the way, Sergio. Feels good to have a target on my back. Russians want a harbor. I'm going to give them a harbor."

"And Director Smith?" I asked. "He's just going to let you?"

"Course he is." Phoenix grinned. "Because his daughter's dying, and we'll do anything for blood, won't we?"

"His daughter?" I repeated. "What daughter?"

"For a hacker, you're really stupid." Phoenix rolled his eyes. "His daughter, Andi, the one you had me trail? Bee's one and only friend?"

I shook my head wildly. "No, no, she isn't his daughter. There's no way I wouldn't have known this whole time. Phoenix, something doesn't add up."

"She is." Phoenix nodded. "Trust me on this."

Something felt off. It was too neatly done, almost like it had been planned, but piecing everything together seemed impossible.

I didn't have to wait long for everything to click.

It was the sound of the door opening and closing that did it first.

And then clapping.

I watched in horror as Pike, Nick, and Director Smith walked into The Space, each of them smiling as if they'd just taken down the five families.

And I had a sinking feeling that's exactly what they'd just done.

CHAPTER FIFTY-THREE

Witnessing the horror of someone you love dying? No words for that.

Bee

I KNEW SOMETHING WAS wrong when I saw Nick and Pike walk up to the building. Weren't they supposed to be dead? Or at least in hiding or something? Panicked, I slumped down in my seat and dialed Mo's number.

"What up?" She laughed on the other end. "This better be good."

"Um, do you think the guys may be in trouble?"

She was quiet. "What makes you say that?"

"I'm at this building on campus, and well, they're all inside, and I just saw Nick and Pike walk in, and I don't think that's part of the plan."

Mo cursed then yelled for Trace. "Hold tight, you're at The Space, right?"

"The Space?" I repeated. "I... I don't know what that is."

"Do you have a gun?"

Holy crap. "No."

"Check the glove box."

I did as I was told and sure enough there was a gun in the glove box. With shaking hands, I pulled it out and nearly dropped it onto the ground. "Yeah, I got it."

"Great, take the safety off."

"What!" I yelled then stared at the gun in my hand. It wasn't the violence throwing me off it was the fact that I may have to do something like fire a weapon and if I missed, if something went wrong, it would be Phoenix's life, maybe my brothers hanging in the balance.

Mo sighed. "Look, we're on the way, point and shoot if any of those bastards gets close to you, got it?"

"Yeah, yeah, okay, I got it."

"Be safe." The conversation ended. I stared at the gun like it was going to actually hurt me. I'd never been trained in how to use any sort of weapon. I might talk a big game, but I honestly wouldn't even crush a bug.

"Crap," I muttered, looking out at the building then back at the gun. I hated not being able to do anything; I felt so vulnerable.

I was so concentrated on my gun that I didn't see anyone approach the car.

Something tapped my window.

I jumped, nearly shooting the steering wheel off and looked out.

It was Andi.

And she'd just seen me with a gun. Great, how was I going to explain that one.

She looked panicked.

I opened the door to diffuse the situation. "I... um, I'm going to a shooting range after school and—"

"Shh." Andi pulled me closer to her and pushed the gun into my hands. "No talking from here on out, alright?"

"What?" I pulled away from her. "What are you doing?" She was walking directly toward the building.

"We all have favors we're owed," Andi muttered. "Stay behind me."

"We can't go in there!" I hissed.

"We don't go in there and they die. Your choice." She pulled a gun from inside her leather jacket.

"Where did you get that?"

"Stop asking questions you really don't want to know the answers to." Her voice had changed slightly. Had she always had an accent? It sounded Russian, not at all like it had before.

Slowly, she kicked open the door and then held the gun to my temple.

And that's what I got for getting out of the car.

"Andi." Director Smith clapped. "And just in time!"

"Yeah, well..." Andi shrugged, her accent getting thicker by the minute. Russian, she sounded Russian. "I had someone to pick up." She shoved me forward.

All the guys were there, including Mil.

Each of them looked calm.

Except Tex and Phoenix.

Tex looked like he was about ready to rip someone's head off, and Phoenix looked so cold, emotionless, haunted that I was afraid he was already dead.

"You should have never raped my sister," Pike spat, holding his gun out toward Phoenix. "Tell them. Tell everyone."

Phoenix shook his head. "I have no idea what you're talking about."

"Yes, you do!" The gun shook as Pike held it in front of him. "You raped her! You killed her! Your father stole her, and you broke her," he raged. "And then when that wasn't enough, you took my cousin."

Phoenix hung his head. "That was a lifetime ago."

"Yeah, well, they're still dead," Pike hissed.

"So what?" Phoenix shrugged. "This is your retribution? Did you ever need a harbor to ship drugs? Did you ever need anything?"

"Yeah." Pike laughed. "Your death. But why stop there? Why not take all the bosses out?"

"Greedy son of a bitch, aren't you?" Tex snorted.

"Shut up!" Nick pushed his gun against Tex's chest. "By this time tomorrow morning you'll be but a bad memory for our families."

With a sigh Tex glared at Nick. "And what? What did Phoenix do to you? Or are you just a power hungry little bitch?"

"I loved her." Nick's voice shook. "I was going to marry her."

"Who?" Phoenix asked.

"Pike's sister, Lana." He sniffed. "We were going to marry, until she was stolen by the De Langes and then sold into prostitution... the same ring run by the Campisis."

"Awesome." Tex nodded. "So you're all pissed."

Nixon let out a chuckle. "And you, Director Smith? What's your story?"

"Oh, that's easy." He pointed his gun at Nixon's forehead. "I take down all five bosses... I become a legend."

"Pretty elaborate planning." Phoenix nodded. "Brilliant, really. You've clearly thought of everything."

Director Smith let out a curse. "Don't patronize me. You can try to fight us, but the odds are against you."

"Are they?" Phoenix tilted his head.

Why the heck did he look so calm?

"I'm calling in my favor," he said aloud.

"Knew you would, you bastard," Andi hissed, shoving me to the side and then firing direct shots into Pike's and Nick's heads. Both men crumpled to the floor.

By the time the Smith guy knew what was going on, Phoenix was already on top of him.

With a grunt and a twist, he snapped his neck. The man fell to the ground.

The room blanketed into silence.

And then the door burst open, revealing Trace and Mo, guns raised.

"Too late." Tex chuckled. "But hot, nonetheless."

"I miss the best fights." Mo pouted.

Trace threw her gun onto the ground and charged toward Nixon. "You bastard! You can't just go and get yourself shot!

"I'm not shot."

"Oh." She looked almost disappointed. "But I thought—"

A gunshot rang out.

And severe pain hit me square in the chest. I looked down as blood stained my white shirt. *What?* Confused, I touched the blood and winced.

"Even in my death," Pike groaned. "I take what is most precious to you."

The gun fell out of his hand just as I stumbled backward, my legs unable to keep me up.

"Bee!" Phoenix roared, running toward me.

Tex was hot on his heels. The room was starting to spin, but all I could think about was the fact that I could be dying and that I would never get to marry Phoenix.

And have our child.

"The baby, Phoenix!" My voice was hoarse. "The baby!"

"Baby?" Tex yelled in confusion.

"You'll be fine, Bee. I promise." Phoenix kissed my mouth, pressing his hands against my chest. "Just try to calm down, alright? Just breathe."

I tried but it was hard, getting harder.

"Untie him." This from Nixon.

Soon Sergio was standing over me, though his form was super blurry. He smacked Phoenix's hands away and inspected the wound. "It looks clean."

"Thank God." Tex rocked back on his heels and sat on the cement.

"But the trauma to the body…" Sergio swore. "Bee, how far along are you?"

I shook my head, my vision blurring even more.

"Bee!" Sergio shook me.

"Phoenix!" I sobbed, and everything went black.

CHAPTER FIFTY-FOUR

It was never about my life — but hers.

Phoenix

SHE WASN'T DYING.

But it felt like it.

And it was my fault, all my fault. I couldn't come to grips with the fact that I'd put her and our baby in danger again, unintentionally.

"Baby?" Tex repeated over and over again, his eyes going from frantic to enraged then back to frantic.

The bullet had gone clean through, missing any vital organs. Luckily, Sergio was a pro at that sort of thing. Otherwise, we would have had to call in another favor or, God forbid, go to the hospital with a gunshot wound.

I was worried about the baby.

Sergio said the only way to tell was if she started to bleed.

I almost lost it right there in The Space. I'd seen a lot of horror in my life. Hell, I was the reason for it, but nothing terrified me more, brought me to my knees more, than the idea of Bee losing our innocent child — and me having to tell her when she woke up.

We moved her into my room. I was the one to hook up the IV and make sure she was comfortable, and Tex refused to leave her side.

She looked peaceful.

"You knew," Tex muttered an hour into sitting by her bedside with me in silence. "You knew all of this?"

"Knew what?" I didn't have the energy to argue. I leaned back in my chair, not taking my eyes from Bee's sleeping face.

"About Smith? Andi? Nick? Did you know it all?"

"Parts." I sighed. "But plans only work so well. In the long run I didn't know if we could trust Sergio. Wasn't sure if he'd hand us over with bells on or try to fight for blood."

"He did the right thing."

I let out a snort. "He was forced to do the right thing."

Tex was quiet then asked, "And Andi?"

"Worked for the Petrov family for years, a bastard blood-daughter to Petrov himself… one of Luca's implants. I didn't know it until I finally opened the folder he'd addressed to me. I sent her a text of our location just in case. Director Smith really had adopted her when she was younger as a favor to the Petrov family. I think, in his own, way he loves her or… did."

I scratched my head. Andi was the least of our worries. She'd been born in violence, trained to do the right thing, and had been approached by Luca years ago. Well, threatened was more like it. Then again, she'd never forgiven her father for giving her up to Director Smith for his freedom.

"Question…" Tex rubbed the back of his head. "Do we… um, all have folders?"

"Oh, yeah," I said in a hoarse voice. "But it's not like I read them before bed or anything. I only opened Sergio's because I had a suspicion he'd been reactivated."

"Great, so mine stays closed until…?"

"Until you piss me off," I growled. What did he expect, really?

"Right, because in this situation you're the one that gets to be pissed off. Tell me, how long have you been screwing my little sister?"

Nixon and Chase chose that inopportune time to walk into the room.

"Great," I hissed softly.

"Story time." Chase pulled up a chair while Nixon stood. "So, Phoenix, when did this love affair start?"

Bee moaned in her sleep. I wanted her to wake up, but I knew she needed to heal, the baby needed her to heal. If there still was a baby.

"Lasagna," I said in a hoarse whisper. "It started with lasagna."

"You started having sex with her because she fed you?" Chase asked with a laugh. "Good thing I never cooked you my ma's favorite dish..."

"She wouldn't stop." I reached for her hand. "The more I pushed, the more she pushed back. I thought I was going to lose my damn mind, and then everything just fell into focus... she..." My voice cracked. "...she's the only one who took the time to look past it all."

The guys were silent, probably because I was close to sobbing all over the girl I loved.

"When Bee looks at me, she doesn't see a monster. Not anymore. She was never afraid, never used my past against me as a way to get back at me, she... she made me want to live."

"So you *slept* with her?" Tex's voice rose. "Look, I'm glad she's your friend and all but—"

"I love her!" I dropped her hand and pushed to my feet. "I love her!"

Tex's eyes widened until it looked like they were going to pop out of his head.

"I want to marry her." I licked my lips. "I want her forever. I love her, Tex. I'm not screwing her. I'm not using her. She — she owns me."

Nixon and Chase both touched my back, and then the door shut behind me.

Leaving me and Tex alone.

The room bent and stretched with tension. I waited for him to call me out; I waited for him to pull out a gun — or any sort of weapon.

"You love my little sister?" he repeated, looking from me to Bee and back.

"A while ago…" I ran my hands through my hair. "The Cappo got on his knees in front of the least likely of men… the most undeserving, and asked for one thing. You remember what it was?"

Tex shut his eyes. "Mo. I asked you for Mo. I asked you to dissolve the contract between me and the Nicolasi family, so I could have her."

"Yeah," I croaked. "I know there's no contract, but I still want your permission… I want to marry her. I want to raise our son or daughter, I want to live and breathe every day for her, for family. I want that second chance more than I want anything, Tex. But I don't want it unless I can have it with Bee. I love her, Tex. I love her."

"I thought Phoenix De Lange didn't know what love was."

"I didn't," I answered honestly. "Until she started cooking for me, teasing me, taunting me, pushing me — I didn't know what love was until Bee walked into my life, and I'll be damned if I have to let her go."

"Don't," Bee whispered from her bed. "Don't leave me."

"Bee!" I rushed to her side and kissed her face. "Baby, are you okay? Do you need anything? Are you in pain?"

"Tex, please." She reached for her brother. "Please… I love…"

"Him?" Tex pointed at me. "You do realize he snores? Likes to kill people for a living? Pierced his own ear when he was eleven?"

I suppressed a laugh.

"I love him," Bee said through a tear-streaked smile. "Please, Tex."

"Well, hell." Tex raised his hands above his head and cursed. "I say no, and I'm pretty sure Mo would hate me forever... not to mention my little sister, who I'm just getting to know."

Tex leaned over and kissed Bee on the forehead then motioned for me to follow him over to the other side of the room.

I didn't have time to prepare for his punch. With a grunt, I fell to the floor, my cheek pounding like hell.

"What?" Tex stood over me, an innocent expression across his face. "You didn't actually think you'd escape without getting injured, right?"

Cursing, I rubbed my cheek and stood with Tex's help.

The minute I was stable on my feet...

He punched me again.

"And that—" He rubbed his knuckles. "—was for getting her pregnant."

I stayed down, even when he offered me his hand.

"Tex!" Bee shouted from her bed. "Don't hurt him!"

"Bastard's just fine." Tex smirked. "Believe me, he'd let me hit him all day if it meant he could be with you."

"True." I winced. "Though I'd rather you not."

"Can't promise I won't feel the urge to punch you again, friend."

"That's fair." I stood and rubbed my face, cracking my jaw to the side, hoping to alleviate some of the pressure and swelling.

The door opened again.

Chase and Nixon shuffled through, both looking absolutely deflated.

"What?" Tex shrugged.

"We missed the fight." Chase sighed. "I wanted to watch

him get a few punches in."

Nixon slapped Chase on the shoulder. "We tried."

"Thanks, guys." I muttered, still rubbing my jaw.

"Well..." Tex shoved me out of the way and pushed the guys out the door. "We should let them talk, but if I hear any sort of... pleasurable noises coming from this room, I'm going to shoot you in the face, Phoenix. That's a promise."

"Noted." I waved them off and made my way back to the bed.

Bee was trying to sit up as best she could, which wasn't all that great, considering it probably hurt her to put pressure on her elbows.

"You okay?" She reached for my face.

I grabbed her hands and kissed them. "Don't worry about me."

"Phoenix..." Her lower lip trembled. "Is the baby okay?"

"Yeah." I was so relieved to be able to say that. "But even if something happens, Bee, I'm here, alright?" I gripped her hands tightly. "I'm never leaving your side."

She started to cry silently.

I pulled her into my embrace and joined her on the bed, letting her cry against my chest. "You should have told me."

"Told you?"

"About your secret keeping." She sniffled.

"Bee..." I sighed and kissed her head. "I didn't even know until I went in this morning... everything was... planned to an extent, but I wasn't sure I could keep you safe. Wasn't sure Andi would follow through with her end of the deal. Hell, I wasn't even sure if Smith would come after the bosses. That's life though... you can try to plan for every possible scenario, but sometimes life surprises you."

"Am I a surprise?" she asked, blinking her eyes up at me.

Damn, she was beautiful.

"The best." I tucked her hair behind her ear. "The best surprise I could ever hope for... and I'll spend the rest of my life trying to deserve you."

"I don't care, you know…" She ducked her head against my chest. "…about the girls, Pike's sister, and cousin. You didn't know."

My gut clenched. I'd forgotten that Bee had even heard that. "Bee, it doesn't excuse what I did, what my family did."

"My father helped."

"Yeah, well, both our dads weren't the greatest." I kept playing with her hair. "Guess I don't have very big shoes to fill."

"They don't even have shoes. You get to start over with a brand new pair." Bee smiled up at me, her eyes shining with adoration. "You're going to be the best dad in the world."

My heart strained and beat wildly in my chest; emotion clogged my throat making it hard to breathe. "You think?"

"I know." Bee reached for my face. "You're going to be incredible."

"You can't drop out of school." I flicked her nose. "That's the rule. We do this, we get married, but you have to stay in school and…" I shrugged.

"Do my homework every night? Drink milk?" she teased. "You still going to boss me around?"

"I'm not bossy," I said defensively.

"Okay then." Bee laughed. "Says the guy who forced my poor ears to listen to Mozart then asked if I had lunch money."

I rolled my eyes and laughed. "Yeah well… I can't help but worry about you."

"If it's a boy…" Bee said, changing the subject. "I want to name him Phoenix."

"What?" I almost pulled away, almost ran out of the room screaming. "Why the hell would you curse a kid with *my* name?"

"It's not a curse…" Bee squeezed my hand. "It's redemption… he's your miracle, Phoenix. Our miracle."

"What if it's a *she?*"

Her eyes twinkled. "Name her Tex to piss my brother off."

We both burst out laughing as a loud banging sounded at the door. "You better not be naked!"

"Quick, put your clothes on!" I shouted.

Tex burst through the door.

"Gross, brother." Bee scrunched up her nose. "I could have been naked!"

"Yeah, well…" Tex turned bright red and scratched his head. "I thought that… um, you see—"

"Go away, Tex." I waved him off then kissed his sister soundly on the mouth. "We're going to be busy for a while."

"And that's how babies are made, boys and girls," Chase said from the door.

Tex shoved past him while Nixon burst out laughing.

CHAPTER FIFTY-FIVE

The story doesn't end happy... not by a long shot.

Sergio

THE COFFEE TABLE FELT too small to be sitting at with Frank. He kept eyeing the coffee cup in my hand like it was going to spontaneously combust and turn into a bomb, killing everyone in its vicinity.

"So..." Frank folded his hands on the table. "...you realize you will be punished."

"Yeah," I croaked. "I do."

"We cannot simply allow this to be looked past. It will appear... weak." Frank licked his lips and took a long sip of his coffee. "And weakness means the family crumbles. It means people start talking. They start asking questions — they start doubting our leadership."

My stomach sank with every word.

"What do I need to do?" The question burned like acid on my tongue.

With a smile his eyebrows rose. "A very long time ago, I promised my brother that I would never interfere with love again — that I'd allow things to progress naturally. I promised him that family would win above all else."

I wasn't sure where he was going with that.

"The Russians have their use."

And that was it.

He didn't say anything more.

Tex charged into the room with Nixon and Chase hot on his heels. They all sat at the table and stared at me.

I didn't belong anymore.

I was the betrayer.

Funny, because in the grand scheme of things, I'd ended up becoming exactly what I hated — a rat.

All because I'd been trapped.

But that's the thing about the human condition; you'll do anything to survive, things you would never entertain, thoughts you'd always pushed away. Hell, I'd judged men for doing what I did. But when put in the position to choose myself over my family? I'd chosen myself.

"Did you tell him?" Tex asked.

"Not yet." Frank smiled. "Not yet."

"Tell me what?"

Nixon spoke in a low tone. "Your new job."

I had a feeling my new job was going to be in the depths of hell — where no one would hear me scream.

CHAPTER FIFTY-SIX

And the Phoenix rose up from the ashes...

Bee

MY GUNSHOT WOUND MADE it near impossible to do anything except allow Phoenix to kiss me — which I was totally okay with.

He kissed.

He touched.

And he made me stay still — which was ridiculously hard to do when he started peeling my clothes from my body and using his tongue in places I wasn't aware were allowed.

His mouth made its way to mine; his kiss always felt like the first time, like he put every emotion he had into that one gesture, ignoring the rest of the world. Letting everything fade into the swirly grey of nothingness — it was only us, our mouths meeting, touching, caressing.

Phoenix pulled back and stared into my eyes. "You make me crazy."

"A good crazy, right?" I whispered.

"Great crazy..." His smile still made my heart jump in

my chest. "The kind of crazy men don't ever get over — the type of crazy I want to embrace every day I have breath in my body."

"You know…" I giggled. "…you're turning into quite the romantic."

He laughed. "And to think… it all started with food."

"The way to a man's heart *is* through his stomach," I said, feeling wise.

"Bee, you know…" Phoenix's eyebrows scrunched up like he'd just seen a really hard math problem and wasn't sure how to work it. "…I'm not perfect."

"You sure?" I looked down. "Because, compared to all those statues you aren't supposed to stare at in the museum, you're pretty perfect… all tight muscles."

"Bee," he warned.

I reached for him. "Hard."

He let out a hiss of air then cursed graphically.

"I'm sorry." I pulled my hand back. "What were we talking about?"

"You." He took my mouth again. "Being the death of me."

"What a great way to go." I licked his lower lip.

"Wait." he pulled back. "I'm trying to have one of those moments here…"

"Oh, my gosh, a magic carpet moment?"

Phoenix rolled his eyes. "Yeah, where we hold hands and bleed our feelings."

"Do tell." I waggled my brows.

"You're impossible."

"You love me."

"Desperately." His voice shook.

"So?"

"I'm not perfect."

"Wait, are we just repeating ourselves now?"

"Bee, please." He gripped my hands. "Let me finish."

"You already did…" I winked and whispered across his mouth, "…twice."

"God forgive me, I've turned you into a sexual deviant." He pulled me into his embrace and rubbed my arm absentmindedly. "I'm afraid I'm going to lose this."

"My arm?"

"And what it's attached to." He sighed. "I'm afraid of feeling. I'm so afraid, Bee, that one day I'll wake up and—" His voice cracked. "—this, what I feel for you, what we have, will either disappear or I'll somehow mess it up. That's all I ever did," he choked out. "I messed things up, made things bad."

My heart clenched.

That's what happens when you fall in love. When the person you share your soul with hurts, you hurt right along with him, only you wish you could take the pain so you wouldn't have to watch them suffer.

"We aren't promised perfect, Phoenix."

"I don't need perfect." He held me tighter. "I just need you. Always."

"You have me."

"Promise not to ever let go." His voice was desperate. "I know it sounds weak, but I'm so sick of trying to look strong, trying to be strong, God, Bee, I just need you to let me be weak in this moment and tell you that you're the reason I'm able to breathe a little easier every day. You're the reason my heart's able to beat without shattering in my chest." He sighed. "I guess what I'm saying is… you've brought me back to life — and after being dead so long — I'm terrified."

My eyes welled with tears. "Small steps, Phoenix… remember?"

"Yeah."

"Small steps… little moments… each second is another one we get together. Right?"

He exhaled. "Right."

"But tell me…" I cupped his face. "Don't ever feel like you have to keep things inside, even if they're scary."

"Bee, I'd never expose you purposefully to the scary."

"But you can." I encouraged. "Because you don't have to do it by yourself anymore."

"A stronger man would."

"A strong man…" I licked my lips to keep myself from bursting into tears at his broken face. "…knows when to ask for help."

"Help." He parroted, his lips finding mine. "That's what you were at first… a lifeline."

"And now?"

"My savior," he said in a reverent voice.

CHAPTER FIFTY-SEVEN
Life... but new life.

Phoenix

IT HAD BEEN A whole week since Bee got shot — and I was still a complete mess. Every time she moaned in her sleep, I was terrified that we hadn't actually gotten the bullet, and she was going to die.

It had taken four doctor visits.

And each of the four doctors had to say to my face, "She's just fine."

"And the baby?" I'd ask in that same panicked voice I'd come to recognize as my own when anything I loved was in jeopardy. "How's the baby?"

"Just fine." They'd patted me on the back and walked away while Bee rolled her eyes and gave me a duh look.

I could always count on her to bring humor into every single situation, either that or drive me insane with her saucy looks and inability to keep her hands to herself.

Ever.

Family dinners would never be the same with her.

EMBER

Nixon cleared his throat. "Good tradition, Mo."

"Why, thank you, evil spawn." She winked and lifted her wine glass while Nixon rolled his eyes and kissed Trace on the head.

Everyone had someone.

But Sergio?

He was still waiting for orders from Tex, and I knew that it was only a matter of time before the guy decided to shoot himself because of the suspense.

"Family dinner..." Tex rubbed his hands together. "...and Chase cooked."

"Because Chase is the only guy here who knows how." Chase scowled and hit Tex's hand as he reached for the chicken. "We pray first."

"Whose turn is it?" Trace asked.

"Phoenix—" Nixon barked. "—you say the prayer."

I'd never been asked to say the prayer at the family gatherings — ever.

It was a thing of honor. Plus, why have the guy who raped girls talk to God? Didn't seem the best way to get the Big Guy upstairs to listen.

I cleared my throat, hands suddenly clammy, and began my prayer while everyone made a cross with their hands.

"Thank you..." I forced the words past my lips. "...for this food..." I squeezed my eyes shut and then opened them and looked around the table. "...for family, for this family."

Nixon's gaze met me across the table as he whispered, "Amen."

Bee didn't let go of my hand.

Which was fine. I was used to her hanging on to me, whether it be my hand, my leg, my hair — now that it was grown out, that seemed to be a personal favorite. She said it was a way to desensitize me since I'd gone so long without any good touching.

At first it made me feel awkward.

Now I craved it.

And missed it when she forgot — not that I'd ever admit that out loud, least of all in front of Tex, who still gave me dirty looks whenever he remembered that I was, in fact, marrying his sister and having a child with her.

Bee released my hand.

I felt the emptiness immediately.

She placed it on my thigh.

Shit, not again.

"So…" Tex said, grinning. "…everything's back to normal for a while."

"Yup." Chase lifted his wine glass then looked down at my lap, his grin widened. "I just love family dinners."

With my free hand, I gripped my knife and pointed it in his direction while he elbowed me, almost making me drop it onto the table.

"You kids alright?" Nixon asked.

"Phoenix is awesome… aren't you, big guy?" He shoved me again.

The knife was looking better and better; one stab, just to jolt him out of his chair and get him off my back.

"Yeah," I answered, choosing peace over violence. Wow, that must be what growing up felt like.

Bee's hand inched closer to the button of my jeans, and then slid, strategically, past the barrier.

Before she could excite me any further, I gripped her hand, shoved her away from my pants, and stood, pulling her to her feet to block all evidence of what she'd just been doing.

"Be right back." I gently pushed her toward the hall.

"Don't break anything!" Chase called.

Tex stood from his seat. "Is Bee okay? Bee, you sick? You need help?"

"Let Phoenix take care of her." Nixon chuckled into his wine. "Clearly that's something he's good at doing."

Tex's eyes narrowed.

I didn't look back.

Simply pushed my soon-to-be wife in the bathroom, locked the door behind me, and said in a raspy voice, "Strip."

She pouted. "Come on, it was funny… getting you all excited over the chicken dish. You love birds."

"I love you." I reached for her shirt, giving it a little tug, and then pulled it over her head. "Now, take off your clothes before I rip them."

"I love it when you get bossy." She held up her hands while I took the shirt off and stared at her naked breasts.

"No bra?" I choked.

"Why else would I use our safe word?" She giggled.

"But you didn't—"

"I did…" She nodded. "Well, in a way, I mean, I pointed toward the chicken, which you should naturally assume meant bird, and then when that didn't work, I took matters into my own hands."

"Literally," I forced out in a dry voice.

"Yeah, well…" She licked her lips and beckoned to me with her finger. "You have really nice hands…"

"Better to tease you with."

"And your mouth?"

"Better to taste you with." I licked the seam of her lips.

"Mmm…" She giggled and threw her head back as I kissed from her chin down her neck. "Keep going, and Tex is going to shoot you."

"It would be worth it." I tugged at her jeans. "Totally worth it."

"Am I?" She wrapped her arms around my neck.

"You were worth it… you still are. And you'll continue to be worth it every single day."

"Love you, soldier man."

"Love you too, little girl."

EPILOGUE

Sergio

THE TABLE WAS CLEARED. The women, all but Mil, were in the other room getting dessert ready.

And I was alone with all five bosses.

Damn, just get it over with already.

Someone knocked on the door.

With a grin, Tex stood. "That must be our guest."

"Guests?" I snorted. "At a family dinner?"

Nixon and Chase shared an amused look with Frank, while Mil patted me on the hand. Hell, if that wasn't a pitiful look I didn't know what was.

Crossing my arms, I clenched my teeth and waited for our guest to enter.

"Sergio..." Tex led someone small into the room. A hooded sweatshirt hid the figure's head and face, but pieces of blond hair poked out from underneath. "I'd like you to meet your new assignment."

The person turned and pulled the hood back.

I choked. "Andi?"

"Told you," she whispered. "One day very soon you'd

regret some things you've said to me."

"What the hell is a Russian whore doing in this house?"

Three kicks, I counted, all from the direction of Mil.

Andi's eyes filled with tears. "Funny you should say that…"

"Sergio." Tex tilted his head, hatred dripping from every single cell in his body. "Your new assignment."

"Her?" I spat.

"Keep her alive," Frank said, "and protected from the Russians. Let her die in peace, son."

"Wait? What?" I shook my head. "You just said to keep her alive."

"Until I die," Andi said softly. "Remember my condition? Leukemia? For my participation in your little shootout… that was the deal."

"Deal?" I was having a hard time breathing. "What deal?"

"With Luca," she whispered. "But I'm sorry it has to be you… I really am."

"What the hell is that supposed to mean?" I shoved away from the table. "I don't understand."

"Protection comes at a cost." Frank stood. "We offer her protection in the only way we know how… blood."

My body went cold.

"Your punishment…" Frank pointed his finger in my direction, his fist shaking. "You will protect her until she takes her last breath. You will protect her with your life… as her husband. We offer her family, since she's lost hers. After all, it was a dying man's wish — Luca's wish — that if it ever came to this, she'd be taken care of."

"My punishment," I repeated.

"Or your reward." Tex angled his head and raised an eyebrow. "It's really all in how you look at it."

Andi chewed her lower lip. "The good news is I've only been given six more months… so your torture won't last that long."

That... My body roared with injustice. ...was what I was afraid of.

PREVIEW
Elude
Eagle Elite, Book 6

Elude: To evade, get away from. Throw off the scent. The process of slipping through someone's fingers. Example: I never knew that in eluding death — I'd be faced with hers.

PROLOGUE

Sergio

THE FLUORESCENT LIGHTS BURNED my eyes. I blinked them rapidly — thinking it would make the stinging go away, but it only made everything worse. The pain was indescribable, like someone had broken my body in half, repaired it, then repeated the process.

"He's not going to make it." I recognized the voice. It was Nixon's. Why the hell was Nixon there? Wasn't he dead? No wait, that was me. I'd taken that bullet.

Memories of the past few days flashed across my line of vision, causing a searing headache to build at my temples.

The fight.

The gunshots.

The agreement.

My wife.

Tears burned the back of my eyes.

Wife...

"I'll do it. I'm a match." I gripped her hand firmly in mine.

"You'll die," Tex whispered. *"Your body... it's too weak from everything else."*

"We're running out of time!" I screamed, my voice hoarse, eyes frantic. *"Do it now!"*

"No." She wrapped her frail arms around my neck. *"No."*

"Yes." I pushed her away. *"If I don't — you could die. The doctor says it needs to be now, so operate."*

Her eyes were sad.

Both Tex and Phoenix looked down at the blue and white tile floor, faces pale. I knew what they were thinking. I'd already lost too much blood, my kidneys were barely working, and I wanted to give her part of my life.

I knew going in I would most likely die.

But I'd do everything within my power to save her.

It's odd, when you face death every day, when you elude it, when you finally come to terms with the fact that you won't be on earth for forever — that's when you think you're at peace.

I thought I was okay with dying.

Until I'd met her.

And then I was faced with someone else's death every damn day — it's harder. People don't tell you that. It's one thing to come to terms with your own mortality; it's quite another to stare down death of the one you love, knowing there is nothing in this world that will stop it.

My vision blurred again.

"He's flatlining," a voice said in the distance.

I tried to keep my eyes open. I saw white blond hair, big

brown eyes, and that tender smile. I reached for it and held onto it, held onto the memory of her. The girl who'd changed my world from darkness to light.

The girl I never wanted.

But desperately needed.

"Tell her I'll love her..." I didn't recognize my own gravelly voice. "...forever."

With a gasp, I felt my heart stutter to a stop.

And welcomed the shade of night that overtook me.

OTHER BOOKS BY RACHEL VAN DYKEN

The Bet Series
The Bet (Forever Romance)
The Wager (Forever Romance)
The Dare

Eagle Elite
Elite (Forever Romance)
Elect (Forever Romance)
Entice
Elicit
Ember
Ember

Seaside Series
Tear
Pull
Shatter
Forever
Fall
Strung
Eternal

Wallflower Trilogy
Waltzing with the Wallflower
Beguiling Bridget
Taming Wilde

London Fairy Tales
Upon a Midnight Dream
Whispered Music
The Wolf's Pursuit
When Ash Falls

ABOUT THE AUTHOR

RACHEL VAN DYKEN is the *New York Times, Wall Street Journal,* and *USA Today* bestselling author of over 29 books. She is obsessed with all things Starbucks and makes her home in Idaho with her husband and two snoring boxers.

CPSIA information can be obtained
at www.ICGtesting.com
Printed in the USA
LVHW092154140319
610738LV00001B/226/P

9 781507 629543